THE SHADOW
messenger

by J.G. SUMNER

Trafford
PUBLISHING®

Order this book online at www.trafford.com/08-1203
or email orders@trafford.com

Most Trafford titles are also available at major online book retailers.

Cover Design by Robert Cox.

Note for Librarians: A cataloguing record for this book is available from Library
and Archives Canada at www.collectionscanada.ca/amicus/index-e.html

Printed in Victoria, BC, Canada.

ISBN: 978-1-4251-8699-9

*We at Trafford believe that it is the responsibility of us all, as both individuals
and corporations, to make choices that are environmentally and socially sound.
You, in turn, are supporting this responsible conduct each time you purchase a
Trafford book, or make use of our publishing services. To find out how you are
helping, please visit www.trafford.com/responsiblepublishing.html*

*Our mission is to efficiently provide the world's finest, most comprehensive
book publishing service, enabling every author to experience success.
To find out how to publish your book, your way, and have it available
worldwide, visit us online at www.trafford.com/10510*

 www.trafford.com

North America & international
toll-free: 1 888 232 4444 (USA & Canada)
phone: 250 383 6864 ♦ fax: 250 383 6804 ♦ email: info@trafford.com

The United Kingdom & Europe
phone: +44 (0)1865 487 395 ♦ local rate: 0845 230 9601
facsimile: +44 (0)1865 481 507 ♦ email: info.uk@trafford.com

10 9 8 7 6 5 4 3 2 1

acknowledgements

Several people deserve thanks for their help in making this book possible. First, there is Dennis Read who supplied the idea around which the entire story was built. Then my SCUBA mentor, Mike Wadel, assisted by providing information and opinions regarding SCUBA equipment and procedures. I also sought his opinions on skydiving procedures. Larry Elmore, my former flight instructor, provided valuable information on aircraft equipment and procedures. The great-looking front cover was designed by Robert Cox, and last but certainly not least, I owe a special thanks to Ron Hamilton for reading the original manuscript and offering constructive comments that were used in the preparation of the final manuscript.

dedications

This book is dedicated to all those who made comments on *The Use of Power* and encouraged me to write a sequel.

Professor Damon Hawker had listened in on many conversations taking place in the White House, but he had never actually been inside before. And, he wasn't actually *inside* now: He had been ushered into the Rose Garden and told to wait there for the First Lady.

He was curious about why she had sent for him. It had to be connected in some way to his nonacademic activities because plain Professor Hawker wouldn't warrant an audience with the First Lady. That would mean she knew about the life he had desperately tried to keep secret. It was reasonable to expect that she *would* know about it, however, because her husband did—*and* had tried to end it.

Hawker stood at the foot of the steps looking out across the garden. It was larger than he would have guessed. To him, it looked more like a small park. There were numerous flower beds and trees, and though the month was October, many of the plants still decorated the scene with eye-catching colors. Many important events had taken place here. It was difficult for him to put into words exactly what he was feeling at the moment. It was some combination of veneration, inspiration and the sense that he was part of something grand. Hawker had not yet been born when President John F. Kennedy hosted the Mercury astronauts in this garden, but Kennedy was his favorite president of recent times, and standing in the spot where his heroes had once stood was more than an honor; it made him want to do something great.

From behind him, a pleasant feminine voice broke into his thoughts, "Welcome to the Rose Garden, Professor Hawker."

Hawker turned to see the First Lady approaching. She was more attractive than she appeared on television. Her medium brown hair was cut about two inches above her shoulders and her green eyes shone with intelligence. He knew she was fifty, but she looked more like early forties. "Thank you, Mrs. uh . . . what do I call you, Mrs. First Lady, Mrs. Bradshaw, or what?"

He thought to himself: *For a physics professor, I'm not showing much intelligence.*

She smiled and said, "Lena."

Hawker smiled back. "I don't think I could get used to addressing you by your first name. I'm still having trouble accepting that you want to talk with me."

She continued past him. "Come along," she said. "Let's take a tour of the Garden." After several more steps, she added, "Relax . . . I'm just as much awed by your presence as you are by mine. I suspect you'd be welcome at any gathering of kings and presidents. That is, if they knew who you really are."

"What're you talking about?" asked Hawker.

The First Lady smiled again. "The hostage rescues in Iraq, the bombings that didn't happen, earthquake victims in Pakistan. . . . Don't be modest, Professor Hawker. I know who you are."

"I suspected you might," he said.

She looked him up and down. "They told me you were tall with blue eyes and blond hair, but they didn't say how handsome you are."

Hawker's face broke into a shy grin. "It's kind of you to say that."

"It isn't kindness. I pride myself in always telling the truth."

The First Lady scanned the Garden and added, "I asked you to meet me out here because I wanted your secret to remain secret. The President and a couple of other people know, but I don't think you have to worry about them."

"And I have you to thank for that," said Hawker. "I never thought I would be able to say this to you in person, but you took quite a load off my shoulders when you prevented the President from attacking Iran. I'm really grateful for that."

The First Lady looked puzzled. "Well . . . it sounds like *each* of us knows the other's secret. How could you know about that?"

Hawker didn't answer. He wondered if he had talked too much again.

The First Lady continued, "But considering the other impossible things you've done, I guess I'm not surprised that you *could* know about it. Who else knows?"

"Nobody," said Hawker. "It's to my advantage to keep that a secret."

She nodded approval; then a questioning look spread over her face. "I'm curious. What would you have done if I hadn't prevented the attack on Iran?"

He certainly didn't want to tell her that his boss, Dr. Ben Huron, had proposed kidnapping the President and Vice President, so he looked away and said, "I hadn't decided."

"I guess I don't really want to know," she said. "Let me tell you why I asked you to come here."

He looked back at her. "Yes. That's what *I'm* curious about."

"There are two very specific things," she said. "But let me start by saying that I believe it would be very advantageous to both of us if we could cooperate on projects of mutual interest. I'll begin the cooperation by giving you some information that I believe you need. . . . Jason Bragg has escaped."

"Who's Jason Bragg?"

"One of the men you marooned on that island. I have reason to believe that he'll make another attempt to obtain your toy . . . but not for the President this time. I had been told that you never leave home without it."

Through a sheepish grin, he said, "I was afraid to bring it. I was afraid this was a trap. I didn't think you were trying to trap me, but I thought the President might be."

The First Lady frowned. "That might have been a really big mistake. I hope it's well secured."

Being in the presence of the First Lady, he had been a little slow to grasp the significance of what he was hearing, but suddenly Hawker realized that the person he loved most was in danger—and he had placed her there. "I'm afraid you're right. I'm afraid I've made a big mistake."

The First Lady could only guess at what he meant. "This is partly my fault," she said. "I now wish I had handled this meeting differently, but it never occurred to me that you would come without your bag. That's why I had Hank meet you out front . . . to make sure nobody looked inside it."

Hank was the Secret Service agent that had ushered Hawker into the Rose Garden.

Hawker was now anxious to leave. "I hope you don't think I'm being rude, but I need to go. I have to get back to Gainesville."

As Hawker turned away, the First Lady said, "Wait . . . I can have you flown back much faster than anything *you* could arrange. But before I do, I want to tell you the other reason I sent for you."

His anxiety was intensifying, but he knew the First Lady was right about the transportation. He stopped.

She continued, "Our intelligence guys have picked up on a plot that's being hatched in Russia. It's a plot that would cause great harm in the United States, but we haven't been able to learn anything beyond that. I was hoping *you* would check it out."

He shook his head. "I think I should tell you up front that I will *not* become a spy for the United States."

"I don't expect that," she countered. "This is about saving lives. According to the information that I *do* have, the civilian population of this country is being targeted. You don't have to report anything back to me. Just check it out for yourself."

"I'll have to think about that later," he said. "Right now, let's get me to Gainesville."

The First Lady did a come-hither wave to Hank, who was watching them, but out of hearing range. Then she reached into a pocket and removed a small object. "This is a special cell phone," she said. "You can reach me anytime of the day or night. Just press the button marked 'FL' if you need help of any kind."

She handed Hawker the phone; then turned to the Secret Service agent. "Hank, get Professor Hawker back to Gainesville by the fastest means possible."

As he and the agent turned to leave, Hawker said, "Thanks. I'll be in touch."

What have I done? he thought. *I've placed a higher value on that suit than on the safety of my own fiancée.*

Since acquiring his special suit, he had carried it with him at all times, stuffed in a small canvas bag. For the visit to the White House, he had made an exception and left it with Teala, his fiancée. The man the First Lady said had escaped from the island was one of the few people who knew about Hawker's connection to the suit. He was also the only person who had ever tried to steal it. Hawker knew the man was ruthless and would stop at nothing to get the suit.

Meanwhile, at the Alachua County Courthouse in downtown Gainesville, Florida, Teala was having her own problems. A friendly deputy clerk by the name of Jackie had mispronounced her name. Trying to be tactful, Teala said, "That's pronounced Tay-AH-lah."

"I'm sorry, Miss Tay-AH-lah," the Deputy Clerk said, mimicking her pronunciation. "But I can't accept this application without your fiancé being present. According to the law, both parties have to appear when making an application for a marriage license."

Showing disappointment, Teala said, "What if I tell you he's in a meeting with the First Lady of the United States?"

"Well that's impressive," said the Deputy Clerk. "And, there are allowances for special circumstances. But unfortunately, that one isn't listed. Surely he can take a little time out of his busy schedule for something as important as marriage."

If you only knew, thought Teala. Aloud she said, "You're right. And you've been very nice about all this. When he returns from Washington, I'll grab him by the ears and drag him down here." Then she smiled. "I'm kidding. It won't take that."

With that, she picked up the canvas bag and left the office. The ladies in the outer office smiled at her as she went through. In the lobby, she passed the security checkpoint again, but didn't have to stop on her way out. That checkpoint had been a surprise to her when she entered the building. She was *so* afraid they were going to open the canvas bag. But they didn't; they just placed it on the belt with her keys and jewelry. The security guard remarked that the bag looked empty as he ran it through the X-ray machine. "It's just a suit," she had truthfully responded.

She knew that Hawker always placed the helmet inside the rest of the suit to achieve maximum radiation absorption. That's why nothing appeared on the screen: The suit had absorbed all of the X-rays. She had briefly considered leaving the bag in the car during her visit to the courthouse, but Hawker had instructed her not to let it out of her sight even for a minute. He had been reluctant to leave it with her, but he was afraid the invitation to the White House was just a ruse concocted by the President to gain possession of the suit.

To avoid feeding a parking meter, Teala had parked in a space behind the Commerce Building, which was located across the street and the next block down from the courthouse. Deep in thought, she walked that distance and arrived at her car without realizing how she had got there. Her parking space was at the back edge of a large area where many other cars were parked. She wasn't even sure this space belonged to the Commerce Building, but she hadn't seen a "no parking" sign. She checked the windshield for a ticket anyway.

The month was October, but in this part of Florida, a car could still get hot inside when parked in the sun. When she opened the door she was surprised to find that wasn't the case this time. It was as if she had left the windows open, which she hadn't.

Before Teala could start the engine, her cell phone jingled. It was Hawker. "Is everything okay?" he asked.

"No," she replied. "You have to go with me to apply for the license."

"That's the least of our worries right now," he said. "Where are you?"

"I just got into my car behind the Commerce Building. I'm on my way home."

"Don't do that," he said. "One of those men that kidnapped you before managed to get off the island where I left him. I guess it's foolish to ask if you've seen him."

"I haven't been looking," she said.

"You should start. The guy's name is Jason Bragg, and I have reason to believe he's gonna be stalking you. In fact, he may be tailing you right now."

"Okay. I'll go someplace where there's a lot of people. How soon will you be back?"

"Soon . . . I'm catching a ride on a Harrier jet."

"What's a Harrier jet?"

"It has vertical take off and landing capability. . . . But let's get back to your situation. Being around other people isn't going to stop that guy. He'll just flash a badge and convince everybody that he's a federal agent and you're a law breaker. And you can't go to the police for the same reason. You're gonna have to protect *yourself* until I can get there. That'll be just over an hour. In the meantime, I want you to drive straight to my house, get my rifle out of the closet and park yourself where you can see both doors. Make sure there's a round in the chamber and the safety's off. Don't take any chances with this guy. If he comes through the door, shoot 'im. Legally, you'll be within your rights under those conditions. I'll be there soon. Can you do that?"

"You're scaring me. What makes you think he's looking for me?"

"He wants what you're carrying. And when he discovers he can't control it, he'll keep you around to use as leverage against me."

"Okay. But hurry up. I don't know if I could shoot a person."

"I'm on my way."

Teala was nervously scanning the area even before she disconnected. During the drive to Hawker's house, she kept a constant vigil in the rearview mirror, but saw nothing out of the ordinary. She felt some degree of relief after turning into the driveway and closing the electric gate behind her. She knew the gate would delay an intruder long enough for her to get situated in the house.

Hawker's house was well buffered from the road. It was at the end of a two hundred-foot driveway and completely hidden by trees. He had cleared an area at the center of a five-acre plot to provide space for the house and a large yard. Most of the yard was behind the house. For the most part, the rest of the property remained in its natural wooded state.

Teala parked in front of the house and switched off the engine. That's when she got a surprise. Suddenly, a man's head popped up over the back of her seat. She screamed.

"Whoa . . . don't do that," he said. "It hurts my ears."

She tried to open her door and jump out, but he held her with his left hand and showed her a gun with his right. "Just be calm," he said. "I don't want to hurt you."

"Who are you? What do you want?" she demanded.

The man feigned a pout. "I'm hurt. After all the time we spent together, and you don't remember me?"

She twisted her body for a better look. "You look different," she said.

"Well, a lot of time in the sun without sufficient food does that to a person. Now I want you to slowly slide over to the passenger's side, and please remember that this gun is on you every second. After what your boyfriend did to me, I wouldn't mind causing him a little grief."

Teala did as instructed, and Bragg leaned the seat back forward and opened the door. Without removing his eyes from her, he slid out and returned the seat back to its upright position. "Now you slide out this way and bring that bag with you," he ordered.

He backed up as she slid slowly toward him.

They stepped onto the wooden deck that ran the length of the front of the house and he ordered her to unlock the door. When she did, he pushed her inside and followed close behind. The room they had entered was long and open, and comprised the living area, dining area and kitchen.

"Turn off the alarm," he said. "And don't worry about me seeing the code. He can change it."

After she did as he ordered, he sat her down at the dining table and handcuffed her to the chair with her hands behind her.

"This is uncomfortable," she said.

"You won't be there long," he responded, as he pressed a button on a small device and shoved it back into his pocket.

He opened the canvas bag she had been carrying and removed its contents. Each item that he lifted appeared as a flat black pattern with no three-dimensional features. "This thing looks weird," he said. "How does he know where the openings for his arms and legs are?"

"He just knows."

"You're gonna have to be a little more cooperative than that, gorgeous. How does it work? How does he make it do what he wants?"

"I guess there's no harm in telling you," she said. "He controls it with thought commands, and it won't respond to anybody but him."

He picked up the item that he reasoned was the helmet. Remembering the shape it had when Hawker was wearing it, he felt along the bottom and found an opening. As he pulled it down onto his head, he felt a band slide into place across his forehead and he could see again. He formed the thoughts of several words such as "fly" and "hover," but nothing happened.

Deciding that he probably needed to wear the entire suit to make it function, he picked up the jacket, but Teala interrupted him. "I have to go to the bathroom," she said.

Bragg removed the helmet and grinned at her. "I'll give you two choices on that," he said. "You can go now and leave the door open, or you can wait until my new partner gets here and close it."

"I can't wait," she said.

As he unlocked her cuffs, he said, "Better grab your toothbrush while you're in there. You're gonna be going with us."

"I don't live here," she retorted. "Besides, I won't be with you that long."

"Suit yourself," he said. "But you're gonna be with me for quite a while. Much longer than the last time. Who knows? You might even start to enjoy my company. You may not think your boyfriend is so special now that he's lost his suit."

As she started toward the bathroom, she countered, "That suit isn't what makes him special. His values . . . his principles are what make him special."

"Principles?" snorted Bragg. "What principles? If he had any principles, he would've used that suit to help end the war in Iraq."

He followed her into the bedroom and sat on the bed where he could see the window but not the toilet.

Teala hoped if she could keep him talking that would help to mask the sound of her tinkling. "He *is* helping to end the war in Iraq, but he's doing it his way. If you're talking about him joining in on the killing, his principles are exactly what prevent that."

"Well your Sunday School Christian had no qualms about leaving my partner on that island to die," countered Bragg.

She had wondered why only one of the men escaped from the island. "I'm sure he didn't intend for your partner to die. If he had wanted that, he could've just dropped him in the ocean."

"He still killed him any way you look at it."

As Teala emerged from the bathroom, Bragg waved the gun, indicating that she should return to the dining area. "Put the suit back in the bag," he ordered.

As she complied, she asked, "So what does the President plan to do with the suit?"

Bragg shook his head. "I don't work for the President any longer. He got religion while I was stuck on that island."

"I thought he already had religion."

"Well he got a different kind. He said he no longer needed my services and didn't want me to contact him again. I thought about exposing him for what he really is, but then I decided the voters got what they deserved. He'll show his true colors again, but I won't be around to help with his schemes. I have a new employer."

"Who?"

"Let's just say we'll be going to Russia."

Teala stopped and shot him a disbelieving look. "You mean you're going to turn this suit over to a foreign government?"

At that moment, they heard the whop-whop-whop of a helicopter approaching. Teala's face lightened: She obviously thought Hawker was coming to rescue her.

"Don't be too happy," said Bragg. "That'll be my partner, not yours. You'll like Luko. He has a strong accent, but he's a ladies' man."

The helicopter landed in the clearing behind the house.

"Grab that pad over there," said Bragg. "I want you to write Hawker a note."

chapter 2

Hawker struggled to obey the speed limits as he drove from the airport to his house. He knew something was wrong; he'd had that feeling before. He hated himself for having left Teala alone with the suit. Sometimes he wondered about his intelligence. He, of course, had had no reason to suspect that Bragg had escaped, but that was no excuse; he should have anticipated it.

On arriving at his driveway he found the gate closed and undamaged. Then at the end of the driveway, Teala's car was the only vehicle parked there. These findings should have relieved him, but he still had the feeling. He yelled to let Teala know who was coming through the door. A key wasn't needed: The door was unlocked. He wondered why she hadn't locked herself in. The reason soon became obvious: She wasn't there. A note on the dining table told him she would be waiting on the island where he had imprisoned Bragg.

He knew that Bragg had chosen the word "imprisoned," and that Bragg obviously wanted him to follow them to the island. He knew why, and he knew that Bragg was not likely to kill Teala until he got what he wanted. But that didn't mean she wouldn't have to endure other ordeals. He cringed at the thought of what those other ordeals might be.

His mind started to run wild, conjuring up images of Bragg as a sexual pervert—or sadist. Then with a vehement shake of his head he blanked out those thoughts. He had to get control of himself. That kind of thinking was not constructive. He had to concentrate on how to get her back.

He knew he had to do exactly what Bragg was counting on, which was to personally follow them to the island. He couldn't involve law enforcement of any kind; that could get her killed in a hurry. A boat to the island would take too long. Bragg had almost certainly used a helicopter. Hawker quickly decided he would have to fly also, but a helicopter would announce his arrival. The only way to arrive quietly would be to parachute. He would have to get somebody to fly him over the island tonight, under the cover of darkness.

Several of his friends were pilots but Dennis was the most logical choice. He already knew about the suit and he owned an airplane. That would make things simpler. The only problem was that Dennis might be out of town. He owned a small trucking company and spent a lot of time on the road driving an eighteen-wheeler. But Hawker got lucky: Dennis answered his cell phone on the first ring and confirmed that he was in town.

After anxiously going through the usual greetings, Hawker said, "It's been a long time since I've flown your Mooney, but can't it fly about five hours without refueling?"

Dennis answered, "If we're talking practicalities here, it would be four and a half hours with a half hour reserve. Why do you ask?"

"I have a big favor to ask of you."

"You know I'll do it if I can."

"I know you will. . . . I need to parachute onto a remote island tonight and I need you to fly me there."

Dennis chuckled. He thought Hawker was kidding around. "That sounds like fun."

"I'm serious, Dennis. Teala has been kidnapped and the kidnapper has my suit."

"You are being serious, aren't you?"

"Yes. . . . Can you do it?"

"I can, but do you realize how hard it is to parachute from a Mooney?"

"Yes. But I need to go as quick as I can and I didn't want to explain things to somebody else."

Dennis was quiet for a second; then asked, "Well how many kidnappers are we talking about? And how do you plan to handle them after you get there?"

"The answer to both questions is . . . I don't know. It's the same guy that kidnapped her and the others before, but I don't know how many men he has with him." After a pause, Hawker added, "I don't know what to expect. I'll have to improvise after I get there."

"I'll go with you," said Dennis. "We'll get Billy to fly us in his Cessna."

"I can't let you do that," said Hawker. "You'd be putting your life in danger."

"I put my life in danger every time I jump," countered Dennis.

"That's completely different, and you know it."

"Maybe, but I'm going with you anyway. Teala is my friend too. You know you need some help. Don't be stubborn."

Hawker was silent for a couple of seconds; then said, "Okay, I'll call Billy and you try to borrow us a couple of dark colored canopies. Black would be best, but dark blue would be okay if you can't find black. I think Mark and Lev both have dark blue. . . . And wear dark clothing."

"What do I say when they ask the reason?"

"Just tell 'em it's for a special night event."

"I assume we're gonna meet at *Skydive Palatka*?"

"Yeah, just as soon as you can get there. I'll be leaving shortly. I have to tell my boss what's happening, and I have to arrange for transportation off the island."

"If you get your suit back, we won't need any other transportation."

"Yeah, but we can't count on that. I don't want to be stranded on that island."

=⇐=

Hawker parked in the lot across the street from The New Physics Building. He would never have found that spot if it had been morning instead of late afternoon. He took the stairs two at a time and almost ran over Myra Wilson who had just started down.

Myra was like a little sister to him. He had known her since she was three and used to baby-sit for her, though she insisted that he wasn't her baby-sitter; he was her playmate. Their play usually consisted of computer games. Even at three, Myra had been as mentally mature as some adults he had known. She was now only sixteen, but was already enrolled at the university as a sophomore and was a student in one of Hawker's physics classes. Her father, Professor Thad Wilson, taught the same course, but she enrolled with Hawker to reduce possible claims of favoritism. Of course if a person knew the close relationship she had with Hawker, they would say: *what's the difference?*

Earlier that year, she, Teala and Ben Huron had been abducted by Jason Bragg and his partner. The rogue agents—who were working for President Bradshaw—were attempting to force Hawker to turn over his special suit, but Hawker foiled their plot and rescued his friends.

Hawker stopped to give Myra a hug and explain why he was in such a hurry.

"Is there anything I can do?" she asked.

"Not right now," he said. "I may call on you later." Then he rushed on up the stairs.

As he entered the outer office, he was relieved to see Ben Huron's door still open. Ben's policy was to be accessible to everyone. He was a good department chair. Everybody said so. He certainly had been good to Hawker. They had served in the Army together and Ben was the one who had introduced Hawker to physics. That was more than eighteen years ago and they had been close friends ever since.

Hawker closed the door behind him as he entered Ben's private office.

"I smell trouble," said Ben. "That's the only time you close my door."

Ben had put on a little weight since Hawker first met him, but other than that he looked pretty much the same. He was about five-ten with short brown hair and bright brown eyes.

"You're right," said Hawker. "They've got Teala again, but this time they also have the suit."

Ben frowned. "You're saying President Bradshaw's goons have her? The same guys as before?"

"Yes, but Mrs. Bradshaw said they don't work for the President any longer. I don't know who they work for now."

Ben shook his head. "Bradshaw can't be trusted, Damon. How do you know you can believe his wife?"

"I just know."

"I hope you're right."

Ben stood and walked around his desk. "Do you have a plan for rescuing Teala?"

"That's why I'm here. I wanted to tell you that I may be gone for a couple of days. *And*, I wanted you to know where I'm going in case you don't hear from me tomorrow. They're holding Teala on that same island where I left them the last time they pulled this stunt. I'll give you the coordinates, and if you don't hear from me tomorrow, notify the Coast Guard. Dennis and I are going to parachute onto the island tonight."

Ben tilted his head to one side. "That sounds risky, but if I were a skydiver, I'd go with you. I know Thad Wilson would want to go."

Hawker shook his head. "I don't want him to go. I wouldn't be able to live with myself if I caused Myra to lose her daddy."

"Well don't worry about things here. I'll see that your classes get covered. I just wish I could do more."

"You do enough," said Hawker. He gave Ben the coordinates and left.

Palatka is almost due east of Gainesville. Hawker figured he could drive it in forty-five minutes or less. He stopped at a convenience store and bought a couple of sandwiches and a bottle of water. He couldn't afford to get hungry in the middle of this operation. As he drove and ate, he asked himself what he had overlooked. Nothing came to mind.

He had decided to accept the First Lady's offer of help. He would use her to get him off the island if necessary. Using a small pouch that had come with his audible altimeter, he had attached the cell phone she gave him to the inside of his left forearm. His sleeve would conceal it there and that would be the spot least likely to get patted down.

He fought to keep the morbid thoughts out of his mind as he drove. He and Teala had begun dating more than ten years earlier when they were both students at the University of Florida. For Hawker, the relationship had been a dream-come-true until Teala graduated and moved back to her home town. They began drifting apart at that point, but the real clincher came one weekend when Hawker borrowed Dennis' airplane to take Teala on a date. He had a problem with the airplane and couldn't meet her as planned. They broke up after that and had no contact for almost ten years. He was devastated at first. That was the second time love had failed him. He didn't even bother to date after that. Then one day about seven months ago he found her sitting in his office. They got off to a rocky start, but she moved to Gainesville and before long they were inseparable.

Darkness was falling as he turned in at Kay Larkin Airport. As he negotiated the narrow road leading down to *Skydive Palatka*, he couldn't help wondering what was happening with Teala at the moment. He scolded himself again for having placed her in danger. This wasn't the first time she had been put in harm's way because of that suit. He hadn't known what he was asking for when he tried so hard to develop it. He mumbled to himself, "Like they say, be careful what you wish for."

As he pulled into the parking area, he saw more cars than he was expecting. Lev's car was there, as was Mark's. Dennis and Billy were there, of course, but he was expecting them. He wondered what Dennis had told Mark and Lev. Lev was the nickname that everybody used for Leverence Prymore. He was a retired Navy pilot and Mark Woodall was a civil engineer employed by the Navy. The two of them plus Billy and Dennis had taken Hawker under their wings back when he began his civilian skydiving career. Over the years, the five of them had become an unofficial team.

Hawker parked and walked through the covered parachute "packing area" that fronted the building. He could see Billy standing behind the counter in the "manifest" office.

As Hawker entered the office and looked around, Lev was the first to speak. "Before you start objecting, let me tell you that you need me. I've had training for dealing with hostage situations."

"And you also need an engineer," added Mark. "You don't know what you're gonna run into out there."

Hawker threw Dennis a questioning look. Dennis grinned and said, "Mark and Lev have their own dark canopies and Billy arranged with the *drop zone* for us to borrow a couple of student rigs that have dark canopies."

Dennis had obviously conspired with Mark and Lev to enlist their help. Lev was clean shaven and kept his dark hair short as one would expect from a military man, but Mark sported a full beard that had begun to show flecks of gray. They were both slender and stood about five feet-eleven. Dennis had short reddish brown hair and a goatee and outweighed Mark and Lev by thirty pounds or more.

Billy Hollingsworth was about the same size as Dennis. He added his bit of information. "And we can use the Caravan if you'll pay for the time we put on it." He was referring to a Cessna Caravan airplane that had been modified for parachuting activities.

"I'll chip in on that," said Dennis.

"We all will," said Mark.

"That won't be necessary," said Hawker. "I can handle it. . . . It looks like the whole gang is here except for Johnny. How did he get left out?"

Johnny was a skydiver in his seventies that jumped with them sometimes.

"He's too old for this sort of thing," said Mark. "We didn't want to tell him about it."

"He's gonna be hurt when he finds out," said Billy.

"It's for his own good," said Mark. "He'll get over it."

Lev stepped to the side and pointed to a box. "And I'll bet, you didn't think about night-vision goggles, did you?"

"No . . . I didn't," admitted Hawker.

"Well I did," said Lev. "You see . . . you're too emotionally involved to do all the planning alone. You need us."

Hawker grinned. He knew he had been overruled even before he could say no. He had been part of this little *band of brothers* for many years. Along with Ben Huron and Thad Wilson, these were his most trusted friends. Their professional careers varied considerably, but they shared similar interests: They were all skydivers, and they were all pilots.

And they were not going to let him do this alone.

"Well there's one thing I want to say up front," said Hawker. "We're not gonna go in there with guns blazing like they do in the movies."

"We know," said Dennis. "I brought a pistol, but it's just for emergencies. I won't use it in any way that will endanger Teala."

Hawker looked back at Lev. "Well, Lev, you're the military man. Do you have a plan?"

"I have a plan for the jump," Lev replied. "But we'll have to see what the situation on the island is before we can do much planning for that. The only thing that comes to mind at present is a diversion. If a couple of us could lure some of them away from where Teala is being held, the other two might be able to sneak in and grab her. We have limited options if guns are not allowed. But even if we manage to free her, they'll still be chasing us and we'll be stuck there. That's the major drawback I see in this plan. I didn't want to involve a backup team to get us off the island until I spoke with you."

"I think I have that covered," said Hawker. "But I don't want to bring in reinforcements until Teala is out of their grasp. What about the jump?"

"Let's deal with the night-vision goggles first," said Lev. "Has anyone used 'em before?"

They all shook their heads. Hawker didn't mention the fact that he had used the night-vision feature of his special suit many times. Of course Lev didn't know he had a special suit.

"I think depth perception will be our biggest problem," said Lev. "And that shouldn't be a problem except when you go to flare for a landing. Let's take the goggles outside in the dark and use 'em to do our 'dirt dive.'"

A "dirt dive" is a simulated jump that is done on the ground. Since the free-fall part of a typical jump is less than a minute, the jumpers practice their moves on the ground where the practice is free. Once they're in free fall, they don't have the time to stop and ask themselves what they're supposed to do.

After explaining the basics of using the goggles Lev moved the group outside and away from the building. Then he had them don the goggles and run toward objects in the dark. Of course, the objective was to stop before hitting the objects. This was the only practice they would get for judging distance in preparation for landing on the island. They continued wearing the night-vision goggles during the "dirt dive" to get maximum exposure to their eerie green images. The actual "dirt dive" didn't take long, however, because what Lev was planning was something this group had done many times.

When Lev was satisfied with the results of the practice, he continued with other details of the jump. "We'll launch the 'four-way' from a high altitude without cutting the engine. That way, it won't sound suspicious if they hear the airplane go over. *And*, Billy won't turn back immediately after we exit. We'll just hold our 'four-way' until it's time to 'track' away. I wouldn't want us running into one another in the dark."

"You *do* know they'll hear the parachutes pop open, don't you?" said Mark.

"Maybe we can reduce the possibility of that," said Hawker.

Hawker was fairly certain the kidnappers would land their helicopter in the same clearing he had used when he left them there earlier that year. He would instruct Billy to make his "jump run" such that they would be upwind and well away from that clearing when their parachutes deployed. They would also open the parachutes higher than usual.

"Maybe they won't recognize the sound," said Billy. "That's not a sound the ordinary person hears every day."

"The guy that took Teala is not an ordinary person," said Hawker. "He probably has experience with parachutes. He's some kind of rogue government agent."

Lev had worked with U.S. intelligence a few times, and even though he was retired, they still called him back to fly special missions at times. He suddenly became concerned about possible conflicts of interest. "Whoa," he said. "Are you saying we're dealing with the U.S. government?"

"No," replied Hawker. "He no longer works for the government. At least not for the *U.S.* government."

"What does he want with Teala?"

"He doesn't want her. He wants me."

"Well what does he want with you?"

"He thinks I have information he needs. But I don't. I might be tempted to give it to him if I did."

"Is this connected to your research in some way?"

Hawker was hesitant as if he didn't want to discuss it. "I suppose you could say that."

Lev gave him a knowing grin. "That's okay. You don't have to divulge any government secrets."

Hawker made a sketch of the island and showed them the location of a large sandy beach where he said they should land. He also marked the spot down the beach and inland a short distance where he expected the kidnappers to be waiting. Then he gave Billy the coordinates and sent him to check the weather and file his flight plan.

"You seem to know a lot about this island," said Lev.

"I've been there a couple of times," said Hawker. "That's why they chose it."

The large cargo door of the modified Cessna Caravan had been replaced by one made with hinged sections of Plexiglas. It opened somewhat like a multi-section garage door except that it had no rollers: It slid along a track. Also, two long bars had been added above the door opening, one inside and one out. They were there for the jumpers to hold onto while preparing to exit. Since there were no seats in the cargo area, they were sitting on the floor.

About an hour into the flight, Lev came back with the news that they were ten minutes from the island. He had been in the cockpit talking with Billy. They donned their parachutes and other equipment without much discussion. They had already done their talking and planning. Now it was time to execute. Lev did mention that it looked as if they would have a cloud cover.

The *standby* light came on. They lifted the door and slid it into its overhead position. Lev stuck his head out; then pulled it back and said, "Man, I can't see a thing down there."

Mark said, "You know . . . we have to trust Billy a lot, to jump out over the ocean under these conditions. What if the island isn't there?"

"It's there," said Hawker. "If Billy's reading his GPS correctly."

"And what if he isn't?"

"Well, you can always stay on the airplane."

"Don't be silly," retorted Mark.

Then the *exit* light came on.

Lev gripped the bar above the door at the front of the opening and slid his backside out, muscling his way against the hurricane-force wind. Mark did the same at the rear and Dennis backed out between them. Mark and Lev gripped Dennis' jumpsuit by the special grippers on his upper sleeves, and Hawker took a hold on his chest strap.

All this maneuvering took less than five seconds; then Dennis gave the count. He rocked his head backward; then forward and backward again. As he moved his head backward that second time, the three on the outside released their grips on the bar and stepped backwards into free fall, pulling Hawker along with them.

They quickly became stable and level and everyone switched to wrist grips. This was a maneuver they had practiced many times just for fun. The usual procedure was to immediately begin moving through a sequence of formations, but this time they held the circle. This wasn't for fun, and they didn't want to risk becoming separated in the dark.

This was the first time any of them had worn night-vision goggles in free fall and they looked weird to one another. They couldn't carry on a conversation, of course, because of the air rushing past their ears at almost a hundred and twenty miles an hour. Since they were used to being very active in this situation, just "lying" there doing nothing made it seem like a long time. In reality less than a minute had passed when they broke through the bottom of the clouds and spotted a light below. That light was a comforting sight. It meant there really *was* something down there besides water.

At that same instant, their audible altimeters signaled *break-off* time. They each turned one hundred and eighty degrees and tracked away from the center of their circle, tracing out a pattern resembling the spokes of a wheel. This maneuver ensured that they would not be close to one another when their parachutes opened. That could be disastrous because they had very little control during that time and could experience speeds relative to one another on the order of fifty miles an hour.

Hawker worried about collisions on openings and landings more than he did about his parachute not opening correctly.

After getting opening shock, Hawker released his toggles and brought his canopy under control; then looked around for the other three. They were all there. He rocked his canopy back and forth a couple of times to identify himself; then headed for the beach. The others followed.

It was now obvious that the light they had seen was a fire. It was in the clearing where Hawker had deposited Bragg and his partner six months earlier. So far, everything was going according to plan. Even the *spot* had turned out good. They had opened over the ocean and let the wind carry them back to the island. The wind also accommodated them by being parallel to the beach when they landed. But just as Lev had predicted, they all had trouble with depth perception and flared either too late or too early. That resulted in ugly looking landings, but fortunately, no one was injured. They were grateful that none of their friends were watching.

They quickly gathered up their canopies and moved off the beach into the edge of the jungle. As they huddled close, Hawker spoke with a low voice and said, "I'm sure you all saw the fire. That's exactly where I expected them to be."

Lev motioned on into the jungle and said, "After seeing this mess, I think we only have one option for approaching their position. Even if we could get through this vegetation, they would be sure to hear the noise we'd have to make. We'll have to hope they don't know we're here. Let's leave our parachutes here and try to get closer via the beach."

Keeping close to the edge of the jungle, they moved down the beach until they were adjacent to the reflections given off by the fire. At about the same time, Hawker spotted a well-worn trail leading away from the beach. He guessed it had been made by Bragg and his partner during their six-month stay here. All of this seemed too easy. But, of course, they still had to deal with the kidnappers. He motioned to Lev that they should follow the trail.

The farther they went the more anxious Hawker became. Sentries could be posted anywhere along here, but he couldn't think of any other way to make their approach.

If he had planned better, they might could have brought some kind of quiet cutting tools for the vegetation. But even if they had, they still didn't know the surrounding area. No, this was definitely quieter than trying to make their way through the jungle. He would just have to see it through now. But everything depended on Bragg not knowing they were there.

Suddenly, about a quarter of a mile from the beach, the clearing, the fire, and some people came into view. They all stopped in their tracks, afraid they had gotten too close before they realized it. Hawker removed his night-vision goggles and saw Lev doing the same. After he got his unaided vision adjusted he could see that Teala was one of the people they had seen. She was sitting on something with her hands behind her, presumably because of handcuffs. A man was sitting near her, but Hawker didn't recognize him. They were too far away for features to be clearly visible.

A helicopter was visible though. The unnecessarily large fire was responsible for that. Though the month was October, it wasn't really that cold; maybe sixty degrees. The fire was meant to make it easy for Hawker to find them. Teala and the one man were the only people he saw and they were sitting well back from the fire. The fact that he couldn't see anyone else concerned him greatly.

They backed away a short distance and huddled close. In a low voice, Hawker said, "That guy could be Bragg. I can't tell. He could probably fly that helicopter himself, but I seriously doubt that he came without reinforcements."

"The helicopter is a Bell 222, or a 230," said Lev. "He could've brought half a dozen men in that."

"I wonder where they all are." said Mark.

"Two of them are pointing guns at you," said a voice behind them. The voice was heavily accented, but its message was clear.

"Just keep walking toward the fire," said the accented voice.

Hawker had known something was wrong. He could feel it. He was going to have to start trusting his instincts. He saw another man emerge from the jungle to the left of where they stood. That man definitely had a gun pointed at them.

Teala and the man with her were seated on pieces of fallen trees. As the group approached, the man stood and said, "Welcome, Professor

Hawker. I see you've met my new partner, Luko."

Hawker recognized the man now. It was Bragg alright, but he looked different; leaner and darker. Teala was wearing jeans and a sweater and had borrowed one of Hawker's jackets. He reckoned she was warm enough, especially with that fire. Her expression seemed to say: *I'm happy to see you. Now get me out of this.*

Bragg continued, "You know, *Professor*," and he emphasized the word "professor." "You are *so* predictable. You did exactly what I expected you would. The only thing that surprises me is that you were stupid enough to involve other people. I'm beginning to wonder just how much smarts it takes to be a professor."

Hawker didn't say it, but he was thinking the same thing. He should never have let his friends get mixed up in this. Two of them didn't even know the whole truth.

"You've just made my job more difficult," continued Bragg. "Now I have to decide whether to shoot these people, or just leave 'em here without food and water the way you left me. I don't know which is worse."

Hawker had been looking at Teala. He turned to Bragg. "You're right, Bragg. My friends didn't know what they were getting into. They have no part in this."

"Well unfortunately, they're here," retorted Bragg. "And another thing, did you really think I wouldn't hear your canopies pop open . . . with all the quiet around here?"

"We were hoping."

Bragg laughed; his two men joined him. Hawker and party didn't see the humor.

Bragg pulled out his own gun and said to Luko, "Go back to where they dropped their parachutes. Make sure they didn't stash anything useful there, such as food and water or cell phones. We'll take care of the chores here while you're gone."

Luko left and Bragg turned back to Hawker. "Now you guys take off those jump suits."

When that was done, Bragg reached behind the log where he had been sitting and picked up a plastic bag. "Now empty your remaining pockets into this bag. And I *do* mean everything. I'll take those night-vision goggles too. They'll make a very nice addition to my collection."

Dennis said, "Just so there's no misunderstanding, I'm pulling a gun to go in the bag."

Bragg moved his own gun in Dennis' direction and eyed him carefully.

By this time, Hawker was assuming that Bragg had only two men with him, and one of them wasn't present at the moment. He racked his brain for a way that he and his three friends could overpower the two men before they could harm Teala.

As if he had read Hawker's thoughts, Bragg stepped over his log and stood behind Teala.

He motioned to the other man and said, "Search 'em."

The man patted Hawker down as if he had training and experience at this sort of thing. He checked under Hawker's arms, around his middle, down his legs, and down the outside of his shoulders and arms, but he did not check the inside of the forearms. Then he did the others.

Dennis, Mark, and Lev had all promised not to endanger Teala, so they remained docile throughout these proceedings.

Bragg said, "I'm gonna give you a choice. You tell me what I want to know, and I'll leave this delicious bit of female flesh with you. Otherwise, I take her to Russia and you can come there to tell us. I kinda hope you let me keep her. I like looking at her."

As if he didn't already know, Hawker asked, "What do you want to know?"

Dennis shifted his position and Bragg briefly glanced in that direction; then back.

"I know you're not too bright," he said. "But don't play dumb. I want to know how to operate your toy."

"The problem is," said Hawker. "I don't know how you would ever be able to operate it. It won't respond to anybody but me, and I don't know how to change that."

Bragg smiled and reached down to Teala's right arm. "I was hoping you would say something like that." As he tugged upward on Teala's arm, he said, "Come on, honey. It's time to go for another helicopter ride."

"Wait," said Hawker. "Taking Teala won't do you any good. I'm the one you want. Take me instead. I promise to cooperate."

"You had your chance," said Bragg. "Truth is, I planned all along to strand you here the way you did me. I want you to get a taste of it."

Hawker knew he had no choice. "How will I find you in Russia?" he asked.

Luko was walking up at that moment. Bragg said, "Luko, tell 'im where we'll be waiting for him in Russia . . . assuming he gets off this island some day."

"Check into the Pekin Hotel in Moscow," said Luko. "We will find you."

As Teala got pulled backwards, she gave Hawker a sad look and mouthed, "Bye."

Bragg and Luko loaded the jumpsuits, the plastic bag, and Teala into the helicopter, and the other man took the pilot's seat. Hawker watched helplessly as the sleek-looking helicopter lifted into the air; then with a tip of its nose, sped away.

Hawker and friends all stood motionless and quiet for a time, feeling the defeat. Eventually, Dennis said, "I hate losing that three-fifty-seven magnum."

"And those night-vision goggles," added Lev. "I borrowed those from the military. I'll have to replace 'em."

Speaking to Hawker, Dennis said, "I hope you made those transportation arrangements you mentioned. I kinda like eating . . . and I'm already feeling thirsty."

Hawker had been slower than the others to come back to the moment. "Don't worry," he said. "There's food and water on this island. I wouldn't have left 'em here to starve. But yes, I did make arrangements."

He then unbuttoned his left sleeve and pulled it up.

Mark was curiously watching him and said, "I'm beginning to wonder what you're not telling us. You've obviously had dealings with that guy before, and he made it sound as if you deliberately marooned him here."

"I had no choice," said Hawker. "But let me make this call first." And he removed his special cell phone from its pouch.

"You still have a cell phone?" exclaimed Mark.

Hawker grinned and pressed the "FL" button. Even though it was late at night, the First Lady answered as she had promised she would.

"I believe you wanted me to go to Russia," said Hawker.

"Yes," replied Mrs. Bradshaw. "Did you find everything okay down in Florida?"

"Not really. Bragg has kidnapped my fiancée and he has my suit. And right now I need a helicopter ride."

"What do you mean? Where are you?"

"Some friends and I attempted a rescue, but we failed. Now we're stuck on an island."

"That's only a minor problem if you can be more specific about your location. Can you?"

"Yes, ma'am." And he gave her the coordinates.

"Okay . . . the Coast Guard will be there to get you, and their orders will be to take you where you say. Now what caused the sudden change of heart about going to Russia?"

"That's where my fiancée and my suit will be."

"I see."

"I'm gonna need your help to get a quick visa. I would like to leave Washington tomorrow afternoon if that's possible. I'll be going to Moscow . . . to the Pekin Hotel. Do you think you can arrange that?"

"Yes . . . I'll have somebody take care of everything. Just give me a call when you know what time you'll be here. Do you have a passport?"

"Yes, ma'am. Do you want to give me the information on the other matter now, or when I get to Washington?"

"I've already told you all we know. You'll have to use your . . . uh . . . special talents."

"I'll do what I can . . . assuming I regain those special talents. And I appreciate your help."

"You've earned it."

"Thanks."

They were all watching him as he put away his cell phone. Dennis asked, "Well are we gonna get rescued?"

"Yes. The Coast Guard is coming to get us."

"I'm glad we had the foresight to leave our wallets and keys back at the *drop zone*," said Lev.

"I've never heard you say 'ma'am' to anybody before," said Mark. "Who were you talking to?"

"The First Lady," replied Hawker.

With surprise in his voice, Lev asked, "The First Lady as in the President's wife?"

"Yeah."

Mark exclaimed, "Man, Hawker, I'm gonna have to start showing you more respect."

Lev added, "Ole Bradshaw turned out to be a pretty good president, didn't he? He kinda changed his tune from the way he had been talking during the campaign."

Hawker nodded. "Considering the way things have turned out, I'm glad he got elected." He didn't tell them that the First Lady was actually running things. He had been using the suit's enhanced hearing feature to eavesdrop the night that Mrs. Bradshaw used blackmail to force her husband into letting her make the decisions. Normally, Hawker would consider blackmail to be a bad thing, but this time it had saved the world from a disastrous war.

Mark added, "Yeah, I voted against him. Now I'm kinda sorry I did."

"Well I didn't bother to vote at all," said Dennis. "What's the point? You know something is wrong with the system when the man that got the fewest votes is the one in office. If I'm gonna vote, I want my vote to count."

Lev said, "You know . . . you've got a point there. Not only does the individual's vote not always count, but the system takes his vote and awards it to the candidate he voted against."

"I agree that the system is flawed," said Mark. "But giving up your right to vote certainly won't improve things."

"I didn't give up my right to vote," countered Dennis.

"If you don't vote, it's the same thing."

"Now, now, boys," said Lev. "We can't solve the election system's problems out here. Let's get on with the situation at hand. I want to hear Hawker's story." He looked at Hawker in the flickering firelight and asked, "How is it that you can just pick up the phone and dial direct to the First Lady? And what is this suit, or toy, or whatever it is that I keep hearing about?"

Hawker glanced at Dennis.

Dennis said, "I think we ought to tell 'em. After all, they risked their lives to try to help."

Hawker knew Dennis was right. He should have told them everything before letting them get involved. "You're right," he said. "Go ahead and tell 'em."

Dennis stepped more into the light, displaying a smug expression. "Guys . . . you know all the TV reports you've been seeing lately about this dude that looks like a shadow . . . the one they're calling the *Shadow Messenger?*" He motioned toward Hawker with an *I-give-you* gesture of his hand. "Well, that's our bud here."

Mark and Lev laughed and looked at Hawker. Hawker wasn't laughing. Their laughter died off and they remained silent for a few seconds.

Eventually, Mark said, "You mean that thing that can fly . . . and bench-press a loaded tanker truck?"

"You make me sound like some kind of monster," said Hawker.

He couldn't quite read the expressions on the faces of his buddies. He added, "And I didn't really lift that much weight. The suit *does* enhance my muscle strength, but I shielded the truck from Earth's gravitational field and made it weightless."

Mark smiled. "You really believe all that stuff, don't you?"

"It's true," said Dennis. "I've seen 'im in action. He even gave me a ride up to altitude for a parachute jump."

Lev's face lit up when he heard Dennis' statement, but Mark was frowning. He said, "You know . . . as an engineer, I'm having a hard time accepting all that. It just doesn't make sense that you or anybody else could fly that fast . . . even with some kind of special suit. I know that a hefty power source is required to cut through the air like they say he does and I haven't seen anything in the pictures that looks like a power source."

"The power source for flight is contained in the material of the suit," said Hawker. "It uses a form of nanotechnology to produce something similar to synthetic nuclear fission. The ejection of millions of high energy particles is what propels me through the air. I should also point out that I'm weightless when I'm flying."

Mark looked at him with an expression that said he wasn't sure he was ready to believe that explanation. Then he turned his attention to

Dennis. "And *you've* known about this all along and didn't tell us."

"It wasn't my place to tell," said Dennis. "I figured if he wanted you to know, he would've told you."

"It wasn't that I didn't trust you guys," said Hawker. "I thought I was protecting you."

"Protecting us from what?" asked Lev.

"The sort of experience you've just gone through," said Hawker. "I didn't want to involve you this time, but you didn't leave me much choice."

Just looking at Lev with his clean country boy appearance, one wouldn't suspect that night carrier landings were just part of a day's work for him and that he jumped out of airplanes for relaxation. This little adventure on the island was nothing. "We're adults," he said. "You don't need to protect us."

Hawker had never known Mark to raise his voice or show anger, but he could be persistent and was somewhat of a maverick. He wasn't quite yet ready to leave the issue of the *Shadow Messenger's* suit. "So you can turn off gravity, huh?"

"Not exactly," said Hawker. "The suit can generate a field to shield certain objects from the effects of gravity."

"Does that mean there are things that it can't shield and things that you *wouldn't* be able to lift?"

"That's correct. The surface has to be electrically conductive."

Mark looked at Hawker in silence for a couple of seconds; then said, "Man, Hawker . . . I knew you had to be smart, but I never realized you were that smart."

"I'm not," said Hawker. "I can't take credit for developing the suit. I suppose you could say I had a hand in designing it, but I had some . . . uh . . . very special technical help in building it."

"Well that's what engineers and scientists do," said Mark. "They do the design work and technicians do the building."

"That's not what I meant," said Hawker. He couldn't tell even his best friends about the scientists who had actually developed the suit. After debating with himself many times, he had decided that *some* secrets needed to *stay* secret.

Lev interrupted them. "Somebody needs to go get our parachutes before the Coast Guard arrives. Dennis can help me do that, and you two might want to stoke that fire. We wouldn't want it to die out before we're found."

Hawker nodded and walked away to look for more wood. He hoped that would be the end of the questions about the suit.

The Coast Guard arrived as promised and ferried the would-be rescuers back to Kay Larkin Airport. To their surprise, they were not asked many questions, a favor for which they were grateful. After the Coast Guard had gone, Lev said to Hawker, "Looks like you're gonna have to go get her without our help after all."

Hawker nodded. "That doesn't diminish the loyalty you guys showed. I'll never forget that." He shook each person's hand and thanked him. "I'll contact all of you when I get back from Russia."

Being anxious to start making preparations for his trip, he left without further ado. He knew the others wouldn't be far behind: They were all feeling tired and dejected.

President Garner W. Bradshaw had overheard his wife talking on the phone. They weren't sleeping in the same bedroom these days. Leaning against her doorway, he asked, "Who were you talking to?"

"A couple of people," she answered. "Professor Hawker for one."

He stepped on into the room. "What've you got going with him?"

"He's gonna help us with that problem in Russia."

"What? I've already told you what I want to do about that."

"I know. . . . But I don't like your solution. In fact, it's no solution at all. Threatening the Russians isn't going to solve the problem. They already feel threatened by us . . . especially after we established missile bases in Poland. That's the problem. Too many people around the world feel threatened by us. We need to change that image. Even animals attack when they feel threatened."

President Bradshaw believed his wife to be naïve when it came to matters of national security. "So you're going to turn the security of our nation over to a school teacher?"

She laughed. "That's laughable, Garnie. Only you could think of him as *just* a school teacher."

"That's all he'd be without that suit."

"That's where you're wrong. Having the power is not what makes the man. It's how he uses that power. Look at you. Look at how you want to use your power . . . and would if not for me."

He frowned. "Just how long do you think we're gonna be able to keep up this charade?"

She tilted her head and smiled. "That depends on how long you want to remain president."

"Well we should at least be sleeping together. I'm sure people are talking already."

Hoping it didn't sound as if she was using sex as a weapon, she replied, "We'll talk about that when I see an improvement in you. And I'll know if you're faking."

"You know I love you, Lena."

"I know you do. That's probably the only reason this is working. Tell me the truth, Garnie. Can't you see how much things have improved since you started taking my advice?"

"You mean, since you forced me to take your advice," he countered.

She let him kiss her on the cheek. Then he went back to *his* bedroom.

chapter 3

Hawker was more than happy to be on the ground again when the plane finally landed at Domodedovo International Airport outside Moscow. Being a pilot, he had spent many hours in the air—and for the most part had enjoyed it—but the twelve hours non-stop from Washington, D.C. to Moscow was a little more than he cared for.

He had little trouble passing through customs. He had been given a currency declaration form on the airplane and had filled that out before landing. Also, his passport and visa were in order, so things were getting off to a smooth start.

The Secret Service agent who had delivered his visa to the airport in Washington, D.C. had told him to take the shuttle train from the airport to downtown Moscow because it was faster than a taxi. Attempting to follow the agent's instructions, he walked from the *Arrivals* terminal through the *Departures* terminal to the shuttle train ticket office, but the ticket office personnel refused to accept his dollars and sent him back to the *Arrivals* terminal to purchase rubles. Fortunately, time was not a problem: The trains ran hourly, and he still had thirty minutes before the next one departed.

Forty-five minutes after leaving the airport, the shuttle train pulled into Pavelets Station which is located just south of the famous *Garden*

Ring. The *Garden Ring* is a region circling the center of Moscow and serves as an informal division between middle class and lower class.

During his flight, Hawker had spent considerable time poring over his map of Moscow and the surrounding areas. Knowing that his hotel was at least ten kilometers from the station, he headed straight for the nearest taxi. He didn't know why Luko had told him to check into the Pekin Hotel, but that was his only link to Teala, so he would follow instructions for now.

The First Lady's people had made a reservation in his name, so check-in wasn't much of a problem. The fact that one of the clerks spoke a little English definitely helped. Hawker asked if a message had been left for him and got a negative reply. After waiting in his room for some time— and not knowing what he was waiting for—he decided he should eat while he had the opportunity. The *American Bar and Grill* was located just over two blocks from the hotel, so he walked the distance and had himself a good American-style lunch.

Shortly after returning to his room, the phone rang. "Professor Hawker," the accented voice said. "You should go outside again and walk in the same direction you just came from. A taxi will be waiting for you at the corner." Without waiting for a response, the caller hung up.

Hawker didn't know what to expect. Was he supposed to take his belongings with him? Would he be coming back to this room? He grabbed his map, passport and visa, but left the bag of clothes and toilet articles.

As promised, a taxi was waiting at the corner. Hawker climbed into the backseat and the driver sped away without speaking. They immediately turned left onto the street that passed in front of his hotel. It was one of several major streets that ringed the center of the city. The street had several different names, depending on what section you were on.

Where it passed his hotel, it was called "Bolshaya-Sadovaya Ulitsa," with the "Ulitsa" part meaning "street." Farther to the south, the same street became a "bulvar," or boulevard.

Suddenly, and without warning, they turned right onto Tverskaya Ulitsa. Hawker was glad he wasn't driving in this city. He had thought American drivers and traffic were bad, but compared to this, they would be a mildly pleasant experience. Again without warning, the driver whipped left onto an adjoining street and parked on the street next to the Marriott Grand Hotel.

Hawker assumed the hotel was his destination, so he opened the door and started to climb out.

"No," said the driver. "You stay. Here I get new passenger."

Hawker closed the door again and said, "I'm glad you speak English."

"Necessary for business," remarked the driver. "How you like Hotel Pekin?"

"It's interesting," replied Hawker. "It looks as if it wasn't always a hotel."

The driver turned toward him and grinned. "Was built for Secret Police headquarters."

"Well that explains a few things," said Hawker. It was then that he saw a slender man with gray hair and a mustache approaching the taxi. The man climbed into the front seat and spoke to the driver in Russian.

The driver sped away again, and after making a couple of turns, was back on that same major street that circled the city's center. About thirty minutes later, they turned left onto Highway M7. Hawker knew from his map that this road would take them past Monino Air Force Museum and on to Vladimir. He didn't know if the new passenger spoke English, so kept quiet.

After more than another hour, they turned left again and soon came upon a fenced complex. The sign beside the gate was mostly unintelligible to Hawker; he didn't even recognize most of the symbols.

The proprietors, however, were apparently expecting a few English-speaking visitors. The company name had been translated for him: *Monino Pharmaceuticals*. The passenger up front flashed an ID card at the guards, but apparently they knew him well enough to ignore it. They waved him through.

The size of the complex was difficult to judge. A large single-story main building and many smaller buildings ringing it were visible. Apparently, the Russians liked their rings. Instead of heading for the main building, the driver turned left toward some smaller buildings that Hawker had not seen at first. As they drew closer, it became obvious that these were residences. When the driver stopped in front of one of them, his front seat passenger turned to Hawker. "Come with me please, Professor." The man had an accent, but he spoke perfect English.

The driver had left the engine running and he immediately sped away once Hawker and the other passenger were out. Apparently, he wasn't expecting immediate compensation from this fare.

Hawker followed his fellow passenger past a couple of golf carts and into the house. In the foyer, the man stopped and called out, "Luko."

Hawker heard a response from down the hall. They continued in that direction and he saw Bragg and Luko enter the hallway at the other end.

His host unlocked a door on their right and said, "In here."

They entered a room that was obviously an office. Bragg and Luko followed immediately behind them. Bragg said, "I'm disappointed. I was hoping you'd spend more time on that island."

"Maybe I'm not quite as stupid as you think," said Hawker. "Maybe I had the foresight to make arrangements for getting rescued."

The man who had arrived with Hawker moved to the other side of a desk; then turned to face Hawker. "I do not have time for casual conversation, Professor Hawker. We want to know how the suit operates. How do we program it to do our bidding?"

"You can't," replied Hawker.

The man studied Hawker's eyes for a second; then said, "I hope you understand that your beautiful lady's life depends on you cooperating with us."

"I *do* understand that," said Hawker. "But like I told Bragg, the suit won't respond to any type of input other than thought commands, and the thoughts have to be mine. It's programmed for *my* brain waves only."

The man displayed a suspicious grin. "I assume you are suggesting that we should let you put on the suit."

Bragg shook his head. "I wouldn't allow that. He almost blinded me once before with a light that appeared from nowhere. We don't know what other little tricks he has tucked away in that thing."

The man gave Bragg a scornful look. "I am not stupid either."

"I want to see Teala," said Hawker.

The man behind the desk was obviously the boss. He studied Hawker again; then said, "Search him. Then put him in with his lady. We will carry the suit to the laboratory."

Bragg turned to Hawker. "You know the drill, sport. Take off your jacket and empty all your pockets on the desk."

Hawker did as instructed and Bragg took the jacket; then patted him down. It was again a good search, but again it missed the inside of his forearms. Hawker thought to himself: *At least I did a couple of things right.*

Luko then led him down the hall to what appeared to be some kind of waiting area. A man was seated there beside a door with a glass panel as its upper half. Hawker could see Teala through the glass. She gave him a nervous smile.

The seated man was obviously a guard. Luko spoke to him in Russian and he got up and unlocked the door.

When Hawker entered the room, Teala rushed to him and they held one another as if they had been apart for years. Hawker heard the lock snap into place again.

"I'm sorry, Hawker," she said. "I'm *so* sorry."

"What do you mean?" he said. "I'm the one who's sorry. I never should have involved you in this."

"I knew what I was getting into."

He stepped back and held her shoulders at arm's length. "Believe me. If I could tell 'em what they want to know, I would. But I can't. I don't *know* how to reprogram that suit. But I'd do it in a heartbeat if I could. I'd do anything they say just to get you out of here."

She frowned. "Don't say that. Don't you know the harm they could do if they had control of that suit?"

He shook his head. "That will never happen. That's *one* thing we don't have to worry about."

"Besides," she continued. "They wouldn't let me go if you *did* tell 'em what they want to know."

"What makes you say that?"

"They've been too careless with their talk. They never *intended* to let me go, or they wouldn't have let me hear some things. They're not gonna let you go either."

He tilted his head slightly and raised his eyebrows. "I wouldn't *want* to leave here without you. In fact, I *won't* leave here without you. But don't worry, we're *both* gonna get out of this alive."

"How?"

"I don't know yet. . . . How did they get you here? I know they didn't bring you in that helicopter."

"They landed on another island . . . a big one . . . and transferred me to a private jet. And we didn't come in at a regular airport. It looked like an old military airfield."

"You said you heard things. What kinds of things did you hear?"

Her beautiful brown eyes were clouded with worry. "A bunch of stuff," she said.

She moved to a small bed at the back of the room and sat looking up at him. "One thing really worries me. Bragg and that Russian creep, Luko, were talking before you and Petrov came in. I think they're contaminating vaccine going to the United States."

"So his name is Petrov, huh?"

Teala nodded. "Yeah . . . Ivan Petrov. Didn't you know his name?"

Hawker shook his head. "Tell me again what you were saying about the vaccine."

"Well, I didn't catch all of it. They grinned and turned away when they saw me watching them through the door. And Luko's English is sometimes difficult to understand, but they were talking about Petrov adding some kind of machines to a vaccine to be used in America."

"Machines? That doesn't make any sense."

He thought about it for a couple of seconds; then said, "A machine that could fit in a vaccine would have to be pretty small. They didn't say 'nanomachine,' did they?"

"In fact, I believe they did. 'Nano' means really small, doesn't it?"

He nodded. "Yeah . . . a nanometer is one one-billionth of a meter. What else did they say?"

"They were talking about how much Petrov hated the United States, and Luko asked Bragg if it would bother him to see all those Americans dying. Bragg said no. It served them right for turning on him after all he had done for them."

"I wonder why the United States would be importing vaccine from

Russia."

"I don't know, unless it has something to do with the bird flu."

"And you're certain they were implying that the vaccine would kill a lot of Americans?"

She shrugged her shoulders. "I don't see how I could have been mistaken about that."

He glanced around. "We've got to get out of here. And we should do it while Petrov and the others are gone." He pointed across the room. "What's behind those doors?"

"The one on the left is a bathroom and the other one is some kind of storage room. There's nothing in it but empty shelves and empty boxes."

Hawker swiveled his head toward the door where the guard was stationed. "That guard appears to be looking in here at regular intervals. See if you can determine the approximate length of those intervals. I'm gonna go to the bathroom and make a phone call."

Teala looked at him in amazement. "You have a phone? How did you get in here with a phone?"

He grinned and pressed the sleeve of his jacket, showing her the bulge.

In the bathroom, he removed his jacket and unbuttoned his left shirtsleeve; then pulled up the sleeve and removed the phone from its pouch. Considering that he was in Russia and inside of a building, he wasn't sure the phone was going to work, but the First Lady quickly answered his call.

"We're not by any chance importing vaccine from Russia, are we?" he asked.

"Yes," replied Mrs. Bradshaw. "I'm sure you've heard that we have a bird flu outbreak."

"But I thought that was only in birds . . . no human infections."

"That's true. But the fear is that it's only a matter of time before it spreads to humans. We're trying to inoculate anyone who has contact with birds. And we hope to include the general population when more supplies become available."

"How many people have been inoculated already?" he asked.

"I don't know. Thousands . . . maybe more."

Hawker groaned, "Oh, man."

"What's wrong?" asked the First Lady.

"You have to stop the use of that vaccine. It's contaminated."

"We haven't had any reports of adverse reactions," she said.

"You wouldn't. He would want to get as many people as possible vaccinated before they start dying . . . and the deaths get connected to the vaccine."

"He who? What are you talking about?"

"Ivan Petrov. He has a hand in producing the vaccine. And he's adding something to it to kill everybody that receives it. He hates America."

"Well that was fast. I knew you were efficient, but I didn't expect results that soon."

"I don't know that this is the situation you wanted me to check on, but it's definitely a serious threat, and I'm not in a position to do anything about it. He's holding me and my fiancée prisoner . . . and it appears that they're planning to kill us."

"I'm sorry, Professor. Maybe the President can intervene in some way to stop it. Do you have any proof of what you're telling me?"

"Not yet. Don't do anything until I contact you again."

He started to disconnect, but then added, "Nothing that is, except stop the distribution of that vaccine."

"That might be easier said than done."

"Well you've got to try. And another thing, don't call *me*. They don't know I have this phone."

With that, he disconnected and put away his phone; then relieved himself and flushed the toilet. The guard was peering through the glass when he emerged from the bathroom. After watching them for a few seconds, the guard returned to his seat.

Teala spoke softly. "That's the only time he's looked in while you were gone. But you flushing the toilet might have triggered that."

"He won't look again for a few minutes," said Hawker. "I'm gonna take a quick look in that storage room."

Just as Teala had said, the storage room contained nothing but empty shelves and empty cardboard boxes. There were no windows, of course, and no openings in the ceiling. That's the same situation he had found in the bathroom.

Teala was still sitting on the small bed when he returned. There were no other seating accommodations in the room. In fact, it was almost bare. He sat down beside her and asked, "What would you say this room was designed for?"

"I don't know," she answered. She nodded across the room to the only other piece of furniture and said, "That heavy worktable and the glass panel in the entrance door make me think it might have been a laboratory."

"Do you think he might have kept human test subjects in here?"

She winced. "Maybe. He might've watched 'em through that door while they died."

The guard looked in again. Apparently satisfied, he returned to his seat.

"That was about five minutes," said Hawker. He stood and lifted the edge of the blanket to observe the structure of the bed. It was a simple metal frame with side rails that attached to the end posts with a wedge and slot arrangement. The rails were essentially lengths of angle iron with wedges welded to the ends. He thought to himself: *A person should be able to lift that side rail out of its slot with his bare hands.*

To Teala, he said, "Here, help me move the bed away from the wall. Not much though. The guard might notice the difference."

They moved it about a foot and quickly returned to their seats on the front side. "Now I want you to examine that glass panel," he said.

"Why?" she asked.

"Pretend you're looking through it to the other room, but your real objective is to determine its thickness and whether or not it has markings indicating it's bulletproof or shatter resistant. If the guard says anything, tell 'im you're looking for something to read. He may not understand you, but that doesn't matter."

"What do you have in mind?"

"I'm still gathering information at the moment. I don't have a final plan yet."

She still had a worried expression, but she kissed him on the cheek and said, "Thanks for coming to get me." Then she got up and went to the door.

He scolded himself again for getting her involved in this mess. He also promised himself that if they got out of this alive, he would never make that mistake again. That promise would probably be easier to keep now that the suit was gone. Maybe it had served its purpose.

The guard noticed Teala looking at the glass and stood up. He said something in Russian and she responded with what Hawker had told her to say; then pretended to be looking through to the waiting area.

The guard pointed to where Hawker was sitting and said something else in Russian. She frowned at him and returned to the bed.

After the guard moved away from the door, Teala said, "There are no markings of any kind. It appears to be ordinary glass, maybe an eighth of an inch thick . . . certainly not a quarter."

"Thanks," he said.

She noticed he had a look on his face she had never seen before. "Are you feeling okay?" she asked.

His response was, "I guess I always knew it would come to this someday."

"What do you mean?"

"I've never deliberately killed a man before. Even with all my trips to Iraq, I always managed to handle things some other way. But this time, I can't think of any other way. The lives of all those people that have already received the vaccine depend on us getting out of here. There's just too much at stake to worry about the life of one criminal."

She gave him a sad look. She knew what an inner struggle he must be going through. "If we *do* manage to get out of this room, then what?" she asked.

"I have to get the details on what he's putting in that vaccine."

"How do you plan to do that?"

"We'll find some place to hide *you* and then I'll come back to his office to look for the evidence we need."

"Do you read Russian?" she asked.

He shook his head. "No."

"Then you need me to stay with you. I do."

"You never told me that."

"You never asked."

"Then you understood what that guard was saying."

She grinned. "I wouldn't go that far. I studied Russian in college, but I never got the opportunity to use it in the real world. Reading it is different from listening to it or speaking it."

"I'll think about it," he said. "In the meantime, as soon as the guard finishes his next peek in here, I want us both to make a dash for the storage room. I'm gonna try to find two boxes the right height and I want you to grab one of those shelves. They're not fastened down. They're just resting on their brackets. Bring one of 'em back here and hide it on the floor behind the bed."

She nodded.

After a short wait, the guard did his thing; then they made their move.

Hawker found his boxes with no problem. From the front side, he slid them under the bed as far as he could; then went to the back side. He positioned the boxes under the side rail and laid the shelf on top of them. Then they returned to their seats for another wait.

The purpose of the boxes and shelf was to support the mattress and foundation after the side rail was removed. Hawker didn't want the guard to notice any change in the bed and he certainly didn't want him to know that the side rail had been removed.

After the guard did his next look-see, they jumped up and went to work again. Teala lifted the thin mattress and foundation while Hawker pulled one end of the side rail out of its slot. One by one, he gently moved that end's slats from the rail to the shelf. They then moved to the other end and repeated the procedure. Hawker lowered the metal side rail to the floor behind the bed; then they reseated themselves on the front.

"This next step is the part I hate," said Hawker.

Teala responded with a look of dread.

Hawker continued, "When the guard finishes his next look-see, let me get into position on the right-hand side of the door, and when I nod, you walk to the other side and flip off the light. The guard will immediately look in again, but this time he'll put his face to the glass and cup his hands beside his eyes so he can see better. The instant he starts to do that, you move backwards along the wall and put your hands over your face."

He hesitated and put his hands over his eyes to demonstrate. "Be sure your eyes are covered and be sure you're hugging the wall. We can't have any hesitation in this. Your step backwards will be my signal to throw that rail through the glass. So give me a good, quick signal. Any problems with any of that?"

She shook her head, still with a look of dread on her face.

As soon as the guard completed his next check, Hawker jumped up and grabbed the bed rail. He placed himself beside the door, probably exactly opposite where the guard sat on the other side of the wall. He held the bed rail in his left hand the way one would hold a spear and placed his right hand farther up front to help guide it. He then nodded to Teala.

As Teala crossed the room, Hawker mentally rehearsed his moves with his spear. His years of skydiving had honed his skills of split second timing and split second reacting, and he had long ago realized the importance of picturing in his mind what he was about to do. But he visualized that thing that was going to be on the other side of the glass as a lifeless target rather than a man.

Teala flipped off the light and the guard reacted exactly as Hawker had predicted. As he positioned his face close to the glass and started to raise his hands, Teala quickly stepped backwards and shielded her eyes.

Hawker stepped out and threw his spear all in one smooth move. He had to see the target, aim and throw, all in a split second before the guard could move. The guard being in a lighted room and Hawker in a darkened one clearly gave Hawker the advantage. He performed his task with wonderful precision. The guard probably never knew what had slammed into his head. And he probably didn't live long enough to feel much pain. Hawker, on the other hand, did. But his pain was mental; not physical.

Hawker flipped the light on again and checked on Teala. Apparently, no glass had hit her, but she was clearly in a daze. He ran to the storage room and grabbed another shelf and cardboard box. He used the shelf to punch out the remaining glass; then ripped the cardboard and placed it over the bottom part of the hole he had made in the door. He turned his back to the door and reached through with both hands to the outside frame above the door. "Come hold this cardboard in place," he said to

Teala. She did as instructed and he pulled himself through.

He didn't have to check the guard's pulse: One glance at the man's head told him all he wanted to know. He retrieved the key from the guard's pocket and opened the door; then took Teala by the arm and led her out past the corpse and the shattered glass. After a few more steps he stopped. "Wait here a minute," he said. Then he went back and got the guards gun.

The room where they had been confined was located in the back part of the residence and Petrov's office was up front. That's where Hawker had been taken when he first arrived. He made a beeline for it. He didn't know how much time he had: It would depend on the amount Petrov would waste before giving up on the suit.

At the office door, Hawker glanced at Teala. She was still in a daze. Surely she had seen many injuries during her nursing career. The up close violence must be what got to her. He tried to lighten the situation by saying, "I couldn't have chosen a better partner-in-crime for this job . . . a nurse who also reads Russian."

She tried to grin.

He tried the door and found it locked. After briefly considering and rejecting the idea of shooting the lock, he said, "I'm going back to get the bed rail. You watch the front door, and if anybody starts to come in just run toward where I am."

She nodded.

But a minute later he was back with the bed rail in hand. He jammed the bloody end between the doorknob and doorjamb and used the rail as a lever to pry against the knob. Because of its angle iron construction the rail was rigid and its length gave Hawker a considerable mechanical advantage. The door popped open with a loud splintering sound and they both looked around to see who had heard it.

Thinking he might need it as a weapon, he carried the bed rail into the office and placed it on the floor next to the desk. The items from his pockets, including his passport and visa, were still on the desk. As he reclaimed his possessions, he said, "You take his paper files and I'll try to get into his computer."

She moved toward the filing cabinet as if she understood what he wanted.

He was encouraged when he looked at the computer: It was the same kind he used at home. It was already powered up, so he pressed a key. After a few seconds, he was surprised to see English words appear on the screen. It was a relief and a disappointment at the same time: The words asked for a name and a password. The chances were very slim that he would ever guess Petrov's password. He began trying every word that he could associate with the present situation. He had no idea about Petrov's family. It could be one of their names. He looked around for family pictures, but saw none. After wasting several minutes he turned his attention to Teala.

She said, "I may have something here."

The potentially good news and Teala's seeming presence of mind half-surprised Hawker. "That's great," he said. "I'm getting nowhere with this computer."

He noticed that she had pulled out several folders and dropped them on the table next to the filing cabinet. She was flipping through the contents of one of them. He picked up a folder and looked at the wording on the tab. "So you can read this stuff, huh?"

"So far I've only been reading the labels and headings, but I think I'll be able to tell you what's inside the folders."

"Looks like Greek to me."

She grinned. "Actually, it's Russian."

"Too bad we couldn't get into the computer files. They may have been in English."

She pointed to the folders he was flipping through. "I pulled those out because they're the most likely candidates based on what's written on the tabs. But this one labeled 'Pavel Project' seems the most promising. Pavel is just a person's first name in Russian so that didn't mean anything to me. The word 'Project' is what caught my eye. None of the other folders have that on the tab. Then when I looked inside, the first thing I saw was 'Bird Flu Vaccine.' It also contains a paper on 'Molecular Machinery' and one on 'Immune System Attacks on Host Bodies.' Most of the stuff in here seems to be related to what we're looking for except for this one on 'Satellites.'" She hesitated and looked at him. "Could those molecular machines be controlled by an orbiting satellite?"

"It's feasible. In fact, I had assumed that they either had a time delay built in or that they would be triggered by an external signal."

"That settles it. Let's take these folders and get out of here. I think we're pushing our luck."

Hawker nodded and grabbed the three folders on the table and the bed rail. "Let's go."

As they walked through the foyer to the front door, he said, "Just act natural when we get outside. Don't get in a hurry. Pretend that we belong here." He peeked through a window and put the bed rail down before opening the door. One of the golf carts was gone.

He stepped outside and said, "We'll take that other golf cart if the key is there."

The key was there, so they both climbed in. They followed the narrow perimeter road away from the main gate, passing other buildings that obviously also were residences. The number of residences made it apparent that only the top personnel lived on site. They also saw other people here and there, but nobody gave them more than a passing glance.

The security fence made this pharmaceutical plant look almost like a military installation or a prison.

Hawker pulled the cart into an open passageway between two buildings. They weren't visible from the road, but they would also be trapped if pursuers approached from both ends of the passageway at the same time.

He gave Teala a thin smile and said, "Okay you can read with relative peace of mind now."

She read quietly for a couple of minutes, and then groping for words, she began slowly reading the contents of the "Pavel" folder aloud.

After Luko delivered Hawker to the room where Teala was being held, he, Petrov and Bragg climbed aboard one of the golf carts and took Hawker's suit to Petrov's laboratory. Petrov drove the cart and Luko stood on the back where golf bags normally ride. It wasn't a long ride, but apparently Petrov didn't go in for much walking. The lab was in the main building along with all the offices and the production room where the vaccine was produced and packaged. They entered the lab by the back door.

Inside the lab, Petrov placed Hawker's canvas bag on the table and began removing its contents. "It still amazes each time I look in this bag," he said. "All I see is a black cavity. There is only one explanation for this. The suit's material does not reflect light. We will start by learning the composition of this fabric." He pointed to an open door. "Luko, you bring a pair of shears from the electronic equipment room and snip off a tiny piece from the cuff of the pants. I want to examine the helmet."

Petrov felt along the bottom of the helmet and found the opening for a head to slip through. Holding it open and under a light, he could see the inside. *That is reasonable*, he thought. *The inside does not absorb light because it is not normally exposed to light.* He could see a lining, and a band configuration for holding the helmet in place. He could also see the inside of the visor and special cavities where the ears fit.

Luko interrupted him. "I cannot cut the fabric, sir."

"Why not?"

"The shears simply do not cut it."

Bragg was eyeing the jacket and gloves. "We know it's bulletproof from all the news reports," he said. "Maybe it's *everything-proof.* . . . Look at these gloves. They look like handprints painted on the surface of the table."

He placed his own hand on top of one of the gloves as if to make sure it was really there.

"That is because they do not reflect light," said Petrov. "One cannot see the three-dimensional features of an object if that object does not reflect light. In fact, you are not seeing the gloves at all. You are simply experiencing the absence of light at that location."

Bragg picked up one of the gloves; then let it fall back to the table. Then he did the same thing again and grinned. He was obviously amused. "It's gonna be awfully tough to find out what this stuff is if we can't even see it."

"We will perform other tests," said Petrov. "As you know, I have a certain amount of expertise in the field of nanotechnology, and I am convinced that is what this suit employs."

He tried every test he could think of without learning anything more.

Actually, he *did* learn that nothing he had could penetrate the suit. After trying everything from acid to lasers—and finding nothing that affected the suit—he tried putting it on. Even though he was smaller than Hawker, he encountered difficulties trying to get it on over his clothes. Bragg informed him that Hawker didn't wear clothing underneath.

"Ah. . . . That makes sense," he said. "His skin would have to be in contact with sensors throughout the suit. I should have thought of that."

He took the suit into the electronic equipment room, removed his clothes and tried again. When he came out wearing the suit, Luko was briefly startled. He recoiled slightly and said, "You look like a shadow."

"That's exactly the way Hawker looked," said Bragg.

Petrov tried to talk to Bragg and Luko, but his voice was muffled and they couldn't understand him. He eventually removed the helmet and said, "Apparently, Hawker was telling the truth."

Bragg said, "I'm curious. I understand your scientific interest in the suit, but what other plans do you have for it? I know you're not gonna let something that powerful lay around and go to waste."

Petrov looked directly at Bragg and said, "Perhaps I should ask you a question, Mr. Bragg. I'm curious about how much of your loyalty still remains with the United States."

"My loyalty lies with the person who is paying me," said Bragg. "I don't owe the United States anything . . . especially not now."

Petrov studied Bragg for a few seconds; then a sly smile crept across his face. "The Americans are so proud of their new hero. What do you suppose the reaction from the rest of the world would be if that hero suddenly went on a rampage and began committing mass murders in the countries of America's allies?"

Bragg nodded. "I think I get the picture. But, of course, you would be the one in the hero's suit."

"Or possibly Luko," said Petrov. "I have no experience with committing violence, but he does."

"Except the suit doesn't work for you," said Bragg. "What now?"

As he headed for the other room to remove the suit, Petrov said, "I think it is time for us to lean heavier on Professor Hawker." Then he stopped and said, "Did I say that correctly?"

"It was close enough," said Bragg.

After Teala had read parts of several papers to Hawker she stopped and said, "He killed three people in that room where we were."

Hawker nodded. "I've heard enough. We need to get this information to Mrs. Bradshaw."

He removed his jacket and pulled up his sleeve. Teala was grinning at where he had concealed the phone. "It may not work in between these metal buildings," he said. "I sure hope it does. I would hate to do this out in the open."

He pressed the "FL" button and was half-surprised when the First Lady answered. "I'm impressed with this phone you gave me," he said.

"I had it made special for you," she responded.

"How long have you been planning this?"

Mrs. Bradshaw chuckled. "I'm teasing. It *is* a very special phone, but you aren't the only person who has one. What's your situation now?"

"We escaped from the building where we were being held, but we're still inside the security fence of the pharmaceutical plant. I don't know how difficult it'll be to get out. We have the evidence you wanted, but you need to go ahead and act on it now without waiting to see it."

"Why?"

"Because I'm afraid that when Petrov discovers we have his files, he'll go ahead and unleash his killing machine on those people that have already been vaccinated."

"What action are you suggesting that I take?"

"Shoot down a satellite," said Hawker.

"What?" the First Lady exclaimed. "What does that have to do with the vaccine?"

"Petrov has synthesized molecules that he calls nanomachines. Those nanomachines have been added to the vaccine. They're undetectable because they're exactly what you would expect to see in a vaccine. After injection into a person's body, they lie dormant until they receive an external signal. They then attach themselves to the body's immune cells and confuse them. They basically tell the immune cells that all of the other cells in the body are diseased, so the immune cells systematically kill every cell in the body. . . . That is . . . until the body stops functioning. That must be a tough way to die. . . . Anyway, that external signal I mentioned comes from an orbiting satellite."

There was a pause at the other end. Finally Mrs. Bradshaw said, "That sounds complicated. The guy must be a genius."

"Yeah," said Hawker. "A *mad* genius."

The First Lady was silent again for a second; then said, "If you were worried about starting a war with Iran, just imagine how much worse it would be to start one with Russia. I'm assuming the satellite you're talking about is Russian."

"It is," said Hawker. "We have a letter giving Petrov permission to place an experiment aboard a satellite that was launched this past April. That experiment is actually a transmitter in disguise. We have enough evidence in these four folders to prove conclusively what he's doing. The transmitter on the satellite has to be triggered from here, so you need to call the Russian president and have this guy arrested before he can send that signal. When the Russians understand why you want to destroy their satellite I'm sure they'll agree that it needs to be done."

"In a simpler world, maybe. But unfortunately, we don't live in that simpler world. Our relations with Russia aren't that good. They don't trust us. On top of that, they're trying to regain the prestige they lost at the end of the Cold War. They would be afraid of what the world would think of them if they allowed the United States to shoot down one of their satellites. No. . . . I don't believe they would okay it. . . . And we certainly couldn't do it without their okay."

Hawker was incredulous. "Does that mean you're not even going to try? You could ask them to destroy it. That wouldn't damage their prestige."

"We could work on that angle, and we can try to convince the Russian authorities to arrest Petrov before he can act. But if we do either of those things it would tie you and us to what you're probably going to have to do."

"What do you mean?"

"Well if it's as urgent as you say, you'll have to handle it on that end."

"I'm not quite sure what you're suggesting, but I'm a little limited without my suit."

"You seem to have done okay without it so far. Besides, you're a physics professor. I'm sure you know how to make things go *boom*."

Hawker took a second to grasp what she had said. "Why would that be any less of an act of war than shooting down a satellite?"

"Because you don't work for the U.S. government. And if you get caught, we'll disavow any knowledge of you. You'll be a disgruntled American acting on your own."

"Wonderful." After a short silence, he asked, "How would you explain the fact that you arranged for my visa and made my hotel reservations?"

"The White House can't be connected to that. It was a backdoor operation."

Hawker went silent again. After a few seconds, he said, "Mrs. Bradshaw, I think I should tell you that I'm beginning to doubt the workability of our relationship. It sounds like you're trying to turn me into a terrorist."

"Let's get something straight, Professor. I know you won't kill anyone unless you have no other choice. Apparently, I have more faith in you than you do in me. I have faith that you will find a way to handle this without harming anyone. That's why I asked you to do it instead of sending our own people. Now consider the alternatives. We do nothing and thousands of our people die. We shoot down their satellite and risk starting a war that would cause death on a scale that we can't even imagine. Or, you find a way to destroy the vaccine making equipment and the ground-based electronic equipment that Petrov will have to use." She paused a couple of seconds; then added, "Now which of those options would *you* choose?"

"I guess you're right," said Hawker. And he disconnected without saying goodbye.

"What was all that?" asked Teala.

Hawker hung his head. "They're not going to do anything. We'll have to do it."

"What can *we* do?"

"We'll have to destroy Petrov's equipment. But even if we manage to do that, it won't be the end of the threat. He can get more equipment, or he could have it already in a different location as a backup. The only way to end the threat is to get rid of that satellite. But for now, we need to make sure he can't send a signal to it."

He moved the cart forward enough to provide a view of the main building and the employee parking lot. "We won't be able to do anything until all those workers leave for the day. That should happen pretty soon. I sure hope they don't have a night shift coming on immediately after the day shift ends."

They watched silently for a minute; then Hawker said, "I was wrong about something. Getting rid of the satellite wouldn't end the threat . . . not as long as Petrov is alive and running free."

"I wonder what made him turn bad," said Teala. "With his knowledge of how to control immune cells he could have been world-famous. Just imagine the good he could have done toward combating disease."

"That's true. But hate is a powerful force. Some people just need something or somebody to hate . . . somebody to blame for the things that are wrong in their life."

"I know you're right," agreed Teala. "I've run into some of those people, but you'd think somebody as intelligent as Petrov wouldn't need to play the *blame* game." She hesitated; then added, "Bragg blames you for the death of his former partner."

"I didn't know his partner was dead."

"He said that you leaving him on that island is what killed him. He called you a *Sunday School Christian*."

"How is a *Sunday School Christian* different from any other Christian?"

"I don't know, but I don't think he intended it to be a compliment." After a short hesitation, she looked at him and asked, "Do you consider yourself to be a Christian?"

Surprised by the question, Hawker thought about it for a second; then answered, "I don't know. I *do* try to be a good person, but that's because it's the right thing to do . . . and *not* because I'm bucking for a seat in Heaven after I die. Is that an acceptable philosophy in Christianity?"

She gave him a strange look. "Well you do believe in God, don't you?"

He sure hoped this wasn't going to lead to one of those controversial discussions that had caused them problems in the past.

"I would have to qualify my answer on that too," he said. "Your concept of God might not be the same as mine. There's a huge difference between the *true* creator of the universe and the one that was invented by man."

"Invented by man? . . ." Their conversation was suddenly interrupted.

He was pointing to their left toward the end of the main building next to the parking lot. "Look. . . . They're leaving. Let's hope the office personnel are also in that group."

A string of people was exiting the building through a door not visible to Hawker.

Teala instinctively glanced to her right, in the direction of Petrov's residence but, of course, couldn't see it because one of the metal buildings blocked the view. "I wonder if Petrov has discovered the dead guard yet," she said.

"I doubt it. Things are too quiet."

They continued watching until the stream of cars exiting the parking lot was gone. Cars were still parked on the lot, but it was impossible to tell what that meant.

"I'm afraid to take you with me," said Hawker. "But I'm also afraid to leave you alone."

"I'll settle that *for* you," she said. "I'm going where *you* go."

He smiled at her and started to move the cart forward.

"Wait," she said. "Somebody's coming out that back door."

Hawker watched as Petrov, Bragg and Luko filed through the door and climbed aboard the other golf cart. He hadn't noticed the cart sitting there until now. "They're still carrying my bag," he said. "I wonder what they learned about the suit."

Teala remarked, "That door must lead to his lab."

"Yeah. We'll try it first . . . as soon as they're out of sight."

As Hawker parked the cart next to the door where Petrov and company had exited, he said, "Bring those folders with you. We don't want to take a chance on losing them."

"I hope it's enough to get us out of jail," she said as she followed him up the steps.

He tried the door and found it unlocked. Cautiously pushing it open, he peered inside. What he saw was a large laboratory but no people. They stepped inside and looked around. "This is definitely a lab," said Hawker. He pointed to an open door on their right. "I wonder what that room is."

Teala walked over and glanced inside. "It's filled with electronic equipment," she said.

Hawker joined her. After a cursory inspection, he said, "Yep. This is the stuff we have to destroy." He turned back to the main lab and scanned the equipment placed neatly about the room. He recognized most of it. Another door on the opposite side of the room held a universal symbol for hazardous material, but he couldn't read the wording. He assumed that was where they stored chemicals and other supplies. After checking the room including a large refrigerator, he turned back to Teala who was following his every step. "Those Bunsen burners out there give me an idea. Let's look for the main gas valve."

They had no difficulty finding the gas valve. It was located on the same wall as the room they had just exited, but toward the outside wall, beyond a workbench and a sink. Hawker opened the valve and said, "I'm gonna check those Bunsen burners to make sure they all have gas running to 'em. I would like you to plug up this deep sink and open the faucet about halfway. Note the time when you do. I want to determine how long it takes to fill."

Using a welder's lighter that was lying next to one of the burners, he lit each of the six Bunsen burners that were located on various workbenches around the lab; then turned them off again and yanked the gas supply hoses loose.

He had seen several items in the electronic equipment room that he would need. Someone had been working on an electronic frequency counter and had removed its metal back plate. There was also a piece of Styrofoam packing material on the floor next to the bench holding the frequency counter. He made a beeline for those items, grabbed a pair of wire strippers from the tool board over the workbench and snipped off the frequency counter's power cord. Then he stripped an inch of insulation from the end of each wire. With the metal plate, the power cord and piece of Styrofoam in hand, he headed for the door, but then turned back to the tool board and grabbed a tubing cutter also.

As he placed his items on the workbench adjoining the sink, he noted that the sink was only about half full. "How long did that take?" he asked.

"Five minutes," said Teala.

"Good. That sounds about right. Turn off the water and unplug the sink. We have to check the building for people. I also need to find the furnace room."

As they headed for the door, he added, "Think Russian. I need you to come up with a phrase that will warn anybody still here that they need to get out."

They left through the door on the opposite side of the lab from where they had entered. That put them in a hallway that ran almost the length of the building.

The building was in the shape of an el, with the hallway running along its front. There was nowhere for them to go to the right so they turned left. The outside wall of the hallway—which was also the front of the building—was now on their right. It contained plate glass windows and provided a view of what appeared to be a picnic area and a couple of smaller buildings. Also, in the distance—and looking between the small buildings—one could see the main gate. The wall on their left was lined with doors leading to offices.

Fortunately, all of the office doors contained glass panels making it easy to determine that the offices did not contain people. The hallway terminated at the entrance to the other leg of the el.

Hawker cautiously peered into that area before entering and saw no one. It was a long room running lengthwise toward the main gate. A long structure appearing to be some kind of assembly line ran along the center of the room and smaller work stations bordered it along the sides. At the end of the room where he was standing were two more doors. He held his forefinger vertically across his lips to signal Teala to be quiet; then cautiously opened each of the doors.

Finding no people, he said, "This is obviously where they produce the vaccine and that other door is the furnace room I was looking for." He took the tubing cutter he had brought along and placed it on the floor by the furnace; then closed the gas valve to starve the pilot light flame.

Teala had peered through the door to see what he was doing. He took her by the arm and said, "Come on. I don't know how long our luck is gonna hold. We need to do this while nobody's in the building. I'm sure Petrov knows by now that we've escaped. They'll be looking for us."

As they hurried along the hallway back to the lab, he briefly outlined for Teala the steps they were about to take.

In the lab, Teala went straight to the sink and again plugged the drain. She then turned on the water and placed the piece of Styrofoam down in the sink so that it floated on the surface of the water. Hawker grabbed a lamp from another bench and plugged it into the electrical outlet by the sink to make sure power was available there. Satisfied about the power, he placed the thin metal plate on top of the Styrofoam that Teala had already put in the sink.

He then took the power cord that he had clipped from the frequency counter and laid it on the workbench so that the bare wires dangled over the sink. After placing a weight on the power cord to hold it in place, he plugged it into the electrical outlet.

He explained to Teala, "In about seven minutes, when the water in the sink is high enough, the metal plate will touch the bare electrical wires creating a spark. By that time, the lab will be filled with gas . . . as will the entire building . . . because we're gonna cut the gas line in the furnace room after we open all the gas valves in here. I'm sure you know what's gonna happen when the spark ignites the gas."

She nodded.

Carefully gripping the wire by its insulation, he bent it a bit more.

"Okay, let's go," he said. He pointed to the Bunsen burners across the room. "You open those three valves on your way out and I'll get the three over here."

They hurried toward the hallway door, opening the valves as they went. Leaving the door standing open, they ran down the hallway and through the door at the end.

He said to Teala, "You stay by this door and keep it closed until I come out of the furnace room. Then open it and make a mad dash for that outside door which I'm going to open now."

He hurried across the room and opened the outside door that led to the parking lot; then went back to the furnace room and used the tubing cutter he had left there earlier to cut the copper gas line. He then opened the gas valve again and beat a hasty retreat.

As he emerged from the furnace room he yelled to Teala, "Okay, open that door and let's get out of here."

He waited for her to run past; then fell in behind. They were almost to that open door leading to the parking lot when Luko walked in.

When they found the dead guard's body, Petrov rebuked Bragg, saying, "I should not have listened to you. This Hawker is obviously very different from what you led me to believe. It is clear from this that he *does* have the stomach for killing. It is also clear that his brain does not travel in such a slow lane after all. Now get out there and find him. They could not have gone very far. Check with the guards at the main gate and check the parking lot. He might be trying to steal a car."

Driving the golf cart they had used earlier, Luko dropped Bragg at the edge of the parking lot and continued on to the main gate. The guards assured him that no one other than the plant workers had passed through the gate. As he was returning to the parking lot to rejoin Bragg, he noticed that the production room door was standing open. He pulled the cart close to the door and peered inside. Seeing nothing, he parked the cart to one side and entered the building for a closer look. That's when Teala and Hawker almost ran into him.

When they saw him, they stopped in their tracks. He already had his gun in his hand, so he leveled it at them without saying anything.

"You can't use that gun in here," yelled Hawker. "This place is full of gas. It's about to blow."

"What does 'to blow' mean?" asked Luko.

Hawker put his hands together; then rapidly moved them apart. "Go boom. Explode."

Luko looked at the file folders Teala was still carrying. "What have you there?" He moved closer to them, but kept well out of Hawker's reach.

Hawker was becoming anxious. "Don't you smell that gas, Luko? I'm telling you we need to get out of here."

Luko held his empty hand out toward Teala. "Give me the folders."

She looked at Hawker and he nodded. "Give 'em to 'im." To Luko, he said, "We're leaving, Luko. If you fire that gun in here you'll kill us all. It'll ignite the gas."

Luko began sniffing and darting his eyes back and forth. Apparently, he had just begun to smell the gas. "Where does gas come from?" he asked.

"The Bunsen burners in the lab," replied Hawker. He took Teala by the arm and said, "Come on. He won't shoot us."

They started running for the open door again.

Luko headed the other way toward the lab. He heard Hawker yell to him to come back, but he ignored it. The smell of gas became stronger and he broke into a run.

The door to the lab was standing open, but Luko stopped anyway and peered inside before he entered. All six valves for the Bunsen burners were open just as Hawker had said. Luko rushed toward the line of valves on his right, attempting to close them on the run. He missed the second one and had to stop and back up. When those three were closed he rushed across the room to the valves on the other side. He slowed down a bit and was more careful.

The last valve he closed was in the corner by the wall adjoining the hallway. When his task was finished, he began easing along the benches toward the opposite wall, which was the outside wall containing the outside door. He was thinking to himself: *What was Hawker doing? What was he trying to accomplish by filling the place with gas. He said the place was going to explode, but he would need a spark to cause an explosion. How would he generate a spark from outside the building?*

Then for the first time, his ears picked up the sound of running water. *Why would water be running in here?* he thought. He followed the sound to the sink on the other side of the room. That's when he saw electrical wires dangling over the edge of the sink and a metal plate floating on the surface of the water just a hairsbreadth below the wires. It took a second for the reality of what he was seeing to register. Then he froze: He was torn between running for the sink and running for the outside door. The outside door was much closer, but he would have to stop and open it. After wasting precious time, he rushed for the door.

As Hawker and Teala ran through the outside door, Hawker had looked back and seen that Luko was headed for the lab instead of following them. He yelled to Luko to come back, but Luko ignored him, so he stopped and told Teala to head for the parking lot. She grabbed his arm and said, "You can't go back in there."

He watched Luko for a split second; then closed the door and said, "You're right. I warned him. Go."

They headed for the parking lot, but saw Bragg coming toward them. "Jump on the golf cart," said Hawker.

They rounded the corner of the building with as much speed as Hawker could coax from the cart; then made a beeline for the smaller buildings where they had been parked while talking with the First Lady. Expecting to hear the boom any second, he steered the cart through the same passageway between the buildings. The boom didn't happen.

He looked at Teala and said, "Luko might have found our homemade spark timer."

He wheeled back onto the same perimeter road he had used before and eased along until he could see the main building again. Bragg was approaching the door where Hawker and Teala had first entered Petrov's lab. The other golf cart they had left there was probably the reason.

Hawker yelled, "Bragg, get back. It's gonna blow."

Bragg gave no indication that he had heard.

At that instant, the door came open and Hawker could see Luko trying to come out. But Luko ran into Bragg who was trying to go in. Then came the wave of fire. It blew through the door and engulfed Bragg and Luko and was followed immediately by the boom. The walls flew outward and the roof flew upward, sending debris in all directions.

Hawker and Teala watched in horror. They had just roasted two men alive. They temporarily forgot that those two men were planning to kill them as well as countless others. They couldn't move at first; they just sat and watched the flames and smoke. Then out of the corner of his eye, Hawker saw Petrov running from his residence toward the burning building. Hawker immediately accelerated the cart toward Petrov.

Petrov saw Hawker coming and changed his direction. He now ran toward the main gate, presumably for the protection the guards could provide.

Hawker stopped. He had realized that none of the three bad guys had been carrying his canvas bag. This might be his chance to regain possession of his suit. Considering the situation they were in, that was probably their only means of escape. He accelerated instead toward Petrov's residence and skidded to a halt barely in time to avoid a collision. "Come on," he said to Teala.

They rushed inside and straight to Petrov's office. The door stood open and there on the desk sat his canvas bag. He unzipped the bag and turned it upside down. The suit fell out. He smiled at Teala and said, "We may get out of this yet."

He began stripping off his clothes and handed his jacket and pants to Teala. "You put my jacket and pants on over your clothes. It's gonna be cold where you're going. Put on my socks too . . . and look around for a hood and gloves."

It wasn't until he put on the helmet that he knew something was wrong.

The suit didn't respond. He removed the helmet and gave Teala a helpless look.

"I couldn't find gloves or anything else," she said.

He shook his head. "It may not matter. It doesn't work. Somebody must have tried to use it."

"Bragg put on the helmet back at your house."

Hawker frowned. "I guess that was enough unless they tried again in the lab. Alex said they would disable it if anybody else tried to use it."

He looked up toward the ceiling and added, "Alex, ole buddy. This would be a really good time for you to be monitoring my thoughts."

Teala instinctively glanced toward the ceiling. "Who's Alex?"

Hawker hesitated briefly, wondering how much he should say. "One of the guys that developed the suit," he eventually answered. "I guess he's a guy. I've never seen him."

Teala looked puzzled. "I thought you developed the suit."

Then they heard the sirens. "We'd better try to find a back door," said Hawker. "They'll be coming through the front one very soon. Bring my shirt. We may need it."

"What about your shoes?"

"Leave 'em."

Wearing the suit and carrying the helmet in his hand, Hawker hurried along the hallway toward where they had left the dead guard earlier. Suddenly, the front door noisily swung open.

Hawker grabbed Teala by the arm and pulled her around the corner to the right, away from the area where they had been held captive. "Try not to make any noise," he said. He opened the first door on his right, but it turned out to be a closet.

As he turned toward another door on the left, he heard the phone signal coming from his helmet. He looked at Teala and saw that she understood what that meant.

The suit had been re-enabled. "Get ready," he said.

He hastily donned the helmet and sealed the flaps around his neck; then lifted Teala into his arms and kicked open that door without bothering to check its status. The room was a bedroom with an outside door and two windows. As he headed for the door, he said to Teala, "Remember to maintain a firm grip on my wrist."

She nodded and gripped his wrist.

Again, without bothering to check the lock, he raised a foot and slammed it into the door. With a loud crashing sound, the door came completely free of its framework and fell to the ground outside.

"I thought you wanted me to be quiet," said Teala.

"That was before," he said, as he sped through the opening he had made. Once outside, he bent his knees and activated the antigravity feature; then propelled the two of them into the twilit sky.

chapter 4

Complete darkness had descended upon them by the time they landed again.

"Where are we?" asked Teala.

"I think about fifty miles west of Moscow," answered Hawker. "I don't know exactly. I needed an unoccupied area to do some planning, and this looked like a good spot."

"I'm glad *you* can see in the dark, because I sure can't see much."

"Yeah . . . the night-vision feature built into my visor comes in handy."

"And I still get freaked out by your computer-generated voice and lack of a face," she continued. "But I'm glad you told me to put on your clothes. It *does* get cool up there." She hesitated; then added, "But you know what . . . I couldn't have worn gloves anyway."

"You could have worn one. It only takes one hand to make good electrical contact. That's one of the things we'll take care of while we're on the ground. After you take your grip this next time, we'll wrap my shirt around your hand. That'll help to keep it warm. . . . Also, you should know that we'll be in the air several hours on this next flight. If you need to tinkle, you should do it now."

"Yeah . . . I guess it *would* be tough stopping in the middle of the ocean."

"We're not gonna be over an ocean," he said.

"Aren't we going home?" she asked.

"Not on this leg. We'll be lucky if we make it to Belarus before we have to land again."

"Belarus? Isn't that the country right next to Russia?"

"Yeah."

"Why don't we just go home? I thought you said you could fly all the way from Florida to Iraq in four hours."

"That's when I'm alone and inside this protective suit. Do you have any idea what a two-thousand-mile-an-hour wind would do to your body?"

"Oh."

"I'm just trying to get you safely out of Russia for right now. When we get to Belarus we'll call Mrs. Bradshaw again and try to arrange for you to go to the American embassy in Minsk."

"Hold it right there, buddy. I don't like the way that sounds. I'm going where you go."

"You can't, Teala. I have to get home fast and find a way to disable that satellite before Petrov can get new equipment set up. It would take over a week at the speeds I have to fly when I'm carrying you."

"Well you can just put that scientist brain of yours to work and come up with a different plan, because you're not leaving me alone over here."

He squirmed. He knew she was right. He had even promised himself that he would never take a chance with her safety again. He owed it to her to make sure she got home safely. "We'll talk about it again after I get some sleep. I haven't slept in more than two days."

"I guess you think I slept like a baby while I was being held prisoner."

"No. . . . I didn't mean to imply that. I know it's been tough for you and I'm gonna try to make sure nothing like that happens again. But you're beginning to sound like that Teala I was tutoring ten years ago."

"Sorry. . . . I guess we're both tired. What's the plan for tonight?"

"Give me that map from my inside jacket pocket. I wrote some coordinates on it that I'm gonna need. And while you're at it, give me my wallet and passport as well. They'll be safer in the tote pouches of my suit."

He turned on the light that was mounted above the visor of his helmet. She handed him the items he had requested and said, "It's a good thing you turned on that light. I couldn't see you at all."

It was easy for him to temporarily forget that the suit automatically stopped reflecting light each time he entered the flight mode. He gave the thought command "reflect light" and said, "Is that better?"

She answered, "A little." She still couldn't see much other than the light and the map that it illuminated, but that was better than nothing at all.

He said, "We'll fly on to Belarus and try to find a warm place to sleep. Maybe I'll be thinking better in the morning."

"I suppose a nice comfortable hotel would be out of the question."

"You need an internal passport to rent a room in Belarus. Besides, considering the close relationship they have with Russia, it wouldn't be wise to take a chance like that. In this country, we are now terrorists and criminals. We've killed three men today."

"*They* were the criminals. Russia should be glad to be rid of 'em."

"I agree. But unfortunately, that isn't the way things work. In our favor, however, is the fact that Petrov wouldn't want much of an investigation. It's possible that he didn't tell the authorities about you and me."

She nodded. "I think that's the more likely scenario."

"The bottom line though, is that we don't know what he told 'em, and without the proper credentials, we're just gonna have to rough it tonight." He hesitated; then added, "I know you're cold, but we really need to get out of Russia."

"Okay," she said. "Give me five minutes."

Three hours and twenty minutes later, Hawker's GPS indicated that they were crossing into Belarus airspace. He immediately began scanning for a suitable place to spend the night. He would have to find it soon or his bladder would force him to land anyway. He was surprised that Teala had not yet complained.

She had turned up the collar on his much-too-large jacket and had pulled it up to shield her face and ears from the cold wind. They had also wrapped his shirt around the hand that was maintaining electrical contact to keep her weightless. And, of course, his pants legs hung down over her shoes. This was all in addition to her own clothing that she wore underneath. Even so, he knew she had to be cold.

En route, he had called Ben Huron back in Florida. Because of the time difference, it was the middle of the work day there. Hawker had explained the situation to Ben and asked for his help in finding a way to disable the deadly transmitter that Petrov had placed in the satellite. He knew if anyone could find a solution, it would be Ben: Most people would call Ben a genius. Ben promised to work on it and said how happy he was that Teala was safe.

With the night-vision feature of his visor, Hawker could see forests, farms, lakes and a river. He even saw a small village with dim lights sprinkled here and there. A lone building set well away from the village caught his attention. It didn't appear to be a home; more like a barn or some other storage structure. He doubted that people would be in it, but it might house animals. In any case, it looked like a possible refuge from the cold for Teala. He wasn't concerned about the cold for himself: His suit provided excellent protection against extreme temperatures of both varieties.

They landed by the building, and he felt Teala jerk and start shivering. "Where are we?" she asked.

"At some kind of storage building in Belarus," he answered.

"We're not close to the area that was contaminated by the Chernobyl fallout, are we?"

"No. That was at the *southern* edge of Belarus. We're well north of that."

"Well I'm cold."

He took her hand. "I know. Come on. I'm gonna see what's in this building."

There was no lock on the door. The building was filled with farm equipment, but no animals—at least none that could be seen.

"We're gonna sleep here," he said, as he closed the door. "So do what you have to do to get ready for bed."

"That's real funny," she said. "Where's the bed?"

She, of course, couldn't see him grin as he said, "I'm going to provide you with the ultimate in sleep comfort tonight."

"I've heard you use that expression before when you were talking about sleeping weightless."

"That's right. But tonight, we're both gonna sleep weightless."

He moved his light around, illuminating the objects and space near her so she wouldn't run into anything when he left her in the dark. "You wait here," he said. "I'm gonna look around for a piece of wire."

He used that opportunity to find a convenient spot and relieve himself. The time alone would allow Teala to do the same.

Fortunately, the owners of the building had coiled leftover wire of several varieties and hung it on the walls. After a suitable amount of time, he selected a piece and took it back to where he had left Teala. He used it to connect their wrists together to be sure they maintained good electrical contact during the night. Then after giving the thought command "degravitize" to make both of them weightless, he pulled her up close and tilted over backwards. They were now suspended a few feet above the floor with his back to Earth and her cuddled up in the fetal position on top of him. Both of his arms were wrapped around her, of course. She, again, pulled the collar of his jacket up around her ears and let his sleeves swallow her hands. Also, his pants legs completely covered her feet as they had before. Then he used the suit's propulsion system to move them higher into warmer air.

She joked about the intimate sleeping arrangement, but he explained that it was necessary. Although her body was weightless, all those clothes she was wearing were not. His body needed to be below hers to support the weight of the clothes. Otherwise, she would be sleeping on the floor with the rats.

Just before he fell asleep, he had the fleeting thought: *What if I dream something during the night that gives the suit a command?* He hadn't worried about that in Pakistan and Iraq because he had been alone and had secured himself to a tree.

They were both so tired—and so comfortable—that they fell asleep almost immediately. Teala was picking up a little heat from Hawker's suit, so even the cold wasn't a problem. They slept soundly there in the dark with the quiet of farm country around them and no unruly mattresses to contend with.

Hawker became aware of the sounds of several voices. Was he still dreaming or were the voices real? Somebody was yelling, "What are you doing in there? We have to prepare the firebreak."

Hawker opened his eyes and was looking at a very close ceiling. He slowly realized where he was. For some unknown reason, the suit had moved them upward during the night and Teala was now in contact with the ceiling.

The voice that had been yelling came closer. "What is going on? What is everybody looking at?"

Another voice said, "That strange looking shadow up there with the bundle of clothes. What is causing the clothes to stick to the ceiling in that manner?"

Still another voice said, "*And*, what is causing the shadow?"

Carrying Teala with him, Hawker rolled over and looked down. Several people were looking up at him. They shuffled backwards as he moved. He gently shook Teala and said, "Teala, wake up."

She slowly opened her eyes and was startled by the unfamiliar surroundings. She let out a muffled cry and attempted to jerk her body into an upright position.

Temporarily forgetting that his translator would not be speaking English, Hawker attempted to calm her. "Easy does it. Everything is okay. I'm gonna take us down."

She scolded him. "Why are you speaking Russian . . . or whatever that is?"

Her words switched the translator back to English.

"Calm down, Teala," he said. "You know how my translator works. The last language it heard is whatever *those* people are speaking."

"What people?"

He began moving them slowly downward and turned her so she could see the group of people gathered by the door. He also switched to the light-reflecting mode, hoping to present a friendlier appearance.

Needless to say, these events looked strange indeed to these farm people. Their talking stopped and they eased backwards through the door. They could now see the thing that had caused the shadow. It was bringing the bundle of clothes down, but why had they not been able to see it before?

As they neared the floor, Hawker said to Teala, "Brace yourself for the surge of gravity."

She had experienced this part several times before, so she knew what to do. It was just a matter of being balanced and leaving the knees so they could flex.

Hawker waited for someone to speak so that his translator would know what language to use. The man that had been doing the yelling was apparently a little less timid than the others. He moved past the group toward Hawker and Teala as Teala lowered the jacket collar, revealing her shoulder-length dark brown hair.

The man eyed them carefully. He did not appear to be afraid. "I have heard of you," he said. "But I cannot remember what it is that I have heard. Please tell me again why it is that you are able to float on air."

Hawker was somewhat relieved by the question: He was half-expecting something else.

He removed the wire from his wrist and answered, "My suit produces a field that shields me from gravity."

Speaking as if he understood exactly what Hawker was saying, the farmer said, "So *that* explains it." Then he looked at Teala as if wondering why her clothes did not look the same as Hawker's suit. "But why do you wear the suit and she does not?"

Hawker had become reluctant to give out too much information about the suit. He attempted an evasive answer. "I wear the suit so that I can do my job."

"And what is your job?" asked the man.

"I help people who are in trouble. Right now I'm trying to get this young lady back to her home."

The man smiled at Teala. "A very beautiful lady, even in baggy clothes."

"Actually, we could use *your* help," said Hawker. "We need some food."

"Food will be arriving here shortly," said the man. "We had to drag all these people out before they could eat this morning. They have to prepare a firebreak or our village will be destroyed."

"I could help with the firebreak in exchange for the food," offered Hawker.

The man began to get fidgety. "We welcome your help, but we would give you the food regardless. Forgive me, but we must take our tools and go. The fire is approaching rapidly."

"You mean there's a fire coming this way right now?"

"Of course. Why do you think we need a firebreak?"

"Good point. I didn't realize you had an existing fire. Maybe I can just put it out and then you won't need a firebreak."

The man gave a disbelieving laugh. "That would be quite a feat."

He beckoned with his hand to the people outside. "Come on in here and get your tools. These people mean you no harm."

Hawker stepped aside so that he would appear less threatening to the people coming in. "I'm serious about putting out the fire," he said. "But I'll need a very large metal container. Where could I find something like that?"

The farmer appeared to be annoyed that this stranger was keeping him from something more important. He stared at Hawker for a couple of seconds; then said, "I do not know of a very large metal container. There is a military equipment graveyard north of here. Perhaps you would find one there. But the fire will be here too soon for that to be of help."

"Where is the fire now?" Hawker asked.

"Do not worry," the farmer replied. "You will be able to see it." He started to leave; then stopped and pointed. "Here comes the food. I will tell the women to feed you. After you nourish yourselves, you may help us if you wish. We must get to work now."

Hawker turned to Teala and said, "Speak to me in English."

She didn't understand all of his words, but she knew that he wanted her to switch his translator back to English. "Did I hear the farmer say something about a fire?" she asked.

"Yes. Apparently one is headed this way. They're going to try to stop it with a fire break, but I'm gonna try to put it out before it gets here.

Will you be okay if I leave you here for a little while?"

"Sure. Go ahead, but while I'm thinking about it, maybe you should go get your shirt. We may need it again."

"Where is it?"

She pointed to the ceiling. "Up there. It snagged on something when we started down."

Hawker "degravitized" himself and pushed up gently with his toes to set him in motion; then activated the propulsion system for steerage. He retrieved his shirt and lowered himself gently back to the floor of the barn.

At that moment, two women came through the door carrying food. They had not been there earlier with the others and so had not seen Hawker and Teala before.

Hawker's suit had automatically stopped reflecting light when he activated the propulsion system. When the women saw him land and hand his shirt to Teala, they gasped. One of them started to turn around, but the other one stopped her. "Sergei said we must feed them."

With a look of dread on her face, the first woman said, "But how does a creature such as that eat. It has no mouth."

The other woman responded, "Then you will not have to worry about it biting you. Take it the food."

The woman slowly approached Hawker and reluctantly offered him food. As much as he wanted everything she was offering, he couldn't take off his helmet to eat it in their presence, so he selected some meat and bread that he could make into sandwiches. Then he stuffed a sandwich into each of his tote pouches. Because the suit was not reflecting light, the women couldn't see the opening of the pouches, so it appeared that the sandwiches had been absorbed into his legs.

The woman jumped back and gasped. "Did you see that?" she asked. "It consumed both sandwiches instantly . . . and it takes food in through its legs."

Her words had switched Hawker's translator back to the Belarusian language she was speaking. He grinned and said, "I'm just a man in a special suit. You need not fear me. I didn't eat the food. I stored it to eat later."

The farmer had been right: Hawker had no problem seeing where the fire was once he was outside. It was coming from the north, the same direction he was headed. Some of the farmers were still eating and others were already walking in that direction. They all looked up when they heard the swoosh sound pass overhead.

Sergei said, "Perhaps I was being too hasty when I dismissed his offer."

Hawker easily found the military equipment graveyard. It was due north of the barn just as the farmer had said. After determining that the place was completely deserted—and had been for some time—he removed his helmet and ate his sandwiches. His inspection had yielded no suitable containers lying around loose, so he needed to make some decisions while he ate. What he needed was something that would allow him to scoop up large quantities of water for dumping on the fire. The chosen container would have to be metal so that he could make it weightless. The water itself was electrically conductive, of course, so it would also become weightless. In fact, all of the water in the lake that he was planning to use would become weightless the instant he touched it. That in turn would reduce the ambient pressure on the wildlife residing in the lake. He hoped that would cause them no harm. He didn't believe it would because the reduction in pressure would be brief.

The metal aircraft hulls he had seen would require too much preparation and the missile nose cones were too small. Most of the other abandoned equipment held no promise at all, but there was a large water tank perched atop a wooden tower. It looked as though it would hold at least five hundred gallons. That would mean a lot of trips to the lake, but it wouldn't slow him down as much as would a larger container. In any case, it didn't look as if he had much choice. He had already killed almost ten minutes. He needed to get moving.

He regretted that he had to take the time to eat, but he also knew it was necessary. He was surprised that his failure to eat had not already made him weak.

He had made his decision. He finished off his food and took a drink from the nearby faucet; then replaced his helmet. *I hope that water isn't too polluted,* he thought.

The tank sitting atop the tower was part of a rainwater-gravity water supply system. The tank collected the rainwater and gravity supplied the pressure to force it through the lines. That meant the top of it was open which was exactly what he needed, but he would have to break it loose from the pipes and from the tower to which it was mounted. He began by yanking on the long metal pipe that ran from the ground up to the tank. It came loose at the tank and he figured a fitting must have broken. Next, he yanked one of the tower legs loose. The tower and tank toppled over, breaking another leg as it crashed against the ground, dumping the water he could have used. He quickly pried the wood fragments and other leg away from the tank and was ready to go.

Gripping the tank for the least wind resistance, he "degravitized" it; then kicked it and himself into the air. The trip back took a little longer because of the air resistance against the tank, but even with that, he had been gone only fifteen minutes.

He scooped a tank of water from the lake and flew directly over the area where the farmers were working. One could only guess what they were thinking when they saw that tank hurtling through the air with a shadow attached to it.

Starting with the flames closest to the village, he simultaneously tilted the tank and began a sweep along the fire line. Nothing happened: No water poured from the tank. He stopped and laughed at himself. Of course no water poured from the tank. For water to pour, gravity was required. He would have to use a method that didn't require gravity.

The water still possessed mass, of course, and would therefore be subject to inertia. He repositioned the tank so that it was to his side with the open end to his rear. Then, as he suddenly accelerated forward, inertia caused the water to stream out behind him and remain suspended in the air until the last of it had left the tank. With the water no longer touching the tank, the electrical connection between it and Hawker was broken. At that point, gravity took over and all of the water fell to the ground at the same time, dramatically extinguishing flames as it hit.

Hawker thought to himself: *This probably works better than pouring would have.*

The farmers had stopped what they were doing and were watching

Hawker. When they saw that long sheet of water suddenly appear in the sky and then drop onto the flames, they let out a cheer. They didn't understand how this was happening, but they knew it was good.

Hawker zipped back to the lake for another tank of water; then used the same technique to douse more of the flames. He repeated his feat many times over the next two hours, though after a time, he did switch to a nearby river for his source of water. By this time, many others had joined in the effort to extinguish the fire. It looked as though it was now well under control, so he went back to the barn to get Teala.

He placed the water tank outside the barn, thinking that the farmers might be able to use it. When he went inside, the two women who had brought the food were there, but Teala was not. When they saw him, they began talking excitedly about the miracle they had witnessed.

Hawker was starting to have an uneasy feeling. "Where is the lady that came here with me?" he asked.

One of the women answered, "The policeman took her."

That was the *last* thing Hawker wanted to hear. "What policeman? Somebody from your village?"

"No, no," replied the woman. "We have no policeman . . . only Sergei."

"Who is Sergei?"

Using a reproachful tone, the woman said, "The man you were speaking with earlier, of course."

Hawker's computer-generated voice wasn't capable of expressing emotion, but he was becoming anxious. "Who is the policeman that took my friend? Where did he take her?"

"His name is Alexandr Lukevsky. He is the head of police in Vistaya."

"Where is Vistaya?"

She pointed to the southwest.

"Is it the next village in that direction?"

"Yes. But it is not a village. It is a city."

"Why did the city police come here to get her? Did you call them?"

The woman looked hurt. "No. They did not come to get her. Alexandr was born in our village. He came to be sure we knew about the fire and to check on our preparations. She was a stranger, so he asked for identification. When she did not produce it, he took her with him."

Hawker thanked her and headed for the door.

The other woman smiled and said, "Do you not want more food?"

Anxious as he was, Hawker was practical enough to know that he should accept that offer. He took more meat and bread and stuffed it into his tote pouches; then thanked them again and left.

Less than five minutes later, he was hovering above what the woman had called a city. He would call it a town, but it was likely that she had never seen anything larger. He couldn't read the writing on the buildings so his only option was to look for a building with police cars parked around it. He flew along the streets scanning for something that looked like police markings. Some of the few people on the streets spotted him and began yelling to others.

Eventually, he spotted what appeared to be two police cars parked in front of a building at the end of a street. The building was two stories high and was one of the tallest in the immediate vicinity.

Hawker's helmet contained a miniaturized and much-improved version of the electronic listening devices used by the world's spy agencies. It allowed him to hear at a distance, through walls and it was directional. He disabled his translator to make it easy to recognize Teala's voice and floated around the building listening to the conversations going on inside. He didn't hear Teala's voice, and unfortunately, without his translator he didn't know what the other people were saying or who they were talking to.

The building had three front entrances and three widely separated doors at the rear. He figured it must be a multipurpose building. It also had a door at each end on the second floor that opened onto a small landing for a fire escape. He was surveying these possible entrance points and contemplating his next move when he noticed that he had attracted an audience. He decided that a direct approach was best at this point.

The police cars were in front of the entrance at the left, so he landed and approached that door. His audience was staying well back and watching his every move. Upon entering, Hawker found himself in a large open room with a counter at the front and three desks spread around behind it. The man at the counter was wearing a police uniform.

This must be the place.

Hawker activated his translator again and listened to the conversation going on at the counter. To his surprise, neither the man in the police uniform or the one in civilian clothes showed any alarm at his presence. Apparently they were expecting him.

Without waiting for them to finish their conversation, he asked, "Where is Alexandr Lukevsky?"

The man in the police uniform simply pointed to the desk in the center.

The desk was located just to the right of a set of stairs and was occupied by a partially bald man with a soft-looking face. Hawker approached the desk and asked the man sitting there if he was Alexandr Lukevsky. The man seemed to be in no hurry to acknowledge Hawker's presence. Eventually, however, he looked up from the paper he appeared to be reading and said, "Yes."

"I believe you are holding a friend of mine," said Hawker. "A young lady named Teala."

"So that is her name," Lukevsky responded. "She has been most uncooperative."

"She doesn't speak your language," said Hawker. "It's probably a communication problem."

Lukevsky gave a faint smile. "You speak my language very well, but your voice sounds strange."

"Because it's coming from inside this helmet," said Hawker.

"Ah, so."

"Now getting back to the lady," said Hawker. "You can turn her over to me and I will get her out of your country."

Lukevsky shook his head. "I cannot do that. She does not have proper papers for travel in our country. It will take some time to process her."

"I don't have proper papers either," said Hawker. "So what?"

Lukevsky grinned. "That is different. You are an international celebrity. I know about you."

"Then take my word for it. She has broken no laws in your country. You have no reason to hold her."

"Oh, but she has broken laws in this country. Being here with no passport, visa, or identification of any type is breaking the law. Furthermore, for all I know, she could have been involved in that mysterious explosion at the pharmaceutical plant near Moscow. We have an agreement with our Russian brothers to cooperate in the apprehension and retention of criminals and terrorists."

"I assure you that she is neither a criminal nor a terrorist. And you will just cause unnecessary problems for yourself as well as others if you hold her simply because she doesn't have identification."

Lukevsky raised his eyebrows. "Is that a threat of some sort?"

"At this point, I'm just trying to reason with you."

Lukevsky stood and let out a sigh. "In any case, I am not personally holding her. She is being processed by others and someone will be coming from Minsk to question her. All of this will take time."

Hawker thought to himself: *I can't let that happen.*

He had been scanning the room, getting the layout of the place without Lukevsky's knowledge since Lukevsky couldn't see his face and didn't know where his eyes were directed. He briefly turned off his translator again to listen for Teala's voice, but still didn't hear it. He would be willing to bet she was here, though.

He reactivated his translator in time to hear Lukevsky say, "Rebels that have been operating in Russia are now infiltrating our borders. They seek to destabilize our government in any way they can. They probably started the fire that you helped extinguish."

Hawker was glad to hear him acknowledge the help with the fire. "I wondered about that," he said. "I would not have thought that wildfires would be a problem for you considering your cold, wet climate."

"You are correct about what our climate normally is, but this past year has been the hottest and driest on record. Still, the fire would not have started without human intervention."

Hawker wondered what he had missed—why Lukevsky was telling him about the rebels.

Lukevsky continued, "You have special methods and skills that the rest of us do not possess. It would be very helpful and we would be very grateful if you were to help us apprehend these criminals."

"I would love to help you," said Hawker. "But I have pressing business elsewhere."

Lukevsky again raised his eyebrows. "I simply thought you might want to speed up the processing of your lady friend."

"You use that word 'process' a lot. Just what kind of processing is she undergoing? If you want my cooperation, harming her in any way will guarantee that you won't get it."

"I assure you that she is not being harmed."

"I hope you understand that I will not allow her to be held unjustly and used as a pawn."

"Does that mean *you* will use the same heavy-handed tactics that your government *always* uses to solve problems?"

"I am not 'government,'" countered Hawker.

"That is what they all say."

"They all 'who,' say that?"

"The spies, the agents . . . the troublemakers your government sends out. When will you people learn that your foreign policy is what causes many of your problems?"

"Like I told you . . . I am not a spy or an agent for any government. Besides, U.S. foreign policy has changed dramatically since the new president took office." He didn't bother to tell Lukevsky that the president's wife—and not the president—was responsible for the change.

"That remains to be seen," said Lukevsky. "He has been president only a few months. Perhaps he will yet do to Iran what the previous president did to Iraq."

Hawker had long ago become annoyed. Now his anxiety to get on to the problem of the deadly satellite was arousing his anger. His computer-generated voice, though, spoke without revealing his anger. "I have an urgent problem to deal with in the United States. I would be happy to come back here and help you with your problem after I finish with my own."

He moved closer, hoping Lukevsky would see that he meant business. "Now I insist that you give me the lady and let me be on my way."

Lukevsky shrugged his shoulders. "It is out of my hands. I told you . . . she is being processed . . ."

Hawker realized that he was getting nowhere with his present approach. He turned off his translator and scanned the upstairs sections with his enhanced hearing, totally ignoring what Lukevsky was saying. Not hearing Teala's voice there, he continued his sweep along the back wall of the room he was in. Then he heard her—just a couple of words before she stopped speaking, but it was enough.

A heavy door with a small barred window at eye level was located just left of the stairs next to Lukevsky's desk. The rest of that southern wall all the way to the eastern wall was blank. The directional feature of Hawker's enhanced hearing placed Teala's voice well left of the heavy door. It was time to end the discussion with Lukevsky.

He enabled his translator again in time to hear Lukevsky say, ". . . higher authority."

Hawker had no idea what Lukevsky had been saying, but he also didn't care. "Maybe I should go check on that fire," he said. "I wouldn't want it to get out of control again."

Leaving a puzzled Lukevsky standing by his desk, Hawker turned and exited the building. His audience was still there, apparently waiting to see what would happen next. He attempted to mislead them by abruptly flying away to the northeast. It took him only a minute to verify that the fire was under control. Then he flew a wide arc to the east and approached Vistaya from the south. That brought him back to the rear of the building where Teala was being held. Fortunately, the building was at the southern edge of the town. Although there were homes beyond that point, he saw no people.

He had noticed earlier before he entered the building that the upstairs door at the east end had no handle on the outside. It was there only for getting out in case of emergencies. Furthermore, it might have an alarm that went off when it was opened. His only options for entering close to where Teala was located consisted of the back door on the ground floor and windows on the second floor. He quickly ruled out the back door, fearing that his presence would be immediately detected.

Hovering weightless outside the second floor windows on the backside of the building, he carefully peered inside. The last window toward the east end of the building revealed an unoccupied office. The window was in two sections such that it could be opened by sliding the bottom section up. But the bottom section slid up inside the top section and there was no way to get a grip on it without breaking the glass, which he was trying to avoid because of the noise it would make. There was also a channel in the casing that would allow the upper section to slide downward. He placed the fingertips of his right hand in that channel and took a grip on the casing and then braced with his feet against the inside of the casing on the opposite side.

With his body wedged in place he used his left hand to push against both window frames where they overlapped near the casing. As he pushed, he visualized the frames moving slowly inward, quietly forcing the casing material out of the way. The visualization constituted a thought command and the suit responded by greatly enhancing his muscle strength allowing him to do exactly what he was visualizing. The destruction of the casing caused some noise, of course, but nothing really noticeable outside the closed-up room. When enough of the casing material had been pushed aside he slid each section of the window to the right and placed it gently on the floor inside. Then he floated himself into the room.

Remaining weightless to avoid making footstep sounds, he zipped across the room to the only door, which he assumed opened to a hallway. His assumption was confirmed when he opened the door and stuck only the top part of his head outside. To his left were more doors on both sides of the hall, and beyond those doors he could see the beginning of a stairwell. That would have to be the set of stairs he had seen near Lukevsky's desk on the ground floor. To his right, the hallway ended abruptly at the fire escape door, but next to that door was another inside stairwell. He hadn't seen stairs at that location on the ground floor. That would mean that they terminated behind the wall he had been listening through when he heard Teala's voice.

The entire surface area of Hawker's suit, with the exception of the helmet, was capable of ejecting propulsion particles. That allowed him to move in any direction with any body orientation. He eased his entire body into the hallway in the upright position and moved sideways toward the stairwell by the fire escape door, while glancing back and forth in both directions. Reaching the stairwell unobserved, he floated downward without touching the steps.

His luck still held when he reached the ground floor. He encountered another hallway, but this one had only one door on the right. It was located close to the other end of the hall and was the heavy door he had seen while standing near Lukevsky's desk earlier. Just beyond that door a uniformed man sat at a desk and was apparently reading or doing paperwork. The entire left wall of the hallway—as far as he could see—consisted of metal bars.

Hawker thought to himself: *Oh man, I hope they're not holding her in a cell behind metal bars. She'll be in a knock-down-drag-out fighting mood.* But even as he had the thought, he knew that would have to be the case.

Remaining in the weightless mode, he eased around the corner and found Teala in the first cell. When she saw him she started to speak, but instead slapped her hand over her mouth. She had quickly realized that he was there without the knowledge of the police.

Keeping a constant vigil toward the man at the desk, Hawker gripped one of the bars with both hands and pulled his knees toward his chest. Then he placed both feet on another bar and visualized them pushing that bar away from him, bending it in the process. The bar bent as visualized, creating an opening large enough for Teala to squeeze through.

Hawker had made no noise and the man at the desk still hadn't looked up. Teala slid between the bars, still wearing Hawker's baggy clothes. She knew the drill, so as he swept her into his arms she gripped his wrist for electrical contact. As that was happening, the man at the desk finally looked up and saw them. He let out a yell, but before he could even stand up, Hawker and Teala were zipping upward through the stairwell, again without touching the steps.

When they reached the second floor, a couple of people were running toward them. Hawker immediately turned his back toward them in case they started shooting. The fire escape door was immediately adjacent to the top of the stairs, so without hesitation he rammed his knees against the bar that opened it and the alarm sounded just as he suspected. But he had hit the bar with such force that the door swung open and banged into the outside wall. He didn't even slow down, but moved right along with the door as it was opening. Unfortunately, his reckless haste had cost him a painful blow to his knees. But that was okay: They were free, and once again were streaking across the sky.

chapter 5

The trip to the military equipment graveyard took much longer this time than when Hawker had gone there looking for a water vessel. The reason, of course, was Teala. Her unprotected body couldn't handle the winds at the speeds he normally flew.

During the flight, she had kept her head tucked inside his jacket and had not attempted to talk. When he placed her on the ground, she said, "Well that was degrading . . . being in jail."

"I'm sorry," said Hawker. "I shouldn't have left you alone."

"Forget it. I understand why you did it."

Was she really going to take it that well? "What did they do to you?" he asked.

"Nothing really. Just asked me a lot of questions . . . and made me take off your clothes. I don't think they were interested in me. I was just a pawn."

Hawker removed his helmet and grinned. "I'll bet they *became* interested in you . . . when they saw you in your jeans and sweater."

If he was expecting her to smile, he was disappointed. "What is this place?" she asked. "Why are we here?"

"This is where I found the water tank that I used to fight the fire. While I was looking for it, I saw something that gave me an idea." He pointed. "See that old airplane fuselage over there?"

"What about it?"

"Well . . . you said you wanted to go back to Florida with me. Think you could handle crossing the ocean in that?"

"Are you being serious?" she asked.

"Yeah. . . . That used to be a small jet that the Russians used to train their new military pilots. It's missing its wings and engine now, but that's actually good. We could do a thousand miles an hour or more if you were enclosed in that."

She studied his face. "Is that the only solution you could come up with?"

He shrugged. "From my perspective, it was the best one. You were adamant about me not leaving you over here, so what choices do we have left? We can't very well walk into an airport and book a flight back. Besides, you were willing to fly all the way back in my arms before. Just think how much more comfortable you would be in that. It even has a seat left in it."

She was silent for a few seconds; then smiled and said, "That might be fun. It's certainly something that nobody else has ever done. How long would it take us?"

"By Florida time, we'd get back about this time of day on this same day."

He had expected her to be awed by that fact and ask how that could be, but she said, "That still doesn't tell me how long."

He knew she didn't like it when he played the role of "professor" with her so he gave her a straightforward answer. "About eight or nine hours . . . depending on how often we stop."

"Well I'm glad to hear that we'll be able to take breaks."

"Yeah . . . when we get to the Atlantic, I'll choose a route that takes us close to some islands."

He hesitated and his face took on a more serious expression. "But I think you should know . . . there's a possible danger associated with this."

"You mean something other than that suit letting us fall to our deaths?"

He laughed. "This suit is probably the most reliable machine on

Earth."

"Then what danger *are* you talking about?"

He grinned. "It might spoil you. You may never want to fly a commercial airliner again."

"That wouldn't be much of a change. I don't want to fly one now."

"But it's not quite as simple as I've made it sound. We can't just go zipping through the airspace of all these countries while we're carrying that fuselage. They'll be able to see it on radar."

She frowned. "You told me you had a transceiver built into your helmet. Couldn't you contact Air Traffic Control and tell 'em who you are?"

"I considered that, but it gets complicated in a hurry. We're talking about the airspace of five different countries including the United States and I don't have frequencies for any of the foreign countries. There's also the question of whether or not they would believe me . . . especially if they think their national security is at stake."

"Are you trying to discourage me?"

"No, not at all. I was just trying to answer your question. I wouldn't have suggested this method of getting you home if I didn't have a plan. Instead of calling Air Traffic Control, I'm gonna call Mrs. Bradshaw. Her people can contact all the appropriate authorities for me. That will simplify things and I won't have to worry about some *controller* not believing me."

She gave a faint smile. "What did you used to do . . . before you had a friend in the White House?"

"I don't know. But most of the calls have been for her benefit."

"Is that it? Any other danger I should know about?"

"Nope. That's it."

"Well, at least I won't have to go through all the security hassles at an airport."

"Does that mean you're up for it?"

She nodded.

"Okay, the first thing we'll do is call the First Lady so she can get her people to work contacting Europe." He hesitated and frowned. "I hate to wake her up. It's three-thirty in the morning where she is."

In order to get to his cell phone, he had to remove the meat and bread he had stuffed into his tote pouch. He handed the food to Teala. Then he had to remove his gloves before he could press the small "FL" button.

As he had expected, the First Lady's voice indicated she had been asleep.

"I'm sorry to wake you," he said.

"That's okay," she responded. "I was anxious to hear from you. Where are you?"

"In Belarus."

"Well I'm glad you're out of Russia. What about your fiancée and the suit?"

"They're with me."

"That's great. I knew you could do it." She hesitated a second; then said, "I got some interesting news late yesterday."

Hawker knew what she was going to say, but he played along. "What news is that?"

"Russia won't be sending us any more vaccine for a while. Seems that some terrorists blew up the pharmaceutical plant that was making it."

"That is interesting. Any word on who the terrorists were?"

"No. The speculation is that it was somebody who hated the United States and they were punishing Russia for supplying us with the vaccine."

"We figured Petrov would handle it that way. . . . But getting on to the reason why I called you, I need you to do something for me. Teala and I are coming home today and we're gonna be bringing a chunk of metal with us. Normally I don't have to worry about radar because my suit absorbs the signals, but that metal changes things. I would like for you to have somebody contact the appropriate authorities in Poland, France and Germany with my intended route and speed. It would be a little awkward for me to try to file an international flight plan."

"Not a problem. Let me get to a pen and paper." A couple of seconds later, she said, "Okay, give me the info."

"We're now about a hundred miles northeast of Minsk. We'll be leaving here in half an hour and traveling a straight line to Nantes near the coast of France. Air Traffic Control usually asks for an exact altitude, but I can't give you that. You can tell 'em we'll be flying at a thousand miles per hour. Also, notify our military and Air Traffic Control that we'll be approaching the coast of Florida around noon today."

"What are you going to do about Belarus?"

"Belarus is relatively flat. We'll fly low enough that they can't see us on radar."

"Okay. I'm glad you're safe and coming home. Anything else?"

"What about that satellite? Any new thoughts or change in your position there?"

"No. We certainly can't tell the Russians why we want it destroyed."

Hawker knew she was right at this point. They would suspect U.S. involvement in the pharmaceutical plant explosion.

The First Lady continued, "I'm banking on you to find a way to disable whatever device Petrov put aboard it . . . and do it without implicating the U.S. government."

"I'm working on it," said Hawker.

He started to disconnect, but then added, "There is one other thing. Could you put out an alert not to let Petrov enter the United States?"

"I think we can handle that."

"Thanks. I'll be in touch." He disconnected and put the phone back in his pouch.

Teala handed the food back to him. "I've already eaten twice this morning. The police offered me food and I took 'em up on it. I figured it would be a good way to stall for time."

He grinned as he took it. "Okay I'll eat it. I wouldn't want hunger to cause us problems during our flight."

She shook her head. "Me neither."

"You said the police made you take off my clothes . . . but you're wearing 'em now."

"Yeah, I pretended I was cold and pointed to the clothes. I knew you'd be there to get me sooner or later and I wanted to be ready."

He smiled. "Thanks for the vote of confidence." Then he added, "But you'll want to take off the extra clothes before you get into the fuselage."

"Are you sure I'm not gonna be cold?"

"Positive. At our speed, the air friction is gonna turn that fuselage into a heater."

He struggled to swallow a bite of dry food. "While I'm eating, how about you scraping everything you can off the hull of your new carriage. You can use that old board over there." He pointed; then added, "Also check the inside to see if it meets your standards for cleanliness. I'll turn it upside down and shake it before you get in."

He finished off the food that Teala had handed back to him and left the rest for emergencies. "I'm gonna have to find some water," he said. "I've only had one drink since yesterday in Petrov's lab. How about you?"

"I drank plenty at the police station," she said.

After a cursory search, he settled on the water standing in the pipe he had broken loose earlier that morning. The vertical section that had been connected to the tank was still standing upright and was about twenty feet in length. He figured that gravity acting on the water would cause a short-lived flow from the faucet he had used earlier. "I don't know how long the water has been standing in these pipes," he said. "I may get lead poisoning, but that won't be any worse than dying of thirst."

"I can't get the canopy open," she said.

"I'll get it in a minute," he responded.

After a satisfying drink of water, he opened the canopy for her; then retrieved his helmet and gloves.

"The inside doesn't look too bad," she said. "But I still want you to shake it. I wouldn't want any critters going for a ride with me."

He rolled the fuselage onto its side and used the board to scrape the dirt from its bottom. Then he held it over his head with the cockpit opening down and shook it vigorously. A couple of items fell out, but they weren't critters.

After placing the fuselage back on the ground, he asked, "Are you ready to start this journey?"

She headed toward the only structure left standing on the property—which was an old shack and it was barely standing. "I will be in a few minutes," she answered. She returned a few minutes later and said, "Okay, let's go."

He lifted her into the cockpit and cautioned, "You should keep the seat belt fastened at all times. We should have no problems, but we should expect the unexpected."

"Where're you going to be?" she asked.

He pointed to the handles on each side of the cockpit. "I'll be above you . . . holding on to these."

"What if I need a break more often than you do?"

"You'll be able to see me and I'll be able to see you, so just point downward if you need to land."

He waited long enough to see her fasten the seat belt; then closed the canopy and floated himself into position. As soon as he gripped the metal handles attached to the fuselage, the whole thing, including all of its contents, became weightless. Actually, the canopy wasn't completely weightless. It, of course, was not electrically conductive, and since the fuselage didn't completely shield it from gravity, it retained a small weight. That weight, however, was almost negligible to the suit's propulsion system.

With his body stretched out above and parallel to the fuselage, belly-to-earth and toes pointed to the rear, he lifted them into the air. Other than his arms, this body orientation insured minimum air resistance. His arms, of course, were reaching down to grip the handles on the fuselage. This placed him in a position looking straight down into the cockpit where Teala sat. It took no effort on his part to maintain that position over extended periods of time: He simply let the suit do the work.

Flying low over the forests and marshlands of Belarus, he accelerated gradually to avoid causing Teala *too* much discomfort. He could see that she was pressed against the back of her seat, but he thought she could handle it. After he reached a thousand miles per hour and stopped accelerating, she looked up at him and mouthed the word "thanks." Twenty minutes later they crossed into Poland.

The terrain they encountered in Poland was a little higher than that of Belarus, but it still wasn't a problem. He was able to maintain a thousand feet above the ground and thirty minutes later they were entering German airspace.

Hawker had never intended for Teala to be his passenger on this flight, but he had intended to do everything within his power to regain possession of his suit. Planning ahead just in case, he had used time during the flight to Moscow to study his aeronautical charts. He knew he would have to climb to at least ten thousand feet to clear some of the mountains in Germany, so he started that climb as soon as he entered German airspace. His GPS was guiding him along a path that took him south of Berlin and north of Frankfurt.

About ten minutes after entering German airspace, he had leveled off at eleven thousand feet and was cruising along at a thousand mph when his collision avoidance system gave him an audible warning. Using a thought command, he displayed a visual on the GPS screen: Something was zooming toward him at more than three thousand miles per hour.

Whoa. . . . I don't like the looks of that, he thought. *That can't be an airplane. The only thing I know that flies that fast is a missile. I guess it's possible that somebody could mistake me for a hostile aircraft from Russia, but surely Mrs. Bradshaw relayed the information I gave her.*

He changed his direction of flight to see what would happen. The fast-moving object changed its direction also. It was coming straight at him again. He had to assume that he was the target and the thing coming at him was a missile. For a brief instant, he perceived the situation as hopeless; then shook that thought and racked his brain for a way out.

He didn't think there was any chance he could outrun it, but he certainly would give it a try. He turned directly away from it and gave the thought command "maximum speed." His speed crept up to twelve hundred miles per hour and stayed there, which meant the missile was gaining on him at the rate of more than two thousand miles per hour. *That's what I was afraid of,* he thought.

If he couldn't outrun it, he would have to outmaneuver it. That was going to cause Teala some discomfort, but not as much as a direct hit from that thing would cause. There was a mountain peak directly in front of him. He would clear it with no problem, but the plan was to use it to try and stop the missile.

Using his telescopic vision, he first checked to be sure the mountain peak had no inhabitants; then just as he cleared the top, he gave the thought command "gravitize." That removed the field that shielded him and the fuselage from gravity, thereby adding a vertical component to his velocity. He now had another force acting to increase his speed relative to the missile—namely gravity.

Teala probably felt the change in direction, but other than that, she most likely didn't notice anything unusual. The reason, of course, was that she was in free fall and essentially still weightless.

Hawker had hoped that the missile would change its direction immediately and slam into the top of the mountain. That didn't happen. It continued on over the peak; then changed its direction. Needless to say, it was coming directly at him again and getting much too close for comfort.

He figured he had only one more chance to save himself and Teala. Knowing that his next move would have to be timed perfectly, he aimed straight for the slope of the mountain on the other side of the narrow valley. At the critical moment, he gave the thought command "degravitize," followed immediately by "maximum climb." That slammed his body against the canopy, stretching his arms back toward his feet. He almost lost his grip on the handles.

The fuselage clipped the tops of several trees before it headed straight up. The missile wasn't quite so lucky: It slammed into the side of the mountain and exploded in a spectacular ball of fire.

Teala couldn't see the explosion below and behind her, but she certainly heard it. And she definitely noticed that sudden upward change in direction. When they landed at a secluded spot on the coast of France for a break, she said, "What was that roller coaster ride all about? Please don't tell me that explosion I heard was meant for us."

He nodded.

"I asked you not to tell me that."

During the rest of the flight, he flew just high enough above the surface of the Atlantic to avoid the waves and swells. They made two more stops: one on the island of Flores in the Azores and the other in the Bermudas. They arrived back in Florida shortly after noon that day.

At about the same time Hawker and Teala were finishing their memorable flight, President Bradshaw was saying to his wife, "I see your man blew up a pharmaceutical plant and killed three people. Tell me again why your methods are so much better than mine."

In less than her usual self-assured manner, Lena Bradshaw said, "He didn't tell me he killed anyone."

"And what do you think the Russians will do if they link *that* act of terrorism to us?"

"They won't," said Mrs. Bradshaw. "Petrov would never reveal the identities of all the people involved in that incident. It might lead to an investigation into *his* illegal activities. . . . And you shouldn't have asked me anything about *Hawker's* activities. You could have honestly denied any knowledge of the incident."

"I won't have any trouble denying it anyway."

"No, I guess you wouldn't."

"But in your favor," said the President. "I'll have to give you credit for taking care of the situation on the ground. There's no way we could've shot down a satellite twenty-two thousand miles up . . . at least not in a timely manner."

"So you did check on the satellite, huh? I wish you hadn't done that. If news of your interest gets leaked to the Russians, it could tie us to whatever happens next."

"What do you mean? What's going to happen next?"

"I don't know, but I do know Hawker won't rest until the danger from that satellite is eliminated. . . . And you shouldn't ask me any more questions about it. I want the U.S. government to be in a position where they can deny any knowledge of it."

He grinned and said, "That's a good idea. Let's talk about us."

She gave him a faint smile.

chapter 6

Hawker hid the Russian fuselage in the woods behind his house. After he and Teala had showered and eaten, she called her office to report that she had been kidnapped and would need a few days off to recuperate, and he called Ben Huron at the University of Florida. He had left his canvas bag in Russia, but fortunately he had another one. He stuffed the suit into *it*, and half an hour later he and Teala were sitting in Ben's private office.

Ben closed the door *this* time and said, "I may have a solution for you, but I want to start with something else. For six months now, we've been skirting around a serious conversation about you suddenly acquiring that suit. I haven't pushed the issue because I knew you didn't want to talk about it. But I think the time has come for you to lay all your cards on the table. I think you owe me that much.

"I appreciate all the good you've been doing and I've done everything I could to help. Now you're asking for my help again . . . and I'm more than willing to give it, but keeping secrets between us won't do either of us any good. We need to clear the air."

Hawker nodded. "You're right, Ben. We should've done this a long time ago."

He had already decided that he could tell Ben most of the story without divulging the one piece of information that was holding him back. "Let me start by saying that I didn't develop the suit. I know you thought I did in the beginning. I don't know if you still think that, but I didn't. Somebody else took my ideas and developed the suit for me. I didn't even know it was happening. Then suddenly one night, the suit was offered to me as a gift . . . no strings attached.

"I've never seen my benefactors and don't know their names. I did speak with one of them, but his voice was disguised to sound like a TV-news anchorman. He told me to call him 'Alex,' but he also said that wasn't his real name.

"I'm not keeping any secrets about gravity from you. You know just as much about gravity as I do and I don't know any more about it now than I did a year ago. I'm also not keeping any results of my research from you. . . ." He felt as though he should say more, but couldn't think of anything else.

Ben stared at him for a full thirty seconds without speaking. Finally, he said, "I believe you, but I'm stupefied. I didn't think anybody was beyond where you and I are with gravity. But I've got to give those guys credit for choosing the right man for the job. They know you well. You said they used your ideas . . . and that's obvious. Who did you give your ideas to? That would be a clue to who developed the suit."

Hawker shook his head. "You're the only person I ever told about my fantasy suit. . . . But Alex said they had thought monitoring equipment. Apparently, they can monitor anybody's thoughts."

Ben frowned. "That's a scary thought. I hope they don't let the government get their hands on it."

Hawker grinned. "I got the impression they were monitoring the government as well."

Hawker was anxious to change the subject. He added, "Ben, if you're satisfied with my explanation, I'd like to get on to your solution for the satellite problem."

Ben nodded. "I need some more information about the suit first. I need to know your maximum possible speed and I need to know about your breathing system."

"I don't really know what my maximum speed is," said Hawker. "I've never taken it to the limit . . . other than today when I was dragging that fuselage along. The air friction limited us to twelve hundred then, but I know I can do better than two thousand when I'm flying alone."

"Is air friction your only limiting factor?" asked Ben.

"Well the suit would obviously be limited as to how much thrust it could develop . . . *and* it's dependent on incident radiation to replenish expended energy."

Teala grinned. "I used to badger Hawker about practical applications for physics. I've got a feeling I'm gonna get an earful today."

Ben smiled at Teala and spoke to hawker. "For what I have in mind, you won't have to worry about lack of incident radiation. . . . Tell me about your breathing system. Does the suit actually produce breathable air, or does it just filter what comes in through that grille?"

"It produces a little breathable air in the form of pure oxygen when it's removing the carbon dioxide I exhale."

"That's another thing I was going to ask about. So it does remove the carbon dioxide, huh? All of it . . . or does some of it have to go out through the filter?"

"I would say all of it. If the filter doesn't allow carbon dioxide to come in, then it probably wouldn't allow it to go out either. Besides, Alex didn't say anything about limitations on the system. He just told me how to clean the carbon out of it. I have to expose the inside lining of the helmet to direct sunlight periodically."

"So the lining is a carbon dioxide scrubber, huh?"

"Yes. It separates the carbon from the oxygen and returns the oxygen to the air inside the helmet."

"What happens if you forget to clean out the carbon?"

"I get a headache that reminds me."

Ben sighed. "Well it's obvious that we'll have to add an oxygen supply to your system for what I have in mind."

Hawker said, "Okay . . . my curiosity is killing me. What do you have in mind?"

Ben grinned and said, "How would you like to go for a trip in space?"

"I've always wanted to go into space. You know that."

"So how well do you think your suit would function as a space suit?"

Hawker shrugged. "It would be a great space suit except for the lack of an oxygen supply. It's well sealed and insulated."

"You don't think the radiation in space would be a problem?"

"No."

"Well that's the only thing I could come up with. I doubt seriously that your original idea of shooting down the satellite would be viable. Even if the President were willing to do it, an operation like that would involve a lot of planning and a lot of time. Based on what you've told me, we don't have that much time. And, we just don't have enough information about the device in the satellite to disable it. The only solution *is* to get rid of the satellite, but since we can't blow it up, we'll have to make it disappear."

Hawker smiled: He was beginning to get the idea. "You mean push it out of orbit and into outer space, don't you?"

Ben nodded. "Yes . . . onto a direct collision course with the Sun. That's why I asked about your maximum speed. It'll be necessary for you to reach at least twenty-five thousand miles per hour."

"Earth's *escape velocity*," said Hawker.

"Twenty-five thousand is a long way from two thousand," said Teala.

"Yes," said Ben. "But the air friction twenty-two thousand miles up is negligible. And since he can shield himself and the satellite from Earth's gravity, there would be nothing to hold him back. He could continue accelerating indefinitely."

"So you're assuming the satellite's in a *geosynchronous* orbit," said Hawker.

Ben nodded. "I'm almost certain of it."

"Okay," said Teala. "I'm gonna have to ask what a geosynchronous orbit is."

Ben smiled. "That's an orbit that always keeps the satellite in the same position relative to the surface of the Earth. Satellite television uses that system. That's why Hawker can always keep his satellite dish pointed to the same spot in the sky."

"What makes you so certain it'll be at that altitude?" asked Hawker.

"Because it's probably a spy satellite disguised as a scientific experiment. . . . But you can bet that the Russian government didn't know the actual purpose of the experiment. A spy satellite would need that orbit if it wanted to keep an eye on the same country constantly. What country do you think Russia would most likely want to spy on? Then there's the question of what Petrov would want for his death ray. Would he want it to be in position so that it could deliver its lethal signal on a moment's notice, or would he be content to wait for it to circle the globe?"

"I see what you mean," said Hawker. "I'm always amazed at your powers of deduction. But I'll still need a means of identifying it. I wouldn't want to take out the wrong satellite."

With disbelief in her voice, Teala said, "You guys are talking like you actually think Hawker can do this."

"It won't be easy," said Hawker. "But it's feasible. We've solved some pretty tough problems in the past." He looked back at Ben. "What did you have in mind on the breathing system? It'll be extremely difficult to attach anything to any part of the suit. We can't drill holes for screws because nothing can penetrate the material."

"What about an adhesive? Great strides have been made in that area in recent years."

Hawker pondered that idea for a couple of seconds; then said, "Maybe. . . . In fact, Mark Woodall does a lot of work with adhesives. I'll ask *him* and see what he thinks. On top of that, he's also an experienced scuba diver. He would know as much as anybody about breathing equipment. He might even be able to help us rig up something."

Hawker stood up. "But I'll have to talk to 'im in person. Today is Friday and he'll be in Palatka with a lot of people around 'im. The *drop zone* has a *Twin-Otter* there this weekend. He wouldn't miss the chance to jump out of that." He took Teala by the arm. "We'll head on over there. In the meantime, do you have any contacts that could provide us with detailed information about the satellite?"

Ben shook his head.

Teala stood also. "Something still bothers me about this," she said. "Why wouldn't the Russians suspect U.S. involvement when the satellite disappears just as much as they would if it exploded?"

"They won't know it's gone in the beginning," said Ben. "They'll just think it stopped communicating. They'll figure it out eventually, but they still won't have any idea what happened to it. It would be embarrassing to admit they've lost a satellite."

Hawker said to Ben, "I assume you've made some preliminary calculations."

Ben nodded.

"Well you've probably thought about this already, but I'll say it anyway. Everything I do will have to be based on time. My GPS won't be reliable beyond a certain point. I won't be able to determine my altitude, speed, or anything else for that matter. My *collision avoidance* system will still work and I'll be able to give a command for a specified value of thrust, but other than that, I'm really going to be limited."

"I'll rig you up a timer," said Ben.

Hawker grinned. "I appreciate all you're doing, Ben."

"Thank *you* for taking on the world's problems."

Hawker started to leave, but then turned back to Ben. "And in your spare time . . . maybe you can get us more information on that satellite, and figure out a way for me to make positive identification."

Ben nodded. "I'll have to. I'll need the exact orbit and mass before I can finalize the calculations."

Walking to the parking lot, Hawker said to Teala, "Would you mind driving? I want to do some calculations."

"Not at all," she answered. "After all, it *is* my car. When are we going to the airport to get yours?"

"After we finish taking care of more pressing matters."

As she unlocked the car, Teala asked, "Didn't you tell me that Lev works for *military intelligence*?"

"He's supposedly retired, but he flies special missions for them sometimes."

Suddenly realizing she needed to exercise a little more discretion, she glanced around; then added, "And wouldn't *military intelligence* keep track of Russian satellites?"

They both got in and closed their doors. Hawker said, "That's a good idea. He might know somebody that can get us the info we need. And, he'll be at the *drop zone* same as Mark."

As they pulled into the parking area at *Skydive Palatka*, the sky was suddenly filled with colorful parachutes. "That sight always amazes me," said Teala.

"Me too," said Hawker. "And I've seen it many times."

By the time they could get parked and get out of the car, some of the smaller, faster canopies were already landing. Hawker watched one of the jumpers do a steep turn, swoop in fast; then level off and glide across the ground with his feet skimming the grass. "Some of these guys get as much fun out of the landing as they do the *free fall*," he remarked.

Most of the jumpers were male, so most of them were looking at Teala as they picked up their canopies and walked back to the *packing area*.

She truly was a beauty, but not in the soft, overly feminine way. Her shoulder-length dark brown hair and her large dark brown eyes accented her flawless face. At the moment, the sight of her was probably the only thing that could take the jumpers minds off the jump.

Dennis, Mark and Lev had seen her, of course, and hurried over as soon as they dropped their rigs. They all had to have a hug.

Lev shook Hawker's hand and said, "We're glad to see both of you back safe and sound."

Dennis said to Teala, "I see the kidnappers let you go."

"They didn't have much choice in the matter," she responded.

Dennis grinned. "I hope you weren't *too* rough on 'em."

With a solemn expression, she replied, "They're no longer with us."

"No longer with us?" Lev asked. "You mean as in *dead*?"

She nodded.

"What happened?" asked Mark.

Hawker broke in. "Maybe we should have this conversation out by the car."

The five of them huddled by Teala's car—away from curious ears—and Teala and Hawker brought the other three up to date. Then Hawker said, "Now I need some help from you guys."

Lev grinned. "You didn't want our help before . . . and now you're asking for it."

"Things change," said Hawker. "And so do people."

"I was just jerking your chain. What do you need?"

"I'll start with Mark," said Hawker. "Because everything else is dependent on what he can do for me." He looked at Mark. "Mark, I need to take a trip into space."

"Whoa," said Mark. "You need to talk to NASA about that . . . not me."

"I can't talk to NASA, or any other government agency. They can't know about it."

"Are you planning something illegal?"

"The Russians would consider it to be a crime."

"So what do you think *I* could do for you?"

"Well I have a perfectly good space suit except for one small detail. It doesn't have a self-contained oxygen supply. I thought with your knowledge of adhesives and composite materials you might be able to help me add one. A major hurdle will be attaching it to the suit. That's where the adhesive comes in. We would need some kind of interface that would have to be fastened over the breathing grille on my helmet."

"Well the adhesive wouldn't be a problem," said Mark. "I have one that would support the weight of an elephant. *And* it's impervious to extreme temperatures, but I don't know how the *radiation* in space would affect it."

"I won't be up there long enough for that to matter."

"How long *do* you plan to be up there?"

"I did some rough calculations on the way over here and I'm estimating that I'll need about two hours."

A questioning look spread over Mark's face. "Two hours . . . to go into space and come back?"

"Don't forget how fast he flies," said Dennis.

Applying her newly-found knowledge, Teala added, *"And* he can fly much faster in space where there's no air friction."

Retaining his skeptical expression, Mark said, "I also have an air tank that would buy you the two hours normally, but we're talking about a situation where there's no room for errors."

"Do I detect a hint that you might be willing to help me?" said Hawker.

"It was never a question of me being willing to help you. The feasibility of what you're asking for is what I question. We can look at what you have and go from there. That's all I can promise."

"That's good enough for me," Hawker said. Then he turned his attention to Lev. "Lev, I need some details about a Russian satellite that was launched last April. Do you know somebody in *military intelligence* that might be able to help us with that?"

Lev puckered his lips. "You're getting into sensitive territory now. Besides . . . I thought you said government agencies couldn't be involved."

"It would have to be an individual that would do it as a favor to you and not involve anybody else. A lot of lives are at stake here. Maybe you know somebody with a soft spot for a situation like that."

"I'll have to give this some thought. I can't promise anything."

"I need the exact orbit, the mass and any identifying markings in case you decide you can help."

He next turned to Dennis. "Dennis, can you take a few days off from work?"

Dennis grinned. "I'm the boss. Of course I can."

"Okay, I would like for you to take Teala home with you and stay with her twenty-four hours a day."

Teala gave Hawker a stern look. "Don't you think you're being a little overprotective?"

"Not at all," said Hawker. "Petrov is not going to let this go. I saw the look in his eyes." He looked at Dennis. "And Dennis . . . *this* time you have my permission to use a gun or any other means necessary to protect her."

Dennis was more than ten years older than Hawker and had been one of Hawker's mentors in the world of flying and skydiving. He frowned at Hawker and said, "What makes you think I need your permission?"

Hawker grinned and continued, "Guys, I hate to take you away from your skydiving, but we need to get started on this like right now. Teala, I need your car, but I wouldn't want you driving alone anyway."

She nodded.

Dennis said, "That was probably the last *big load* of the day anyway. Besides, some things are more important than skydiving."

"I don't know," joked Mark. "It's hard to beat the thrill of a good skydive."

"I can imagine," said Teala. "I get a thrill out of just watching you guys. I'll never forget that first time I went up as an observer. Just watching all of you exit amazed me. Everybody was lined up down the aisle of the airplane . . . then somebody yelled and all twenty-one of you were gone just like that." She snapped her fingers. "I know it couldn't have been more than five seconds. It's hard to believe that all of you . . . with all of your equipment could get out of the airplane that fast. Airline passengers should take lessons from you guys."

"I don't know about the five seconds part," said Dennis. "But what's even more amazing is that we all flew to the same point in the sky and built a formation. And we did all that in less than a minute."

Mark couldn't resist getting in a little dig. "Actually, not all of us flew to that point in the sky. Some of us just hung out there and waited for the others to fly to 'im."

Dennis grinned. "The base is the most important part of the formation. Without it, the rest of you wouldn't have anything to fly to."

Hawker broke in again. "At the risk of being seen as a party pooper, I'm gonna drag Mark away from this. I want to get him started on his part of this venture."

Dennis kept his grin. "You can count on Mark to take care of all the tiny details. He's the ultimate engineer. Remember all the faxes he used to send us when we were doing demo jumps for the Navy?"

Everybody, including Mark, chuckled. They had a vivid memory of all the faxes.

Hawker handed Lev one of Ben Huron's business cards. "If you get the info on the satellite, call Ben directly. It doesn't matter what time of day or night." Then he gave Teala a kiss and said, "Don't be too rough on Dennis."

He started to leave, but then turned back to Lev. "One other thing, Lev. I would like to know the whereabouts of Ivan Petrov. He used to live and work at *Monino Pharmaceuticals* near Moscow until they had the little accident we told you about."

Lev pocketed Ben's card. "You know I can't promise anything on any of this, don't you?"

Hawker nodded. "I know. Just do what you can." Then he turned to Mark and said, "I'll follow you, Mark."

Much like Hawker's homesite, Mark's was also nestled in the woods, but it was located near Green Cove Springs instead of Gainesville. Half an hour after leaving Kay Larkin Airport their two vehicles pulled up in front of what appeared to be a garage attached to Mark's house. Hawker knew the garage was actually a sophisticated workshop. He had been inside it a few times over the years and had always been amazed at its contents. Mark was actively engaged in all the things that other men dreamed about.

Before taking the suit inside, Hawker removed the contents of its tote pouches, including the cell phone the First Lady had given him. He placed the cell phone in the glove box and then locked the car and followed Mark in. Once inside, Hawker donned the suit long enough to switch it to the light-reflecting mode so Mark could see what he was working with—at least that was the original intention.

Mark watched the process in amazement. "Well that was interesting," he said.

He was referring to Hawker's transformation from a featureless shadow to a man wearing a bulky body suit.

Mark added, "How about demonstrating some of the other things you can do."

Hawker activated the antigravity feature and lifted himself a few inches off the floor. Then keeping his body in the standing position, he zipped about the room.

"That must be some kind of fun," said Mark.

Hawker grabbed Mark's wrist, making him weightless also. Then the two of them darted about, flipping their bodies into every imaginable position, playing games as if they were children. Hawker had never seen Mark this playful before. He was pleased to see his friend having fun, but he was also anxious to get to work. He eased them back to the floor and cautioned, "Brace yourself for a return to gravity."

Being a skydiver, Mark was better prepared for that event than most of Hawker's passengers: He staggered but didn't actually fall.

Mark said, "I'm still curious about how you did that shadow thing."

"It's all in the beholder's eye," joked Hawker. "Actually, the suit normally absorbs all electromagnetic radiation, but I have the ability to turn off the absorption of the visible frequencies."

Hawker held out his arm and said, "The suit has another feature that I think you will find interesting. Grip my wrist and squeeze."

Mark squeezed Hawker's wrist and exclaimed, "Why that's like a section of metal pipe!"

"Now use both hands and try to bend my arm at the elbow."

Mark again followed instructions. "It's as rigid and unbendable as steel," he said.

"It isn't steel," responded Hawker. "But it's even stronger than steel. That's the neat thing about nanotechnology. You can actually control the properties of a material."

Mark nodded. "Yeah, I've tried to keep up with nanotechnology." Then he shook his head. "But I had no idea it was this far advanced."

Hawker continued, "I can effectively enclose my body in a rigid shell. I'm sure there are other uses for that property changing feature that I don't know about yet. That's something I'll have to experiment with when I get the time."

"I'd like to help with that," said Mark.

Hawker nodded and converted the material of the suit back to its flexible state. Then he removed the helmet and pointed to a square-shaped grille that supplied his air. "We need an interface that will fit over this and form an airtight seal."

Mark took the helmet, looked at it and then measured the grille. "I remembered something during the drive here that I had almost forgotten. I started a project some time ago that would have involved attaching an interface similar to what you're talking about to the outside of a small submersible. I was planning to expand my underwater exploration capabilities, but I got sidetracked and never went back to it." He placed the helmet on a workbench, began rummaging through a drawer and extracted an odd-looking item. "Here's what I was looking for."

The object he was holding appeared to be some form of plastic and was shaped like a small, shortened loaf of bread with a coupling for an air hose in the center of its curved top. When he turned it over, a rectangular opening revealed that the device was actually a hollow shell with slightly curved edges at two opposite ends.

Mark placed it over the grille on Hawker's Helmet and examined the fit. "This is made of a strong composite material," he said. "I'll have to grind off some of the material along the inside walls on two sides and reshape the curvature on the end walls, but this project of yours is beginning to look a little more doable."

"That's encouraging news," said Hawker. "You said you had an air tank, and I know I'll need a regulator, but what else will I need?"

"Yeah . . . I have a tank with a capacity of a hundred and five cubic feet. That would provide two hours of air here on Earth if we were talking about scuba diving, but I can't say how much time it will give you in space, breathing pure oxygen. I think I have all the other components we need for a very basic breathing system. You obviously can't use a scuba regulator, but I have another type that I picked up at a NASA surplus sale. I was going to use it on my submersible along with some other components I got at the same sale."

"I didn't know NASA had surplus sales."

Mark corrected himself. "Actually, it was a government sale . . . not exclusively NASA. But the guy that was helping me said the stuff came from NASA. The general public doesn't usually get invited to those sales. I knew about it because I work for the Navy. Anyway, in answer to your earlier question, I think we have everything we need other than the oxygen. We'll have to take the tank somewhere and get it filled."

"Maybe I can do that while you're working on the helmet. Do you know of a place nearby?"

"Actually I don't . . . not tonight. Everything will be closed."

"I'll take it to the university. I need to talk with Ben again anyway. Mind if I use your phone to call 'im?"

"No, but let's talk about a couple of other things before you do. How much air pressure do you want inside the suit?"

Hawker took a second to visualize the actions he would have to perform in space. "Five psi," he answered. "I'll need to keep it low enough that I can manipulate my hands and arms without too much trouble. The suit won't be able to enhance my muscle strength in space because the pressure differential will prevent sensors from making contact with my skin."

"I figured you'd use a reduced pressure. . . . I'm sure you're aware of the consequences of going from a higher pressure to a lower pressure too rapidly . . . in the world of underwater exploration we call it the *bends*."

Hawker nodded. "Yeah . . . I'll go on pure oxygen several hours before I launch."

"Okay. . . . The other thing I'm thinking about is testing the helmet for air leaks once the adhesive cures. I assume you have a vacuum chamber at the university."

Hawker nodded.

"Since you're going there to get the oxygen, you might want to wait until I finish the helmet. We might be able to save a trip."

"Okay, but I still want to call Ben. I'll need his okay to get the oxygen and use the chamber. Besides, I want to find out if he's learned anything new about the satellite."

Ben had learned something new. "I checked with an acquaintance who's conducting a study involving man-made objects orbiting the Earth," he said. "And it turns out he's been tracking that satellite. He faxed me a diagram of its orbit."

"That's great," said Hawker. "Mark is working on adding an oxygen supply to my suit and we're gonna need to use some of the physics department's resources. I don't yet know what time we'll be there, but I was hoping you could meet us."

"Well let me tell you something else that might affect your planning. The ideal time for you to intercept the satellite would be tomorrow morning at seven forty-nine. Actually, seven forty-nine plus thirty-seven seconds. Its instantaneous velocity vector will be pointing directly at the sun at that time. If you don't push it out of its orbit at that instant, you'll have to wait another twenty-four hours to get the same conditions."

"I need to do it as soon as possible," said Hawker. "I don't know how long it'll take Petrov to get more triggering equipment set up."

"Have you considered the possibility that he could have already done that and has already sent the triggering signal?"

"Yes, but I'll have to assume that he hasn't . . . and act accordingly."

"Can Mark have the suit ready by tomorrow morning?"

"Yes. He wants to test it tonight using our vacuum chamber."

"Okay, that can be arranged. What are your plans for avoiding decompression sickness?"

"I'll have to flush the nitrogen out of my body by breathing pure oxygen for several hours before I launch."

"I thought as much. In that case, you shouldn't wait for Mark. You should come on in now and get your oxygen. I'll contact a local company that offers twenty-four hour emergency service on oxygen equipment. I should have it by the time you get here. What do you plan to use as your launch site?"

Hawker pondered that question for a second. "We'll do it here . . . at Mark's house. I know that involves a lot of traveling, but we need a secluded spot, and all of Mark's tools and supplies are here. I would hate to be preparing for launch and discover that we needed something that was an hour's drive away."

"Okay," said Ben. "I'll be waiting for you at the physics department." Then he disconnected.

After discussing the new plans with Mark, Hawker left him grinding away on the helmet interface and headed for Gainesville, taking with him the large air tank to be filled with oxygen. Realizing that one of his long-held dreams was about to come true, he was filling with anticipation. At one point, he had considered applying for the astronaut program, but in the end had decided that would interfere with another dream, namely that of developing an antigravity device. But finally, he was going to fly in space. He just wished it were under different circumstances.

Earlier, while Mark and Hawker had been in Mark's workshop discussing the helmet interface, the First Lady had been engaged in a conversation with her husband. Following that conversation, she pulled out a cell phone and pressed a button. It was the button dedicated to the cell phone she had given Hawker. After waiting through ten rings and getting no response, she closed the cell phone and considered her options. She really didn't want to involve other people so she decided to wait five minutes and try again. But Hawker still hadn't answered after several tries, so she called Hank, the Secret Service agent. "Hank, I need for you to contact any known associates of Hawker's. I've been trying to reach him by phone but failed. I know that he works closely with another scientist but I don't remember the name. I also know that he has a fiancée, but I don't know her name either. Be discreet. It would be better if you could talk with him personally. Tell him I need to speak with him."

Half an hour later Hank called back with the results of his efforts: "I found the names of the two people you mentioned and called their homes . . . no answer at either place. I called a contact in Jacksonville who is going to contact the university police. He'll go to Gainesville if necessary. Nobody answers the physics department phone at the university."

"Thanks. Keep trying. I'll wait up for your call."

The drive to Gainesville took Hawker just over an hour.

Ben was waiting as promised. "I failed to mention something earlier," he said. "I still don't know the mass of the satellite. We'll need that before we can determine how much thrust to apply. I can guess at it if necessary, but it would be much better if we had accurate information."

"I have Lev Prymore working on that," said Hawker. "Maybe he'll call you in time. If not, go ahead and guess. I trust your guess as much as I do most people's facts."

Ignoring the compliment, Ben pointed to a box containing several small oxygen bottles. "You should take that oxygen and go back to Mark's place now. You need to start on it as soon as possible. I'll wait here to help Mark with the testing. And you can leave that air tank with me. I'll get it filled. I also need to finish some other preparations, but you should concentrate just on yourself from here on. Prepare *yourself* for the trip. Mark and I will take care of everything else."

Hawker grinned. "Yes, boss."

Hawker had been gone close to three hours and Mark had finished attaching the interface to the helmet. "You're not gonna be very pretty in this thing," he said as he showed Hawker the helmet.

"I wasn't very pretty before," responded Hawker. "So it won't matter."

The helmet already had a protrusion running across the top and back that resembled a Mohawk haircut. It also had round bulges on the sides over the ears. A three-inch-square breathing grille had been visible below the visor originally, but now it was completely covered by the interface Mark had added. The interface was almost the same color as the helmet—a dull black—and its loaf-of-bread shape had an air hose connection protruding from it. He truly would look like a monster now.

"I was getting ready to leave for Gainesville," said Mark. "Make yourself comfortable."

The workshop had a couch placed against one wall. Hawker sat on it and opened up a take-out tray he had picked up at a fast-food restaurant. "The first thing I need to do is eat," he said. "Then if you don't mind I'll take a nap on this couch. I've been getting shortchanged on my sleep lately."

"That's fine," said Mark. "I'll be back as soon as I'm sure this thing is air tight." Then he placed the suit and helmet in a box on top of some hoses and fittings and left.

Hawker finished eating and went to the bathroom. Then he extracted an oxygen mask from the box Ben had given him and connected himself to one of the small oxygen bottles. He was asleep within minutes after relaxing on the couch.

Meanwhile, the First Lady had decided there was no real reason for her to remain awake: The phone would wake her if someone called. But before lying down she tried contacting Hawker one more time through the cell phone she had given him. He still didn't respond.

———

Hawker didn't feel as if he had been asleep very long when Ben shook him awake. "Okay, sleeping beauty . . . time to get up and take advantage of our labors."

Hawker sat up and stretched, held his oxygen mask and asked, "Did the test go okay?"

Ben nodded. "Yep . . . and we have to get you prepared if you're going to launch by seven o'clock this morning."

"What time is it now?"

"Six-thirty. We decided to let you sleep as long as possible."

Hawker stood. "Okay . . . let me go to the bathroom first."

When he returned, he asked, "Did Lev Prymore ever call you?"

"Yes," said Ben. "He came through for you. He confirmed the orbit and he gave me the accurate mass. I've already adjusted my calculations to take that into account."

Then Ben asked, "How long will it take you to get to two hundred miles altitude and come to a complete stop?"

Hawker thought about it for a couple of seconds; then said, "About six minutes."

Ben came back with, "About isn't good enough. I need exact numbers."

"Okay . . . five minutes and fifty seconds."

"That's better. We'll round that off to six minutes."

"Like I said, six minutes."

Ben checked his notes and said, "You need to launch at two minutes and twenty-four seconds before seven."

Hawker grinned. "Can we skip the 'seconds' part and round that off to either two or three minutes?"

Ben looked up and smiled. "I guess I am taking myself a little too seriously. I didn't get any sleep last night. I'm all tensed up."

Hawker lifted the bottom of his mask slightly and exhaled. "I appreciate all the effort you've put into this, but you know . . . I think you kinda enjoy being involved in my extracurricular activities."

It appeared for a second that Ben was going to respond in the affirmative, but instead he looked back at his notes and said, "Now that the niceties are over, are you ready for your briefing?"

"Ready as I'll ever be."

Mark entered the workshop and said, "I trust you slept well."

Hawker nodded.

Ben continued, "Okay, like I said earlier, you'll launch at three minutes before seven. Your launch angle will be fifteen degrees from the vertical and twenty-five degrees north of west. You'll need to maintain that vector all the way up to twenty-two thousand miles.

"I brought you two timing devices, one for each wrist. One is a digital clock and the other is a digital timer. The only thing you have to do with the clock is read it, but you'll have to start the timer when you come to a complete stop two hundred miles up."

Hawker grinned and said, "Yes, boss."

Ben ignored him and continued. "I've designed the plan to give the fewest numbers possible that you'll have to memorize."

"That was kind of you," said Hawker.

Ben ignored him again. "The time of intercept with the satellite is written on the band that attaches the clock to your wrist. You will need to memorize only two values of thrust, one for when you're accelerating just yourself and the other for when you're accelerating yourself and the satellite. For just yourself it'll be five hundred and seventy-six pounds, and when you add the satellite, three thousand and seventy-six. And a word of caution . . . those values should be considered upper limits. Try not to exceed them. I know your body could handle more acceleration, but those numbers will produce two-point-five times Earth's gravity. Let's be safe."

Again, Hawker grinned and said, "Yes, boss."

"Well I don't want you blacking out up there and blowing the whole mission."

"Don't worry," said Hawker. "I don't dare mess up. Mark would never let me forget it if I died while using equipment he rigged up."

"Very funny," said Ben.

He flipped a page in his notebook and continued. "The other numbers you have to remember, of course, are times. The first one is the time from two hundred miles altitude to the halfway point. I'm rounding that off to twenty minutes and twenty seconds exactly because I'm assuming you'll kill a couple of seconds giving the thrust command after you've started the timer."

He hesitated and asked, "You do know why you have to come to a complete stop at two hundred miles, don't you?"

Hawker nodded. "I'm assuming that's a reference point. Since I told you the only measurable quantity I could rely on would be time, you would want very precise initial values of position, time and velocity. You would then combine those with a precise value of thrust to effectively turn my timer into an altimeter. And you chose the two-hundred-mile point to keep the atmosphere from being a factor."

"I see I taught you well," said Ben. "Now let's get back to that half-way point I mentioned. As I said, you will arrive there at twenty minutes and twenty seconds. At that instant you will reverse your thrust, but keep the magnitude the same. You don't have to remember this, but your speed will be more than sixty-six thousand miles per hour at that point. The reversed thrust will act as a brake to slow you down at the same rate you were accelerating before. That will bring you to another complete stop at the satellite's orbit at the end of exactly forty minutes and thirty-eight seconds. You'll have to remember to turn off your thrust at that instant.

"Actually, you should use your telescopic vision and look for the satellite before you reach that point. It should go zipping past just before you get there. Let your timer play out all the way though to make sure you have the right orbit. Then immediately fall in behind the satellite and apply your maximum allowable thrust to catch up with it. You don't have to remember this either, but that will take a little more than three and a half minutes. That should be enough time to make positive identification. Then you just match its speed and wait for the appointed time."

Hawker adjusted the oxygen mask and said, "Sounds easy enough."

"At seven forty-nine and thirty-seven seconds you grip the satellite to shield it from gravity and it goes flying off into space. But on top of that you also apply maximum allowable thrust and hold it for five minutes and thirty seconds. That will accelerate the satellite to twenty-five thousand miles per hour, guaranteeing that it's well on its way to the sun.

"Now the order in which you do these next steps is very important.

At the end of the acceleration period for the satellite, be sure to reduce your thrust to zero before releasing the satellite. If you release the satellite first, the sudden acceleration will kill you."

"I'll try to remember that," said Hawker.

"Immediately after you release the satellite, apply maximum allowable reverse thrust. That will eventually stop your forward motion and reverse it. You won't know when your direction reverses because you'll feel the same constant force going backwards that you felt going forward. You'll even feel that same force during the brief instant that your velocity is zero. That will occur at thirteen minutes and six seconds after you first touch the satellite.

"At that point, you should turn around and look for Earth; then head straight toward it. Although it won't be exact, you can use the same value of time to get to the halfway point that you used going up. That will save you having to remember another number. Obviously your speed would reach zero before you got back to the two hundred-mile reference point, but your GPS will be working again by then. You should have at least twenty minutes of air remaining when you get back to the atmosphere."

Ben smiled and said, "Any questions?"

Hawker feigned an inquisitive look. "What did you say that first number was that I had to memorize?"

"You'd better start getting serious about this," said Ben.

Mark had been listening to all this but had kept quiet. When it appeared that Ben had finished his briefing, Mark said to Hawker, "Sounds like you're in for a little fun. Wish I could go with you." He hesitated briefly; then added, "By the way, you'll be happy to hear that I wrapped your air tank with a special web material that should help to impede the reflection of radar signals."

As launch time drew near, Mark and Ben helped Hawker get dressed for his mission. He was somewhat handicapped by his need to keep the oxygen mask in place and carry the oxygen bottle everywhere he went. He had donned most of his special suit without help, but was waiting until the last minute to put on his helmet. There were two reasons for that: He wanted to save the oxygen in the SCUBA tank for the trip, but he also wanted to purge as much nitrogen from his system as possible before he went to the lower air pressure. Mark and Ben were now helping him with the rest of his equipment. They lifted the SCUBA tank onto his back and made sure the conducting strap connected to the tank was wedged against the suit. Then Mark fastened the tank's supporting harness in front and routed the hose with the pressure gauge over Hawker's right shoulder.

As he attached the gauge to the harness on Hawker's chest, he proffered a warning: "One more time . . . this gauge shows the remaining pressure in the tank. When this needle gets to this red mark, it's time to head for home . . . regardless of what you're doing."

Hawker glanced down to be sure he could see the gauge's face. "I got that part," he said. "But thanks for your concern."

It didn't take long for Hawker to begin feeling the weight of the tank on his back. He had become spoiled by spending so much time weightless.

Then Ben signaled it was time for the next step.

Hawker took a deep breath of oxygen and held it; then removed the mask and handed it to Ben. Ben in turn handed him the helmet. The helmet had looked weird enough before, but now it had a hose dangling from it.

Still holding his breath, Hawker donned the helmet and sealed the flaps. Mark quickly connected the loose end of the hose to a three-way valve attached to two tanks resting on the floor next to them. Then without hesitation, he reached down and opened the valve on the tank containing a vacuum. Most of the air inside Hawker's suit was immediately sucked out, and Mark moved the three-way valve to a new position. This new position connected Hawker to the other tank which contained pure oxygen under thirty pounds per square inch of pressure. The oxygen's pressure was reduced to twenty psi as it escaped the tank and inflated Hawker's suit.

Hawker's arms were now down at his sides. As soon as he felt the new air pressure, he gave the "degravitize" command followed immediately by another which converted the suit to a rigid shell. When Mark felt the suit become rigid, he quickly disconnected the air hose from the three-way valve and moved it to the pressure regulator atop the SCUBA tank on Hawker's back.

Throughout the thirty-five-seconds procedure, Hawker had been holding his breath. Mark said, "Okay, you can breathe now."

The procedure they had just executed had been worked out by Mark and Ben while Hawker slept. They had briefed Hawker following Ben's briefing on the activities to be carried out in space. If they had not gone through this routine, the ambient air pressure on Hawker's chest would have been three times as great as the pressure on the oxygen he was trying to breathe. He would not have been able to expand his lungs. When the suit was inflated and then made rigid, an air space was created between it and Hawker's body. The pressure then was the same on his chest as in his lungs. The problem they were counteracting would go away once Hawker was above Earth's atmosphere and he would be able to return the suit to its flexible state. Until then, his arms were going to be pinned to his sides.

Mark and Ben were observing Hawker to determine his reaction to the lower air pressure. "How do you feel?" asked Ben.

"Fine," said Hawker.

"Well we're about out of time. We'd better move outside."

Mark wasn't expecting observers, but he opened the door and scanned the area anyway. "All clear," he said.

Being in the weightless mode, Hawker glided effortlessly through the door and to the designated spot in Mark's front yard.

"Are you still feeling okay?" asked Mark.

"You two quit worrying," said Hawker. "We took all the necessary precautions."

Ben said, "Ten seconds."

Hawker said, "Thanks, guys. See you later." Then on Ben's signal he gave a thought command for the vector Ben had given him and thrust himself skyward.

At exactly two hundred miles up, Hawker came to a complete stop and changed the suit back to its flexible state. Then he started the timer Ben had attached to his wrist and gave the thought command "thrust-same-direction-five-seven-six." The sudden acceleration definitely got his attention. In an instant, he had gone from weighing nothing to suddenly feeling as if he weighed almost five hundred pounds. On top of that, the air tank that had been a minor discomfort on the ground now felt two and a half times heavier. Fortunately, the acceleration force was spread out over his body and not concentrated just on the soles of his feet. But he still had to endure this discomfort for twenty minutes before the force would be shifted to different surfaces of his body.

As he was well above any appreciable atmosphere, there was no longer any need to streamline his body, so he opted for the most comfortable position. The situation reminded him of some of the trips he had taken in his airplane where a good bit of time passed with nothing to do but wait to arrive at the destination airport. There were major differences, however: When piloting his airplane, he always wore his headset and kept his transceiver tuned to Air Traffic Control. That provided him with an almost constant source of sound. He didn't do that while piloting his suit because of the need to carefully control his thoughts.

Also, this time there were no clouds or any other nearby objects to give him a sensation of relative motion. He was looking into the blackness of space with only the distant stars to tell him his eyes were open. He could see the Sun if he looked far enough to his right, and he could see the timing devices on his invisible wrists. But when looking straight ahead, the distant stars were the only visible things in the universe. The lack of nearby visible objects—plus the fact that there was no air to provide a sound of rushing wind—completely robbed him of the sensation of motion. The sensation he *did* have was that of a very heavy person sitting completely still in a totally darkened, soundproof room.

At twenty minutes and twenty seconds he gave the command "thrust-reverse-direction-five-seven-six" and immediately felt the pressure change from his backside to the front of his body and upper shoulders. Since his helmet didn't participate in the propulsion process, his head felt nothing, but his neck felt the change in acceleration because of the mass of his head. He kept the same body orientation because he wanted to be looking in the direction of motion even if he couldn't see anything.

When his timer indicated he was getting close to the satellite's orbit, he began looking for it. Its speed as it zipped past exactly according to

Ben's prediction amazed him. Though he had no way to observe it directly, he knew that *his* speed now was almost zero, so he turned immediately and started chasing the satellite. After a few minutes he had caught up and was matching its speed. He identified the markings Ben had told him to look for; then moved in close to a point that would provide an easy grip. At the appointed time he gripped it, causing Earth's gravity to lose its influence. That immediately changed its motion from a circular path to a straight line—straight toward the sun.

He would need both hands for this next part, so he took a grip with the other hand also. Then to reduce the chances that the sudden acceleration might break something loose, he reoriented the strongest axis of the solar panel supports along the direction of motion. He wasn't concerned about damaging the satellite; he just didn't want any more trash roaming about in space. With the satellite positioned the way he wanted it, he converted the suit to its rigid state and prepared himself to become heavy again. Then allowing the satellite to pull him along in order to establish a direction, he gave the command "thrust-maintain-direction-three-zero-seven-six."

He had enjoyed that brief interval with no acceleration stress on his body. Now he was back to two and a half times his earthbound weight. The rigid suit was pushing the satellite, so he felt no additional force from that. He accelerated the satellite for five minutes and thirty seconds as per Ben's instructions; then gave the command "thrust-zero." The welcome weightless feeling returned. The satellite was now pulling him along at a constant speed. That was his signal to release it. He converted his suit back to flexible material again and let the satellite slip from his grip.

As he watched the much greater mass move away from him, he gave the command "thrust-reverse-direction-five-seven-six." That command applied the brakes to his forward motion and began decelerating him at the maximum allowable rate.

That's when he heard the sound; the first sound he had heard since leaving the atmosphere. It sounded different with the reduced air pressure inside his helmet, but he still recognized it. It was the audible alarm of his collision avoidance system.

He summoned a visual of the situation: Something to his left front was coming at him with a relative velocity of more than thirty-seven thousand miles per hour. He knew his own velocity had been twenty-five thousand when he released the satellite. It would be less now, but that object would still be traveling at almost thirty thousand mph relative to space. It certainly wasn't a satellite of Earth. And it couldn't be a missile from Earth unless it had been launched from a satellite in *High Earth Orbit*. But the image looked strange.

Regardless of what it was, he had to do some fast thinking on how to avoid it. It would be too dangerous for him to slow down enough: His body couldn't handle that extra deceleration. He couldn't make sharp turns because of his high momentum. If he reversed his thrust again that would just speed him up straight toward the path of the unknown object. Maybe he could start a turn to his right, and after his direction changed enough, switch to maximum allowable forward acceleration. That would at least reduce the object's velocity relative to him. And if he had enough time to get in a complete U-turn, he might avoid the collision altogether.

He had to do something and that's all he could think of.

As he started the turn, he scanned the space to his left front with his telescopic vision and the object came into view. It wasn't a single object; it was many objects. He was just before being hit by a menacing swarm of meteoroids. He didn't know what his speed was but he couldn't wait; he had to reverse the thrust and accelerate away from the meteoroids. Violating Ben's rule for maximum allowable acceleration, he reversed the thrust and gave the command for three gravities instead of two and a half. That command immediately halted the braking and began accelerating him away from the meteoroid swarm. But it wasn't enough to avoid the encounter: Small meteoroids began pelting his body. They hurt more than the bullets he had felt in the past. His thought now was to increase forward acceleration again, but before he could give the command, something hit his helmet with a force that sent shock waves through his entire body and sent his mind into the depths of blackness.

When she awoke that morning, the First Lady had continued her efforts to contact Hawker, but without success. The Secret Service agent, Hank, also had not called again. She called him.

"We're still working on it," he said. "The university police went to Hawker's house and to Ben Huron's house. Nobody was home at either place. Same for Hawker's fiancée. And that was after they had already been to the physics department. After all that failed, an FBI agent from Jacksonville drove down there. I'm still waiting to hear from him."

"How can that many people just disappear like that?"

"I don't know, but it's the weekend and they're all close friends. Maybe they all just took a holiday together somewhere."

"Hawker doesn't take holidays. Are we sure he made it back from Russia okay?"

"Yes. He and his fiancée were seen at the university yesterday."

"Well keep trying . . . and keep me updated a little better. I'm becoming very concerned about this situation . . . especially with the promise the President made."

Then she disconnected and went looking for her husband.

When Hawker regained awareness, he had the feeling he hadn't been out very long. The meteoroids were gone, but he didn't know how far off course they had moved him. In fact, he didn't even know what his course had been at the time of the collision. He also couldn't remember the last command he had given the suit. He was literally *lost in space.*

He knew one thing though: He didn't want to accelerate in any direction until he figured out what that direction should be. He gave the command "thrust-zero" and immediately felt the pressure removed from his body. That certainly felt better.

The only thing he could see at the moment was the blackness of space. *Did I get blown so far out into space that I can't even see Earth?* he thought. Curious about how long he had been unconscious, he glanced at the clock on his wrist. It had survived the encounter with the meteoroids and indicated that only four minutes had passed since his release of the satellite. That confirmed his feeling that he hadn't been out very long.

Knowing that he couldn't have moved too far from Earth, he began a slow rotation of his body to find it. It didn't take long. It was hard to miss that huge blue and white globe—just hanging there in all of its splendor. It took up a large portion of his field of vision and he thought it was truly the most impressive sight he had ever seen. There was no longer any doubt about which direction he wanted to go.

He wondered if the air tank's pressure gauge had been damaged. It was firmly attached to the harness on his chest, but he reached up and moved it as much as he could in each direction. The gauge appeared to be undamaged and the pressure was reading close to where it should be. He might have consumed a tad more oxygen than he would have expected, but certainly not enough to be alarmed about. Still, he had the nagging feeling that something was wrong. He just couldn't put his finger on it.

In any case, it was time to stop thinking and head for home. His next move would take two commands because up here the suit had no way of measuring absolute values of acceleration. He looked straight at Earth and gave the command "accelerate-eyes-direction-minimum." A small force directed toward Earth was immediately applied to his body, but he didn't know if he was actually moving in that direction. In fact, he probably wasn't because it would have taken him seven minutes and thirty-six seconds to come to a complete stop if he had continued under reverse thrust. Since he had changed the thrust and then turned it off completely, he was probably still moving away from Earth. Oh well, it didn't really matter. His next command would eventually send him accelerating toward Earth.

Still using Ben's numbers, he gave the command "thrust-maintain-direction-five-seven-six." That would get him close to the halfway point in twenty minutes. He could then apply reverse thrust and begin slowing down. It wouldn't be necessary to come to a complete stop at two hundred miles altitude because his GPS would be working again by then and he would know his speed and altitude.

His reasoning was good, but unfortunately he didn't have all the facts. As he approached the halfway point as measured by his timer, he again checked his air pressure gauge. That's when he got a nasty surprise: The gauge was reading dangerously close to that all-important "go-home" mark. In fact, it was reading what it should have read once he was safely back in the atmosphere. That meant he had a leak. The meteoroid encounter had damaged something after all. It was impossible to know exactly, but he guessed he would run out of oxygen within fifteen minutes. The only problem with that was that it would take more than twenty minutes to get to Earth's atmosphere.

It would take that long, that is, if he followed the original plan, but this situation definitely called for being flexible. According to Ben, his speed would be about sixty-six thousand miles per hour at this point. Instead of applying the brakes as had been planned, he turned off the thrust and transitioned to a constant velocity. The removal of the acceleration force from his body also removed the feeling that he was racing toward his doom.

He needed a few seconds to think: *What's the distance to the halfway point between here and the atmosphere? Half of eleven thousand is fifty-five hundred miles. How long will that take at sixty-six thousand miles per hour? Sixty-six thousand in one hour . . . thirty-three in half an hour . . . sixteen in fifteen minutes . . . eight in seven and a half . . . four in three and three quarters. Okay, six thousand miles in five minutes is close enough considering I don't know my actual speed and position anyway.*

> *That leaves me ten minutes to slow down enough to enter the atmosphere. I have half the distance and half the time of the original plan, so that means I'll have to double the deceleration. That means five gees. At two hundred and thirty pounds for me plus the air tank, ten gees would be twenty-three hundred pounds. Half that would be eleven-fifty. So when the five minutes are up, I'll apply eleven hundred and fifty pounds of reverse thrust.*

I wonder if I can handle five gees for ten minutes without blacking out. I guess I'll find out. If I run out of air up here, I'll black out anyway. So what do I have to lose?

Then he thought to himself: *Why did I rush through that? Now I don't have anything to do for the next four minutes.*

He looked longingly at Earth. He had always wanted to take a trip in space, but right now he would much rather be safe at home.

His five minutes of weightless bliss ended and it was time to get heavy. He looked at Earth and gave the decelerate command "thrust-re-verse-eyes-direction-one-one-five-zero." Out of habit, his arms had been at his sides in the position used by skydivers when "tracking." Suddenly, they were thrown out in front of him in the direction of motion and he felt a force five times his own normal weight. But the force wasn't act-ing on his feet and legs; because of his body orientation, it was directed against the tops of his shoulders and upper chest. He felt as if all of his insides were being pushed into his throat.

It didn't take long to realize he needed to make some changes. He visualized his body rotating to place his stomach out in front. That es-sentially oriented the lengthwise axis of his body perpendicular to the direction of motion. With the force spread out over the entire front of his body, he felt some better, but it wasn't enough. He then tried con-verting the suit to a rigid shell, but that just made things worse. He quickly changed the suit back to its flexible state and considered his op-tions. Actually, he was having difficulty thinking now, but he was lucid enough to realize that he would have to reduce the deceleration. Maybe he could handle something closer to four gees. His thinking was getting fuzzier: *How much thrust will give me one gee? It doesn't matter, man. It doesn't have to be exact. Two hundred is easy to work with. That's close enough to one gravity.* He gave the command "thrust-maintain-direction-nine-five-zero."

That was better, but he still felt like a seven hundred and forty-three-pound man lying on his stomach too weak to turn over. Because of his hampered thinking ability, he endured his misery for several minutes before it occurred to him that he would be traveling faster than his hastily-put-together plan called for, and would therefore reach the atmo-sphere sooner. That could be a real problem. If his speed was too great when he hit the atmosphere, the air friction would create more heat than he could handle.

It then occurred to him to check his GPS: *Oh, man . . . I'm coming up on my two hundred-mile reference point at over twenty-eight thousand miles per hour. I can't hit the atmosphere with that kind of speed.*

His only choice was to circle the Earth until he could slow down enough to enter its atmosphere. He was having trouble concentrating: *How long would that take? It doesn't matter how long. It has to be done.*

His speed was much too great for his own body weight to hold him in orbit. He would have to use part of his deceleration thrust to curve his path. He tried to mentally calculate how much centripetal force he would need, but it was no use. He had to act now or it would be too late. Then he scolded himself: *What's the matter with you, man? The GPS is working. The suit can make the calculations.* He changed his direction, attempting to achieve an instantaneous velocity that would be tangent to the two hundred-mile orbital path at the instant he reached that altitude. He wasn't sure he made it, but when his GPS read two hundred miles he gave the command "maintain altitude." That gave him a force component pushing him toward Earth as well as one slowing his forward speed. The result was a path that always curved toward Earth. Unfortunately, his mental state prevented his enjoyment of the beauty that was passing below him.

There was nothing else he could do at the moment, so he glanced at his timer. Seven minutes and thirty seconds had passed since he started decelerating. He would soon be out of oxygen. He looked at the air pressure gauge. Correction: He was already out of oxygen. The gauge was reading zero. Either the gauge was wrong or he was breathing the oxygen produced by the suit. If that was the case, it wouldn't last long.

He had barely released the pressure gauge when he became aware of his air hunger. *I shouldn't have looked at that gauge,* he thought. *I was doing fine before that.*

Then it occurred to him that part of his problem was due to his body position. He was having difficulty expanding his lungs because of the extra pressure on his chest from the deceleration. He scolded himself for not thinking of that earlier; then pulled his knees up and leaned backward and toward Earth into a reclined sitting position. That transferred most of the pressure to his backside and legs—a definite improvement.

He checked the GPS screen again. His speed was steadily coming down, but was still much too great to enter the atmosphere. He had to stop glancing at the patches of clouds below: It was making him nauseated.

Then his air hunger took a turn for the worse. *Maybe that's why I'm nauseated,* he thought. *But I don't know of anything else I can do. I'd be roasted alive if I entered the atmosphere at this speed.*

Then he spotted something, well ahead and lower. *What's that I'm coming up on?* He thought. *I must be hallucinating. I know my mind isn't working right. No, wait. . . . That's the International Space Station. I wonder if they'd let me inside. That's my only chance. If they don't help me, I'm gonna die up here.*

Even in the mental state he was in, he could still see that he was rapidly gaining on the Space Station and that it was several miles below his altitude. He checked his speed again: *Eighteen thousand . . . too much . . . got to decelerate more while I can still think.*

He visualized his body taking a direct path to the Space Station; then matching their speed once he got there.

Then in a brief moment of renewed awareness: *But don't know how to get their attention . . . don't know their frequency. . . . Gotta think . . . but without giving commands.*

He realized the astronauts would need to see more than a shadow, so he switched to the light-reflecting mode. *What else? Think . . . Hawker . . . think . . . your last chance . . .*

He almost missed it, but just before his thinking process failed him, he removed the field that was shielding him from Earth's gravity. Gravity would be necessary to keep him in the same orbit with the Space Station.

His chest felt like the deceleration pressure was on it again, but it wasn't. There just wasn't enough oxygen left to inflate his lungs. Through blurry eyes he saw movement outside the Space Station: *Is that somebody in a space suit? Gonna run into 'em . . . gotta slow down . . . no . . . gotta turn off thrust.* He somehow managed to give the command "thrust-zero."

He wasn't certain, but he thought somebody was close to him—looking at him. Slowly, and with great effort, he grasped the air pressure gauge and attempted to present its face to the person he thought he saw. But his oxygen starvation won out: The increasing grayness suddenly turned to blackness.

Meanwhile back in Florida, Mark Woodall and Ben Huron were

waiting for Hawker's return. "It's about time for Damon to get back," said Ben. "I'm anxious to hear about this trip. For everybody's sake, I certainly hope we didn't make any mistakes."

At that instant his cell phone jingled. "This is probably him," he said.

But it wasn't Hawker; it was Professor Thad Wilson.

"Where are you?" Professor Wilson asked.

"I'm with Mark Woodall at his house."

"I didn't know you knew him that well."

"We're working together on a project for Damon."

"That's why I'm calling," said Professor Wilson. "Is he there with you?"

"Not at the moment, but we're expecting him soon."

"Well there's an FBI agent here that wants to talk with him. I'm gonna turn you over to the agent. Hang on a minute."

The voice on the other end said, "This is Special Agent Ross Miller. Do you know how to contact Professor Damon Hawker?"

Ben had become leery about being too cooperative with government personnel since his experience with President Bradshaw's goons earlier that year. "He doesn't own a cell phone," Ben replied.

"That's not what I asked you," said the FBI agent. "Do you know how to contact him?"

"Why do you want to know?"

"The Secret Service wants to speak with him. It's urgent."

"Give me the name and number," said Ben. "I'll pass it on when I talk with him again."

"Are you always this cooperative with law enforcement?"

"People employed by the government don't always have the interest of the people at heart."

There was a brief pause before Special Agent Miller said, "You know Dr. Huron, for something as urgent as what I'm dealing with, I could take measures that you probably wouldn't like. Why don't you make it easy on yourself and be a little more cooperative?"

"Look," said Ben. "He's not at home and he's not here at the moment. I don't know exactly where he is and he doesn't carry a cell phone. I told you I would relay a message as soon as I talk with him. What more do you want from me?"

There was another pause; then Agent Miller gave Ben the Secret Service agent's name and number and disconnected.

"I wonder what the Secret Service wants with Damon," Ben said to Mark.

Then he immediately punched in the code for Hawker's helmet phone, but the call wouldn't go through. He tried again with the same result.

"This is not good," he said. "If he's still outside the range of the communications satellites, he's in trouble."

At that moment, his cell phone jingled again. "Maybe this is him," he said.

But it was Professor Wilson again. "The FBI agent is gone," said the professor. "Maybe you should tell me what you and Hawker are up to."

Professor Wilson was one of Hawker's closest friends and already knew about the suit, so Ben told him about Hawker's trip into space and the fact that he should have returned by now.

Hawker slowly became aware that he was still alive. The last sensation he'd had before losing consciousness was the terrible feeling in his chest. Now that feeling was gone and he was breathing without difficulty. He opened his eyes and a blurry space helmet came into focus. He didn't have to ask where he was; he knew he was inside the airlock of the International Space Station. But the hatch was still open. How was he breathing? He adjusted his position to get a better look at the astronaut and his surroundings. Then he saw that his air hose was connected to a coupling on the compartment wall.

The astronaut was holding them both in position by gripping a bar attached to the wall with one hand and Hawker's wrist with the other. He hadn't been able to see through the visor of Hawker's helmet, and so didn't know Hawker was conscious again until he saw the movement.

When Hawker completed his brief scan of the airlock and returned his eyes to the space helmet, it was obvious the astronaut was trying to speak with him. But even if the astronaut's voice could penetrate through his helmet, there still wasn't any air in the airlock to conduct sound waves. He obviously was trying to communicate via radio transmission.

Hawker pointed to the side of his helmet where his ear would be and shook his head. Then he held up a finger and traced out a question mark followed by a sine wave.

The astronaut placed Hawker's gloved hand on the bar that he had been gripping; then held up his own fingers giving Hawker a series of numbers.

Hawker activated his transceiver and tuned it to the frequency the astronaut had given him. "Can you hear me now?" he asked.

The astronaut replied, "Yes. Didn't they give you a frequency for contacting me?"

Hawker wasn't sure who "they" was, so he said no and left it at that.

"That's odd," said the astronaut. "But what's even odder is that they sent you into space with scuba equipment. What's the idea behind that?"

"We needed to get me up here in a hurry and that's what was available."

Hawker could see the astronaut shaking his head inside his helmet. "It is really hard for me to believe our engineers couldn't come up with something better than that," the astronaut was saying. "That rigged up job jeopardized this whole mission. You came close to losing your life out there . . . and Gregor could have died as well."

"Who's Gregor?"

"Gregor Ulitsky, our Russian roommate. Didn't they tell you anything?"

"Not really," said Hawker.

The astronaut's tone indicated he couldn't believe what he was hearing. "Gregor is the reason we sent for you. He has acute appendicitis and needs immediate surgery. If he doesn't get it soon, his appendix could rupture and kill him."

Hawker, of course, hadn't known the astronauts had sent for him, but he quickly recognized the opportunity given him and played along to conceal his real reason for being in space. "It was certainly lucky for me that you were outside waiting for me. Thanks for saving my life."

"Don't mention it. I suited up and got ready after the President promised that you would be here. Then when we saw you coming I moved on outside. I was supposed to guide you in and make sure you didn't damage anything. As it turned out, I had to pull you in and that wasn't easy. I was afraid you would die before I could get you connected to our emergency oxygen station." Then his face broke into a thin grin. "Our guys did at least one thing right. Your air hose connector mates perfectly with those on our oxygen lines."

Hawker thanked his lucky stars that Mark had attended that surplus sale. "I'll definitely remember to thank the guy responsible for that," he said.

"By the way, my name is Ned Beckett." When Hawker didn't respond with his own name, Beckett asked, "What on earth possessed you to start this trip without sufficient oxygen?"

"I had plenty of oxygen when I left the ground, but I collided with some unexpected space debris and wound up with a slow leak."

"A leak? Oh, man . . . this isn't going well at all. . . . Look, I'm gonna have to check in with *Mission Control*. You just hang out where you are and I'll be back with you shortly."

Beckett turned his back to Hawker and used a handle on the opposite wall to propel him a short distance away where he was doing something that Hawker couldn't see.

Hawker looked at Beckett's huge space suit; then at the round black hole that was the hatch opening. *It looks so small*, he thought. *I'm amazed he got me through it in time.*

After several minutes, Beckett moved to a new position, opened a storage compartment and pulled out a hose. Then he closed the compartment and "floated" back to Hawker's position. "Here's what they want us to do," he said. "I'm gonna connect your air tank to a high pressure oxygen line and recharge it. Then we'll reconnect you to your tank and monitor your loss of pressure for a few minutes. If we decide your leak is slow enough, we'll go ahead with our plan to have you transport Gregor back to Earth. How long do you estimate it would take you and Gregor to get back into breathable atmosphere?"

"That would depend on how much deceleration Gregor can handle."

"The less, the better . . . but no more than one gee for sure."

Hawker did a mental calculation: *I'll have to bleed off about sixteen thousand miles per hour of velocity. That'll convert to about twenty-four thousand feet per second. One gee is thirty-two feet per second per second which means I'll need about eight hundred seconds or something over twelve minutes.* To Beckett, he said, "At one gee, about fifteen minutes."

As Hawker was doing his calculation, Beckett was cautiously gliding past him. Hawker could feel a tug on the air tank as Beckett connected it to the high pressure oxygen line. "How long has Gregor been sick?" he asked.

"I suspect he was having pain long before he let it be known. He first admitted it about eighteen hours ago. Doctors on the ground came up with the diagnosis within two hours after he started complaining."

"Wonder what caused it?"

By this time, Beckett had moved back to Hawker's front and was inspecting the air hose and interface attached to his helmet. "We don't know," he said. "It could be a number of things . . . stress associated with the trip up here . . . poor bowel habits . . . diet. . . . In any case, the problem is that it would take much too long to get a spaceship up here and back to the ground. That's why we asked the President to send you."

Hawker wondered what made them think the President had any control over him. To Beckett, he said, "I thought they kept a Soyuz space pod here all the time."

"They do, but it's not operational at the moment. It developed a serious safety problem during the flight up here and is undergoing repairs."

Beckett backed off and took a grip on the opposite wall. "I don't see any damage to the equipment that's been added to your suit," he said. "Maybe there's a tiny hole in the suit itself."

"That's not likely," said Hawker. "It's probably somewhere along the adhesive seam on the interface. My helmet took quite a blow." It was obvious to him that Beckett was familiar with the former appearance of his helmet.

"*Mission Control* was a little confused. They weren't aware that anyone from there had talked with you or that you were on your way up here."

Hawker let that ride without giving an explanation.

"We've rigged up a carrying strap for Gregor," said Beckett. "It's electrically conductive and it's attached to the aluminized Mylar of his space suit. It should allow you to carry him in a way that will be most comfortable for both of you."

"Sounds like somebody has done their homework. How long have you been working on this?"

"More than twelve hours, but I already knew what it takes for you to make a person weightless. Actually, I'm the one who got you into this predicament. I've read every news article that's been written about you and knew you were the best hope we had for saving Gregor."

Beckett pushed off gently from the wall and "floated" over to Hawker. He tilted the air pressure gauge on Hawker's chest for a better look. "That's the maximum pressure we can give you." Then he moved around to Hawker's rear and Hawker again felt a tugging on his air tank.

Beckett moved Hawker slightly and disconnected his air hose from the airlock's emergency oxygen station. Then he immediately reconnected the hose to the tank on Hawker's back. "Now we'll see how bad your leak is," he said.

Hawker reset the timer on his wrist to zero.

They both watched Hawker's pressure gauge for several minutes before Beckett said, "Scuba diving is one of my hobbies. That's how I knew immediately that you were in trouble out there when I saw your pressure gauge. Based on what I'm seeing here, I think we can proceed with this operation. Your leak seems to be very slow. Even if it's leaking at the same rate you're consuming, it would still last about forty-five minutes. What do you think?"

"Let's do it," said Hawker.

"Okay, I'll put you back on the airlock's oxygen supply until you're ready to go."

After he finished that, Beckett closed the outside hatch and said, "Gregor is in the next compartment, all suited up and ready to go. He's been on oxygen for some time . . . in anticipation of this move. We'll have to partially pressurize the airlock before we bring him out. Then we'll have to depressurize it again before we open this outside hatch." As an afterthought, he added, "By the way, the President wants you to deliver Gregor directly to Walter Reed Hospital in Washington."

"Walter Reed, huh? That's an interesting twist."

Beckett was now moving toward the hatch that connected the two compartments. "What? You mean a Russian in a U.S. Army hospital?"

"That too . . . but what I was thinking was that the man the hospital was named after died there from appendicitis."

Although Beckett couldn't see Hawker's face, he turned and gave him a quizzical look.

"Just a bit of trivia," said Hawker. "Nothing else intended."

Standing outside in Mark Woodall's front yard, Ben Huron had tried several times to reach Hawker by phone, but always without success. "I'm really worried now," he said to Mark. "Even if Damon had decided not to come directly back here, he would've called to let us know he was okay."

And at the White House, President Bradshaw was asking his wife, "How did you finally get word to Hawker about the astronaut?"

"I didn't," she answered. "I don't know how he knew. But when I was talking with him in the Rose Garden a few days ago I found out he knows stuff about you and me that nobody is supposed to know, including the fact that I'm running the show around here. We have to assume he knows the same dirt on you that I do. Apparently, he has some skills we don't know about yet."

President Bradshaw flinched. He almost hated her when she brought up the dirt she had on him. "That suit is what gives him his skills. You made a big mistake when you prevented me from gaining control of it."

She scoffed. "Somehow I doubt that you would ever have gained control of it even if I hadn't interfered. You probably don't want to know what he would've done to prevent you from attacking Iran. You're lucky I stepped in to prevent it before he had to act."

"Maybe you should move in with him."

President Bradshaw had mixed emotions about the situation he was in. On the one hand he deeply resented having to take orders from his wife, as well as the verbal abuse. But at the same time he was jealous of her devotion to Hawker, which she made no effort to conceal. He believed he should be the recipient of that devotion—and he desperately wanted it.

Changing the subject, he said, "And I'm appalled at your insistence on treating a Russian spy in a U.S. Army hospital."

"He's not a spy," she countered. "He's an astronaut." Then she smiled. "Just think of the headlines. The press will love it. I hate to be one to take advantage of a bad situation, but this could go a long way toward improving relations between our two countries . . . and Heaven knows we need that."

Back on the Space Station, many minutes had passed and the hatch to the adjoining compartment was now open. Beckett was presumably preparing Gregor for the trip, but Hawker couldn't see what they were doing. Also, because of not being privy to their other frequency, he couldn't hear what they were saying. He could hear sounds at times, but the sounds were not familiar; probably because of the unfamiliar environment.

He'd had some prior knowledge of the airlock's construction and furnishings from his readings, but seeing it firsthand was an eye-opening experience. The concepts of up and down had no meaning here because of the microgravity. Likewise, there was no need for a floor or ceiling, so everything was wall. And every square inch of that wall was being utilized. Where equipment, cables and pipes were not attached, there were doors to storage compartments. Under different circumstances he might ask for a tour of the entire station, but not this time.

The airlock was constructed of aluminum which he knew blocked electric fields, so he didn't think his phone signals would penetrate to the outside, but he decided to try anyway: He knew Ben would be worried about him not returning on schedule. As he suspected would happen, his call to Ben didn't go through. He wished Beckett and Gregor would hurry: He had been in space more than two hours now and his bladder was beginning to tell him it would need relief before too long. He might have to go inside his suit if they didn't get underway soon. He'd never yet had to do that and wasn't looking forward to the prospect.

Fortunately, a space suit came through the open hatch shortly after that thought. It was followed by another that most certainly contained Gregor Ulitsky. Hawker arrived at that conclusion because of the strap "floating" above the second suit's back.

The hatch was closed and Beckett moved on past Hawker. "I'm going to reconnect you to your tank now," he said.

After the airlock was depressurized they opened the outer hatch and eased Gregor out.

Hawker followed and took in his first fully-conscious close-up of the exterior of the Space Station. He was awed. Then he turned back to Beckett and said, "Thanks again for saving my life."

"My pleasure," said Beckett. "Stop in again sometime."

Hawker took a grip on Gregor's carrying strap so that he could slow their forward speed, but he did not "degravitize" them at the beginning of the trip. He used gravity to pull them toward Earth as they decelerated. When he was satisfied that things were going according to plan, he converted the suit to a rigid shell to permit breathing once in the atmosphere. The plan was to be down to a thousand mph when they reached an altitude of fifty miles. He also wanted to do most of his lateral traveling while still in the sparse atmosphere above fifty miles. That would put less of a strain on Gregor's body from air friction.

His plan would have put him about fifty miles north of Washington, D.C. at the time he reached fifty miles altitude. He would have then continued his descent at a forty-five degree angle while bleeding off more speed. The atmosphere would obviously be helping to slow his speed at this point. He had chosen to approach from the north because Walter Reed Hospital was in the northern part of Washington, D.C. and he didn't want to fly through the restricted air space surrounding the White House. Although the authorities were expecting him, his recent experience with the missile over Germany made him want to take every possible precaution.

As it turned out, storm clouds caused him to detour farther north and he and Gregor were forced to traverse the entire state of Maryland at about a thousand feet. That prolonged the trip because of the need to fly slower in the atmosphere for Gregor's benefit. If he had still been in space, the added time would have caused him to deplete his oxygen again. But in the atmosphere the pressure outside the suit was almost three times as great as inside, so the leak was into the suit rather than out. The leak contaminated his pure oxygen environment but that was okay because the contaminant was what he normally breathed anyway.

Because of gravity acting on the unshielded parts of Gregor's attire, he was now hanging below Hawker supported by the carrying strap Beckett had devised. Authorities were swamped with calls about an alien invasion. No doubt, the sight of a fully suited astronaut flying across the sky under his own power was confusing to some people.

Medical personnel plus an audience greeted them when they arrived at the hospital. Hawker had now held his bladder as long as he could. He urgently needed relief so he gently lowered Gregor to the pavement, dropped the carrying strap and flew away.

First Lady Lena Bradshaw was informed that Hawker had just delivered the Russian astronaut to Walter Reed. *I still wonder how he knew,* she thought. *That guy never ceases to amaze me. I'm anxious to see what he'll do about the satellite.*

She didn't know the satellite was already on its way to a fiery collision with the Sun.

chapter 7

Hawker's welcome-back committee was larger than the one that had seen him off: Professor Thad Wilson and his daughter, Myra, had joined Mark and Ben in their vigil after Thad learned of his friend's incredible mission. They already knew he was okay, though, because he had called Ben shortly after leaving the Space Station.

Myra waited patiently while Mark disconnected Hawker's air hose from the tank and lowered the tank to the ground. Then when Hawker got his head free of the helmet and dangling hose, she moved in for her "little-sisterly" hug.

"Welcome back," she said, as she squeezed him. "We were worried about you there for a while."

"I had to make a detour by the Space Station," he responded. "I tried to call while I was there, but I was enclosed within metal walls and my phone wouldn't work."

"That must have been when I tried to call you," Ben said. Then he added, "So the mission was successful, huh?"

Hawker nodded. "Yep. The satellite's on its way to a fiery death."

Thad Wilson stepped in and shook Hawker's hand. "The crisis was over almost as soon as I learned about it," he said. "I'm glad it's finished, but I wish you guys would start including me in these things. I'm really disappointed that you didn't let me in on that night jump onto the island."

Hawker gave him a sheepish grin. "Your wife would've shot me if I had taken you along on that."

"I guess you're right," said Thad. "She's not real pleased that I'm still jumping at forty-eight. She thinks that's a young man's sport."

Mark came back to retrieve Hawker's helmet. "That's not old in sky-diving," he said. "I know guys in their sixties and seventies that jump on a regular basis. In fact, I know a couple in their eighties that are still jumping."

"I know," said Thad. "But Moira is very protective. She won't even let Myra go to the *drop zone* unless she's along. She's afraid Myra will jump."

Myra smiled. "I'll soon be old enough that I won't need her permission."

"Don't sell your mother short," said Thad. "She's the one who nursed you through diabetes until you could take care of yourself."

"I know."

Then Thad looked back at Hawker. "Anyway . . . this calls for a celebration. I want you and Teala and everybody that was involved in this project to come to my house for dinner tonight. It'll be a welcome home dinner and a celebration of the completion of a successful mission."

Ben grinned. "Have you checked this out with Moira?" he asked.

"Not yet, but it'll make her happy. She loves to entertain."

"I think the dinner is a good idea," said Hawker. "But the mission isn't over yet. I still have to deal with Petrov. The only evidence we had against him got destroyed in the explosion. I don't like the idea of appointing myself judge, jury and jailer, but I also believe I have a responsibility to protect innocent people from someone I know is a threat. Lev is trying to determine his whereabouts for me. I'll probably be leaving for Russia again tomorrow morning."

"Okay," said Thad. "It's settled." He took Myra by the arm and started toward their car. "We'll call Lev and Dennis and invite them. The rest of you know about it, so we'll expect to see you tonight. Be sure to bring your wife, Ben."

Ben waved and said, "She's out of town . . . visiting her mother. But

I'll be there. I need a good meal." Then he headed for his car. "See you two later," he said to Mark and Hawker. "I need some sleep."

Hawker turned to Mark. "Do you have a solvent that will dissolve the adhesive you put on my helmet?"

"As a matter of fact, I do," said Mark.

As Mark was removing the interface from the helmet, Hawker said, "I don't know if it was sheer genius on your part or just plain luck, but those NASA components you used saved my life."

True to his character, Mark smiled faintly and remained quiet.

Hawker added, "I hope you'll save everything for me. I might have to make another space trip someday."

Mark nodded and handed him the helmet.

He stuffed the suit into its bag and thanked Mark again for making his space trip possible. "See you tonight," he said. "I need some sleep too."

Then he drove Teala's car back to his house, showered and checked for bruises; then had lunch and took a much needed nap.

That evening when Mark and Lev arrived at the home of Thad and Moira Wilson, Myra was the one who answered the door. Lev had never seen Myra, so he was surprised when Mark introduced her as the daughter of Thad Wilson.

"You're not Teala's sister?" he asked.

"Of course not," she said. "Why would you think that?"

Mark chuckled. "She's teasing you, Lev. She knows she resembles Teala. I think she's proud of it."

Myra smiled and led the two through a short hallway past a door that opened into a formal dining room. At the end of the hallway was a great room, but nobody was in it. In fact, it looked as if it wasn't used very often. She led them on through the great room to an adjoining room where the others were gathered. That room contained two couches angled at ninety degrees to one another, two computer stations, a piano, a television set and two easy chairs. Hawker, Teala and Dennis were sitting on one couch and Thad and Moira Wilson on the other. They were all watching news on television.

"You just missed Damon carrying an astronaut," said Moira.

"Don't worry," said Thad. "They'll show it again. They always do."

Lev had never met Myra's mother either. When he was introduced to her, he said, "Well I can see where Myra gets her big brown eyes."

"I'll take that as a compliment," responded Moira.

"Absolutely," said Lev. "They're beautiful."

"Thank you."

Thad had been right: Before they could finish introducing Lev to Moira, the spectacle at Walter Reed Hospital was shown again. The camera captured the shadowy form of Hawker approaching the hospital with the fully suited astronaut dangling beneath him. Then it showed Hawker gently lowering the astronaut to the pavement and dropping the carrying strap. He hesitated briefly as if trying to decide what to do. The movement of Hawker's head could be seen, but it was impossible to tell which direction he was looking or what he was contemplating. Then he flew away without further ado.

"I love to see you fly away like that," said Myra. "It's just like in the movies when the hero does a good deed and then leaves without waiting to be thanked."

"He *is* a hero," said Moira. "But he's not in the movies. He's for real."

Teala playfully punched Hawker on the shoulder and said, "Don't give him the big head."

Hawker flinched and said, "Whoa . . . easy on the shoulder."

Moira smiled and said, "Dinner is ready. We can eat when Ben gets here."

At that moment the doorbell rang. "That must be him," she said.

Thad stood up. "I'll get it this time."

Speaking to Hawker, Teala said, "Is something wrong with your shoulder?"

"Just a little sore," he said.

"What happened to it?"

"It got hit by a piece of space debris."

"Did that happen at the Space Station?" Myra asked.

"No," he answered. "Much higher up . . . right after I released the satellite."

"I wouldn't have thought there'd be a lot of space junk that high up."

"This wasn't man-made debris," said Hawker. "It was actually a whole swarm of meteoroids. They hit me in several places."

Moira, Myra's mom, said, "Oh . . . I'm sorry you got hurt."

Myra grinned. "Don't feel sorry for him. He aged less than the rest of us today."

Ben Huron had just entered the room. He smiled and said, "*Time dilation* might not work for Damon. He doesn't believe in Einstein's *theory of relativity.*"

Hawker smiled. "I hope everybody knows that Ben is kidding. It's not that I don't believe in the theory. I just think it leaves some questions unanswered. I know most of the scientific community takes the attitude that we now know what gravity is . . . Einstein told us. But I'm not convinced that we do. We have a mathematical model sure, but it's one we can't grasp in the context of the real world we live in. We can visualize the bulge in the two-dimensional plane that's always used to explain the concept, but that's a far cry from grasping a warp in four-dimensional space-time. Furthermore, that warp in the two-dimensional plane extends into a third dimension in which the plane does not exist. Does that mean that the warp in four-dimensional space-time extends into a fifth dimension in which space-time does not exist? And if it doesn't extend into a fifth dimension, what *does* it extend into?"

Mark and Lev had both studied physics as part of the curriculum for their engineering degrees, so they were quickly drawn into this conversation.

Lev said, "I had never considered the need for a fifth dimension. What you're saying seems to be reasonable, but what about all the discoveries that support relativity?"

"Don't get me wrong," said Hawker. "I'm not discounting all of *relativity*. I've just never been able to fully accept that gravity is just a warp in space-time. Gravity is a very real entity whereas that warp is a mathematical concept. I think math is great . . . I couldn't get along without it, but we have to remember that math is a tool invented by man. It is not a cup of God-given truths."

"Four dimensions make a lot of sense to me," said Mark. "How would you locate a person or object at a given point in space at a given time if you didn't use four dimensions?"

"I agree," said Hawker. "That system is absolutely essential. My problem is with combining the concepts of space and time to create a new entity called *space-time*. Space and time as separate concepts could claim existence because they existed intuitively in the mind of man, but space-time cannot make that claim. When we talk about space-time curving or having a shape, we are essentially making time into just another spatial dimension. I think it's a mistake to do that. Consider the differences. Each of the space dimensions has exactly the same properties, and in fact, could be interchanged. The orientation of the spatial coordinate system can be arbitrary. Each of those objects or persons that you mentioned occupy a distinctly different point in space, but they all occupy exactly the *same* point in time. If man had some way of relocating a given point in space, he could revisit it many times, but he could never revisit a point in time because any point that he has previously visited no longer exists. I think that time has to be weighted differently."

"So what's your solution to the problem?" Lev asked.

Hawker shrugged. "I don't have a solution. I just have questions. But I will say I think it's possible that some of the interpretations of the theory are flawed. We know that was the case early on. Initially it was thought that Einstein's equations predicted a static universe, but we now know that the universe is expanding. In fact, relativity had predicted all along that the universe could not be static . . . it had to be either expanding or contracting. Then fast-forward to more recent discoveries. We now believe that the expansion of the universe is actually speeding up. But that leads to a problem, namely that of distant galaxies moving away from us faster than the speed of light. One of the conclusions from *relativity* is that material objects cannot travel faster than the speed of light. We get around that problem by saying that the galaxies are not traveling at that speed through space. We say that space *itself* is expanding at that speed. We have now given space all kinds of magical properties. It can curve and it can stretch and it can expand under its own power at rates that would take enormous amounts of energy. . . . I still tend to think of space as the emptiness in which everything else exists. Looking at it from that perspective, it would be meaningless to say that space is expanding. It would be like multiplying zero by some non-zero number. When you get finished nothing has happened. You still have zero. . . ."

Teala broke in. "You're lecturing again, Hawker."

"I want to hear this," said Myra. "He won't say things like that when we're in class."

Moira broke in this time. "Now that Ben is here, let's continue this conversation over dinner. I don't want everything to get cold."

As everybody followed Moira into the dining room, Ben said, "Who's driving that rental car down the street?"

Nobody answered immediately. As they began taking their seats, Thad asked, "How do you know it's a rental car?"

"I've driven enough rentals to know one when I see it."

They all looked at one another and shook their heads.

"That reminds me," said Hawker. "I've been meaning to ask you, Lev, if you found out anything about where Petrov is."

Lev shook his head. "The information I got is that he isn't at his house and nobody seems to know where he is."

Ben said to Hawker, "Did you ever call that Secret Service agent?"

Hawker nodded. "Yeah . . . he said I had already done what he wanted."

"That makes sense," said Ben. "I had two messages from the FBI when I got home. The first one said they were trying to contact you and the second one said to ignore the first one."

As they were passing the food around and helping their plates, Hawker looked at Myra and smiled. "The first time I sat at this table Myra was on a booster seat and her hands were too small to help her own plate."

Thad smiled and nodded. "A lot of things have happened since that night."

Myra added, "I certainly won't forget the day you parachuted into the swamp to bring me my insulin."

"That's when we first started dating," said Teala.

Moira looked at Hawker. "I have to admit it's been interesting knowing you. I don't have many friends who've bumped a satellite out of its orbit and then dropped in on the International Space Station . . . or for that matter, any of the other unbelievable things you've done."

"I've had a lot of help," said Hawker.

Teala grinned and said, "I guess you felt right at home in the Space Station with the weightless astronauts around you."

Hawker smiled.

Myra corrected Teala's statement. "The astronauts aren't weightless. In fact, they're about ninety per cent as heavy in orbit as they are on Earth. It just looks like they're weightless because there isn't anything restraining them. They're actually in free fall of a sort. Earth is still pulling on them with a strong force, but their speed through space balances that force and keeps them in orbit. As a matter of fact, Damon would have had to reestablish gravity on himself while he was inside the Station. Otherwise he would have been forced against one of the interior walls."

Teala looked at Hawker and he nodded.

Moira smiled and said, "How do you put up with her in your class, Damon?"

Hawker grinned. "I let her teach the class and I just take it easy."

Myra shook her head. "He's kidding. He doesn't really do that, but he does let me help him sometimes."

"Are you still planning to go to Russia tomorrow?" Mark asked, as he looked at Hawker.

Hawker had his mouth full, so he nodded. After swallowing, he said, "I'll never feel comfortable as long as Petrov is running loose. He could have agents here right now. Every one of you could be in danger simply because you're my friends. Petrov himself is not likely to be here because I made arrangements to keep him out of the country." Then he thought to himself: *But I also made arrangements to avoid being attacked by missiles. Look how that turned out.*

Then he looked at Dennis. "Dennis, I'd like for you to continue guarding Teala at least until I come back from Russia."

Dennis nodded.

Teala jerked her head to the side toward Hawker. "Don't I have a say in this?" she said.

Hawker frowned. "Teala, you've just come through an experience that could have cost you your life a couple of times. Do you really want to repeat that?"

She grinned sheepishly and shook her head.

Then Hawker looked at Thad Wilson. "And Thad, I don't think Myra should be left alone until I get this thing settled. I know it sounds as if I'm being paranoid, but I've learned the hard way that I should trust my inner voice."

Before Thad could respond, Moira said, "Tomorrow is Thad's day to go flying. I'll keep her with me all day. We're going to Jacksonville Beach to have lunch with a friend of mine."

"And I'll drive her to the university on Monday for your class," said Thad. "Are you going to be back in time to teach it?"

Hawker nodded. "I hope to."

"I may have to ask you to take it if he isn't here," Ben said to Thad.

Thad nodded. "We'll get together tonight before he leaves and talk about what should be covered."

At the same time in Washington, D.C., President Bradshaw and Mrs. Bradshaw were having their dinner.

President Bradshaw was saying, "I hate it with people around all the time. I like it like this much better when it's just you and me."

She smiled. "You asked for this job."

"I know . . . and I like it most of the time. I just don't like people bugging me all the time."

"Just think how much tougher it would be if I were not helping you," she said.

He frowned. "Don't rub it in." There was a brief silence as he took another bite. Then he said, "The Russian president called me this afternoon. He wanted to thank me for bringing his astronaut down for surgery."

"That's the result I was hoping for," she said. "Did you talk about anything else?"

"A couple of things, but the satellite didn't come up if that's what you're wondering about."

"Good." She hesitated before adding, "I'm anxious to see what Hawker does about it, but I doubt he'll confide in me. He doesn't like to think he's working for us. I'll probably have to find out through the news media the same as you . . . and that's probably best."

"What happens when Hawker starts doing things you don't want him to do and you have no control over him?"

"Hawker's a good man. He'll always do what's right."

"What makes you think you know so much about him?"

"I've looked into his eyes."

President Bradshaw didn't know exactly how to interpret that statement. He decided to change the subject. "Okay, what's this *phase two* you say you're ready to implement? . . . And for that matter, what was *phase one?*"

"I thought that was obvious. *Phase one* started when we began listening to other countries. When we opened up the lines of communication and started trying to convince them that we value their opinions. It's when we tailored our actions and our rhetoric to back up our claim that we are not the threat. It's when we changed our strategy in Iraq and began using more diplomacy and less military might. Haven't you learned anything from all this?"

Acting unimpressed and a little bored, he shoved his plate away and signaled the server that he was ready for dessert.

She continued, "In phase two we begin implementing non-military defense strategies."

He gave her a puzzled look. "What exactly does that mean?"

"I may not have stated that exactly the way I intended. I probably should have said that in *phase two* we begin *viewing* certain non-military actions as part of our national defense strategy. We're already doing some of what I'm talking about. What I want to do is expand what we're doing and view it differently for funding purposes. I want some of the funds that we're shelling out to foreign countries for military aid to be channeled into economic development and construction projects that will provide jobs and improve living conditions. I'm talking about projects that will provide water, electricity and other basic necessities for the poorest of people and give them jobs helping to construct those facilities. I'm talking about building and staffing medical clinics and schools. And I'm talking about viewing all this as part of our national defense strategy."

He laughed. "And you actually think those countries are going to spend the money the way we tell 'em to?"

"They won't have any choice. If they want any military aid at all, they'll have to accept our conditions."

"And how does that mesh with the notion that we value their opinions?"

"I don't expect you to be your usual self. I expect you to use diplomacy. You have to convince those governments that these projects are in their best interest . . . that they can claim the credit for bringing them to their countries. We can't just turn the money over to them, though, and expect them to carry out our plans. We'll have to set up organizations in those countries—staffed with our own people—to handle the money and oversee operations. We'll deliberately seek out managers here that have lost their jobs to downsizing and offer them the opportunity to work overseas or coordinate operations stateside."

She hesitated and smiled. "This is going to put a lot of people to work . . . including Americans. So that's the second phase of our master plan."

He huffed. "What do you mean *our* master plan? You don't ask my opinion about anything. You just dictate what you want done."

She gave a faint smile and raised her eyebrows. "Don't you want to take credit for the progress we've made in Iraq? Violence there has gone down dramatically since we changed our focus from military operations to reconstruction and diplomacy. Don't you want to tell the world that was part of your master plan?"

He remained quiet.

She continued, "In fact, you're going to have to claim that if you expect them to go along with this new undertaking. You'll also have to hold it up to congress as a model . . . as proof that your new defense strategy is sound."

"Just what does all this have to do with our national defense?"

"Like I said, use what we've done in Iraq as a model for . . . I was going to say the rest of the world, but I should narrow that down and say . . . the countries that are most likely to breed terrorism."

He scoffed. "Any country can breed terrorism."

"I know that . . . and we'll address that in *phase three*, beginning right here at home. But for now, I want to concentrate on our greatest threats."

"Iran is our greatest threat. That's what we should concentrate on."

She shook her head. "I don't believe that. In fact, I don't believe any government will attack us directly. Some of them may support terrorism to get at us, but even that will be done with great caution. None of them will want to put their military up against ours. No . . . for the time being, our greatest threat comes from terrorism. That's why we have to strengthen our procedures for rooting it out at our borders and at the same time, work on its root causes overseas. Those root causes are the target of our economic development and construction projects."

"What exactly is it in your background that makes you such an expert on national defense?"

She ignored his question. "And since you've brought up Iran, that's where I want you to start making changes. I want the hundreds of millions of dollars that we're spending on covert operations to destabilize Iran's government redirected to construction projects in the tribal regions of Pakistan. That's where our greatest threat lies . . . not in Iran. We have to win over the hearts and minds of those people. We have to show them that we can offer them a better way of life than the terrorists can."

"What do *you* know about covert operations against Iran?"

"I have my sources."

"Then you should know that members of congress are pushing for those operations as well as much tougher sanctions."

"I do know that, but I also know that our own actions in that direction are where the real danger lies in regard to Iran."

He stood. "You can't blame me if congress doesn't go along with your plan."

She stood also. "I'm counting on you to convince 'em. Besides, you have the final say on how that money is used. I do so hope you choose to use it wisely."

He knew her final statement was a threat.

chapter 8

Moscow is eight time zones east of Gainesville. Muscovites were already winding down their day when Hawker began his. His trip was uneventful and he flew directly to Petrov's residence at the pharmaceutical plant—that is, at what *had* been a pharmaceutical plant. Only a couple of days had passed since the explosion and apparently no cleanup had started yet.

He arrived at the plant about nine o'clock local time, so it had been dark for some time already and lights were on in some of the remaining buildings. No lights were on, however, in Petrov's place. Unless he had gone to bed very early, he wasn't home. That would be consistent with Lev's information.

Hawker kept to the shadows and landed softly in the backyard near the door he had destroyed. The door was still lying on the ground and the opening had been covered with a tarp. He gently pulled the tarp loose at the bottom and eased himself inside. Then he stood silently, listening for sounds. The house was completely quiet, so he began retracing the path he had used during his exit the previous Thursday. Not wanting to attract attention, he was using the suit's night-vision feature rather than turning on a light.

The guard's corpse was gone, which was to be expected. He hadn't had much time to think about that since it had happened—the only man he had ever deliberately killed—but every time he did, he felt a deep sense of loss. He tried to put it out of his mind.

He didn't have a clear notion of what he was looking for, so this was definitely an exploratory mission. Two things in general came to mind: evidence proving what Petrov had been planning, and clues as to his whereabouts. The most logical place to find either would be in the office where he and Teala had previously found evidence. But Teala wasn't here to read Russian for him this time, so he was undeniably operating under a severe handicap.

Even though the place appeared to be deserted, he knew it would be a good idea to make sure before he did anything else. A door directly across the hall from the office stood open. That turned out to be another bedroom with nobody in the bed. He moved on toward the front of the house and opened two more doors without finding anyone.

After satisfying himself that he was alone, he returned to the office. With the light above his visor preset to a low intensity, he turned it on and scanned the desk. Petrov was apparently a slave to neatness: Nothing cluttered his desk. The computer was still on, so Hawker moved the mouse, hoping that Petrov had left a file open. No such luck: It asked for a password again. He didn't waste his time with the computer; instead he went for the desk drawers. One of them was locked. After finding nothing he could use in the other drawers, he gripped the handle of the locked drawer with his fingers and pressed his thumb against the desk. The drawer popped open with some noise, but otherwise no problem. Everything in the drawer was in Russian.

He turned his attention to the filing cabinet. As he moved his head in that direction, he noticed through the window that lights were on in the house next door. He quickly jerked his head away from that direction, fearing that his light might be seen. He started with the top drawer and worked his way down. Most everything was in Russian, of course. Much to his surprise, one of the folders was dedicated to news clippings about him—or to be more precise, about the *Shadow Messenger*. He did find a file containing articles on immunology and nanotechnology that were written in English, but so far, nothing he could use as evidence. His total attention was focused on the papers in that file when suddenly the room filled with light. He whirled around and saw a woman standing in the office doorway.

"Have you returned to the scene of the crime?" the woman asked.

Hawker had been caught in the act and didn't know what to say.

She continued, "You certainly are an interesting-looking creature . . . a shadow with a light beam coming from its head."

Hawker remained silent, contemplating how he should handle this situation: *Who was the woman? She was younger than Petrov but old enough to possibly be his wife.*

She took a step into the room. "Do you not understand Russian, Mister Shadow?"

Hawker found his voice. "Yes, I understand Russian."

"Ah so . . . a computer-generated voice," she said. "Why does a computer speak for you? Are you a robot?"

"No . . . I'm not a robot. . . . Are you Petrov's wife?"

The petite and attractive lady smiled and shook her head. "No. I am his neighbor and coworker. I knew he was not at home, so I came to investigate when I saw the strange light."

Hawker turned off his light. "Do you know where Petrov is?"

"Why? Do you want to ask his permission to plunder through his office?"

"Petrov is a dangerous man. I need to find him."

"What will you do when you find him?"

"I had hoped to find evidence in his papers that would put him in jail, but unfortunately I can't read them."

She flashed him an amused grin. "My, my . . . an *illiterate* shadow. What is this world coming to? Perhaps you are the one who should be put in jail. Ivan did not destroy our place of work. You did."

"What makes you think I destroyed it?"

She took another step forward. "I saw you and the lady depart soon after the explosion. It does not take much thinking to know who caused it. Ivan did not tell the authorities you were here. I could tell he did not want them to know. I wondered why."

"Did you know the lady was a prisoner here?"

"Of course not. She was a guest. He had other guests also. She arrived with another American and one of Ivan's Russian friends. They are now dead and you are the one who killed them."

Hawker thought that for someone who thought he was a murderer, she didn't seem to be too afraid of him. "I didn't intend to kill them," he said. "In fact, I told them the building was going to explode and warned them to get out."

"That does not change the fact that you are responsible for their death," she said. "Why should Ivan go to jail rather than you?"

Hawker *did* feel responsible but that didn't erase the danger that Petrov represented. "Petrov was contaminating the vaccine being shipped to America with molecules he had synthesized. He was planning the mass murder of many Americans and possibly others as well."

"Don't be silly. Of course he was adding his synthesized molecules to the vaccine. They greatly improved its effectiveness. Why would you think he was planning murder?"

"Because the lady I rescued from here overheard conversations to that effect and because we found undeniable evidence in his files."

"That is impossible. I am also a scientist. If the vaccine had contained anything harmful, I would have known about it. . . . And if you already have the evidence you say, why are you searching for more?"

"Unfortunately, that evidence was destroyed in the explosion. And if I were you, I'd be careful about claiming knowledge of what was in the vaccine. Everybody associated with this place is going to be investigated before this is over. If you're truly innocent, I would hate to see you share Petrov's fate."

"If you believed Ivan was committing a crime and you had the evidence, why did you not present your evidence and let the investigation take its course. Do you know how many people you have caused to be unemployed by your act of terrorism?"

"They would have been unemployed even if the plant hadn't been destroyed. The United States would have immediately canceled any and all orders for the vaccine and would have refused to pay any outstanding debts from past orders. On top of that, they would have demanded refunds and investigations, and would have warned all other countries that their citizens were at risk from this vaccine. Production of the vaccine would have stopped and all of you would have been out of work anyway."

"We could have made adjustments and produced a different product. You and your government are responsible for the loss of income for many people. What are you going to do about that?"

The disbelieving expression on Hawker's face was, of course, hidden by his helmet. "Do you really think anyone would buy your products after they learned what you were doing here? These workers were producing a product to kill Americans. Why would I want to do anything to help them?"

"They did not know that . . . assuming that what you say is even true. They were simply honest people trying to feed their children. Do not transfer Ivan's guilt to them."

"So you acknowledge that Petrov is guilty. You know he is dangerous."

She sighed and wearily seated herself in a nearby chair. "Perhaps I suspected something, but I did not know what. Ivan has been a troubled man for some time, but do not judge him too harshly. Your own countrymen helped to make him what he is."

Hawker put down the folder he was holding and seated himself on the edge of Petrov's desk, an act that would have produced an interesting sight for a curious eye. "Why do you say that?" he asked.

"How much do you know about Ivan's family?"

"Nothing."

"Ivan's wife died while giving birth to a son. Ivan had loved his wife passionately and transferred that love to the son she had given him. Even though Ivan was a true genius and deeply involved in his research, he still found time to give his son much attention. They were the closest father and son pair I have ever known."

"So you've known Petrov a long time, huh?"

She smiled. "Yes . . . a very long time. I was jealous when he married his wife, but he was already in love with her before he met me. I have waited a very long time but he has never been unfaithful to her."

"And you're still in love with him?"

She shrugged. "I do not know if one can still call it love."

"I feel sorry for you, but what does all that have to do with my countrymen?"

"Do not waste your pity on me. Ivan is the one who needs it." She lowered her head as if remembering something painful; then raised it again and continued, "His son eventually grew up and went into the Russian military. About ten years ago when Kosovo was seeking its independence, terrible atrocities were being inflicted on its civilian population. NATO intervened and was launching air strikes against Serbian military targets. Ivan's son was part of a Russian team monitoring the situation on the ground. The Russian team was not involved in the fighting. They were gathering information for the United Nations. A NATO fighter jet—or more specifically, an American fighter jet—attacked the Russian convoy killing several of its members including Ivan's son. The pilot claimed that the similarity between the Russian and Serbian flags had caused the attack. He said he thought he was attacking a Serbian convoy. It was deemed a tragic accident of war. It almost destroyed Ivan. All of the love he felt for his son was converted into hatred for Americans. He has been obsessed with his hatred for years. I watched a loving, gifted scientist turn into . . . It was not easy to watch."

They were both silent for a few seconds; then Hawker said, "Okay, tell you what I'll do Miss uh . . . what's your name?"

She had lowered her head again. She lifted it and said, "I am Anna Korkorov."

"Okay Miss Korkorov . . . as far as I know, Petrov hasn't killed anyone yet. If you help me stop him before he does, I'll do what I can to help him. I have contacts that can get him into a treatment center in the United States. He'll be confined, but he won't be in jail. We'll try to keep this whole thing quiet so maybe no one will know you were producing a killer vaccine here. The U.S. government might even be able to offer financial help to the plant employees until they can secure new employment."

"Ivan will never submit to treatment. He is much too proud."

"He really won't have a choice in the matter. And if you don't help me stop him before he starts killing Americans, nobody will be able to help him after that."

"He will think I am a traitor if I help you."

"He doesn't have to know. But consider this . . . I'll find him eventually with or without your help, and if I don't have the evidence to guarantee that he's permanently confined, then I'll have to deal with him in my own way. I cannot allow him to run free."

"So you will kill him also . . . as you killed his friends. Perhaps what I have read about you is not true."

"No, I won't kill him, but I'll put him someplace where he can't harm anyone. . . . And if you think I'm a murderer, why are you not afraid of me?"

She ignored his question. "Do not take this as a yes, but if I agreed to help you, what would you have me do?"

"Go through all of his papers. As a scientist who worked with him, you should be able to spot the evidence easily if it is there. We need proof that his nanoparticles are intended to make the body's immune system attack the body, eventually killing it. We also need proof that an orbiting satellite was going to provide the external signal that would start the process. . . . Did you know that he had an experiment on the Russian satellite that was launched this past April?"

"Yes. He was studying the effects of the space environment on molecules he had synthesized."

"I think you will find that is not all he was doing."

Hawker rose to his feet. "The other thing you can do is help me find him. Tell me where he is if you know."

She didn't respond to his statement; instead she said, "If I were to find evidence supporting your claim, how would I contact you?"

He had already been reaching for a pad on Petrov's desk when she asked the question. He handed that and a pen to her and said, "I'll have to contact you. Write your phone number for me."

She wrote her name and number on the pad and handed it back to him. He tore off the top sheet, folded it and slipped it into one of his tote pouches. He had not switched his suit to the light-reflecting mode during their conversation, so to her it appeared as if the folded sheet of paper moved itself down the front of his body and was then absorbed into his leg.

She looked amused. "That is quite a trick. I would like very much to know what just happened."

It was his turn to ignore her remark. He said, "And unless you want to see our two countries engaged in a devastating war, I suggest that you don't mention to anyone else that I destroyed the pharmaceutical plant.

. . . Now can you tell me where Petrov is?"

Her expression became more serious and she nodded. "Yes, I will tell you where he is. I think I now understand his last statement to me. I fear he is going to do something terrible."

About an hour before Hawker arrived at Petrov's home, Myra Wilson and her mother were arriving at their friend's home near Jacksonville Beach in Florida. It was, of course, the noon hour there and the Sun was shining bright.

The house overlooked the Atlantic Ocean and directly adjoined the Beach—truly a prized location. Myra was driving. She turned into the driveway and followed it through a ninety degree turn and parked in front of the garage door.

Moira said, "You'll be blocking *her* car if you park here."

"We'll be leaving before she does," responded Myra.

The house had two levels with a brick exterior boasting a southwestern desert tone. The overall structure—and especially the steps—suggested that the main entrance was on the second floor. Myra and Moira climbed one set of steps that was perpendicular to the driveway; then turned left and climbed another set that was perpendicular to the first. When they turned left again and started up the final set, Moira said, "She almost needs an elevator."

"This is a really cool place," said Myra. "We should come during the summer and go to the beach."

Moira nodded. "Maybe we will next summer. I didn't want to bother Harriet this year because it's been really tough on her . . . losing Barry . . . and the way she lost him."

"I didn't know they sent men to war when they're *that* old."

Moira smiled. "I guess you *do* think of us as being old, don't you. But he was in the National Guard. A lot of older men have suddenly been uprooted with this Iraq thing."

The steps terminated at a wooden deck that ran the length of the front of the house. The deck was stained with a brownish tint that gave the appearance of natural wood and again suggested southwestern.

There were two entrance doors: one at the extreme left end of the deck and the other slightly to their right. They hesitated briefly, wondering which door to approach.

Harriet Simms answered that question by opening the door on their right. Harriet was about the same size and age as Moira, but had blue eyes, unlike the brown of Moira and Myra.

"I'm glad to see you two," said Harriet. "Thanks for coming."

"Our pleasure," said Moira.

Harriet hugged both her guests and said, "Come on in."

They stepped through the door into a large room that ended any lingering doubt about the southwestern motif. Where they were standing just inside the door was actually the dining area and the kitchen was immediately to the right. There were no walls separating the areas; the one large room encompassed the dining and kitchen areas as well as the living room. Just beyond the kitchen on the right was a huge stone fireplace with a thick wooden mantle. The mantle held the family photographs and the walls were adorned with pictures of horses, cowboys and Indians. The coffee table, end tables and anything else that could support them, held ornaments of horses, cowboys and Indians.

Moira moved toward the mantle over the fireplace. "I assume that's Ed's wife and children in the picture with him. I haven't seen Ed since before he got married."

"It *has* been a long time then," said Harriet. "His two boys are four and five now."

"He has a beautiful wife."

"Yes he does. He met her in college."

Moira turned away from the mantle toward Harriet. "You say he has his own business now, huh?"

Harriet nodded. "In fact, he's had his own business since he was nineteen. He takes after his dad like that. I hesitate to use the word *genius* since he comes from my own flesh, but he is super smart. He's even smarter than his dad in some ways. He wanted no part of that shameful war that killed his dad. He sided with me in trying to convince his dad to get out of the National Guard. He could have, you know. He had over twenty years in including his active duty time."

Harriet fell silent and looked as if she was going to start crying.

Her friend's expression made Moira want to cry, and she knew that wouldn't help so she quickly changed the subject. "I'm dying to see the rest of your house."

Harriet attempted a smile. "Tell you what . . . let's eat while everything is still hot. Then I'll give you the grand tour."

As they began eating, Myra looked around the room and grinned. "Do you like horses?" she said to Harriet.

The question elicited a full smile from Harriet. "What was your first clue?"

They all laughed at that.

"Actually, that was Barry's thing," said Harriet. "He was into everything western when I met him. He even used to go to the firing range and practice his fast draw with a six shooter. Over the years we spent a lot of quality time together while on the backs of horses. We own a couple of horses, you know." She hesitated. "I guess I should say I own a couple of horses. I just couldn't bear to sell his."

This time she *did* start sobbing.

Myra and Moira stopped eating, but they didn't know what to say. Almost anything they could say would sound patronizing. Eventually, Moira said, "You don't have to talk about this if you don't want to, Harriet."

Harriet straightened up and dabbed her eyes and nose with her napkin. "Actually, it's probably better for me to talk to someone about it rather than keeping it bottled up inside." She noticed the others weren't eating so she took a bite to encourage them to continue.

They took the cue and began eating again but they were afraid to say anything. It appeared that all conversations eventually led to her dead husband.

But she apparently wanted to get it off her chest. She said, "Barry thought he was doing a noble thing . . . staying in during his country's time of need. I tried to tell him there was nothing noble about participating in an ill-advised, unjust war, but he saw it differently. You want to know if I'm bitter? Yes, I'm bitter. I've often wondered how a president could start a war like that debacle in Iraq and then live with himself afterwards. How can he sleep at night . . . knowing that he is directly responsible for the deaths of thousands of his own countrymen plus tens of thousands of innocent Iraqis? Do you suppose he deludes himself into believing that he *isn't* responsible?"

Myra and Moira kept silent and listened with sympathetic expressions on their faces.

Harriet continued, "If it had been something like World War Two, or even like driving Saddam out of Kuwait, I could have understood, but this was aggression on our part . . . plain and simple. We unleashed our military might on a weak country that had done nothing to us. To me, that's unforgivable. I could never understand why Barry wanted to be a part of that. When he first enlisted in the National Guard I thought it might be for the extra income, but Heaven knows, we haven't needed that extra income for many years now. I began to suspect that he was disappointed that he had never served his country in combat. Why are men like that? Why do they need to prove themselves?"

Anxious to get Harriet off the subject before she started crying again, Moira said, "I don't know. I've wondered that same thing about Thad. I know it isn't like going to war, but I think he's doing the same thing with his skydiving. I keep telling him that he's already proved that he's brave. After all, he's been doing it for ten years. I've asked him to stop. I tell him that he doesn't need to prove anything anymore."

Whether or not Myra understood what her mother was doing she couldn't contain herself after hearing that last statement. "Mom . . . Dad isn't trying to prove anything. He jumps because he loves to jump. He loves the feel of flying his own body through the sky. Just imagine what that must feel like. Just imagine the skill it takes to dive from an airplane with complete control and fly your body at a hundred and eighty miles an hour and then slow down enough to gently dock on a free-fall formation. That's why he does it. He loves to fly and flying his own body is the ultimate flying experience."

At that instant, the doorbell rang.

"I wonder who that could be," said Harriet. "Excuse me just a minute."

They were sitting only a few feet from the door. Harriet took a few steps and opened the door to a distinguished-looking gentleman who appeared to be about sixty.

With an accent that Harriet didn't recognize, the man said, "Good afternoon. I saw Mrs. Wilson's car out front and wanted to say hello to her. Is she here?"

Moira heard this but she couldn't yet see the man and didn't recognize his voice.

Harriet said, "Yes, she's right here. Come on in."

A slender man about five-ten with gray hair and a mustache came through the door and headed straight for Moira with an outstretched hand. As they shook, he said, "It is so good to see you, Mrs. Wilson. Please introduce me to your lovely hostess."

Moira searched her memory for some recollection of this man but couldn't find it. "Her name is Harriet Simms, but I'm afraid you have me at a disadvantage. Please forgive me, but I can't remember yours."

Instead of giving his name, the man turned to Harriet and said, "And where is your husband Mrs. Simms?"

Still thinking this man was a friend of Moira's, Harriet said, "My husband was killed in Iraq."

The man bowed slightly and said, "You have my sympathy. And do you live here alone?"

Harriet slowly nodded. "Yes . . ."

Moira was becoming suspicious that something wasn't right. "Do you work with my husband in some capacity?" she asked.

Harriet had closed the door after the man entered. He now walked over and locked it; then turned back to them with a gun in his hand.

All three recoiled in shock.

The man said, "Actually, Mrs. Wilson, we have never met. Nor have I met your husband, but we do have a mutual acquaintance. Perhaps I should say we have two mutual acquaintances. The gun is to encourage you to do as I say without question. It would be unwise on your part to act recklessly."

"What do you want?" Moira asked.

The man gave a faint smile. "That is the attitude I want to see. I want you to call Professor Hawker and tell him that you need him. Tell him that your life is in danger."

Their fears were confirmed.

"He isn't at home," said Myra.

"Where is he?" the man asked. "Does he work on Sunday?"

Myra hesitated; then answered, "Yes, he's working."

"Then call his office. I do not care where he receives the call."

"He isn't *in* his office and he doesn't own a cell phone."

The man frowned at Myra. "Are you taking charge here, young lady? Are you refusing to cooperate?"

Moira broke in. "No . . . she isn't refusing to cooperate. It's just that she's closest to Mr. Hawker. She knows him better than we do. We'll dial the numbers if that's what you want." She rose to her feet. "Let me get my purse. It's on the counter behind you." She pointed to a granite counter that—with its accompanying bar stools—was the only thing separating the kitchen from the dining area.

The man wasn't actually pointing the gun at anyone; he was simply making them aware that he had it and would use it if necessary. He turned sideways to them and motioned toward the purse with the gun. "Do not reach your hand into the purse. Open it and empty its contents onto the counter."

She did as instructed; then picked up her cell phone and carried it to Myra. "You do it, Myra. I don't know the number."

Myra rose, took the phone and walked around the table toward where the man stood. She punched in the number; then handed the phone to him. "Do you want to hear his answer machine?" she asked.

He took the phone and listened; then handed it back to her. "Now dial his office."

She punched in the number for Hawker's office and once again gave the man the phone.

He listened as before; then lowered the phone and said, "I am quite certain that Professor Hawker has a means of communicating at all times. I would now like for you to contact him by whatever means are necessary to accomplish that."

Myra looked at him with a scornful expression. "Believe me, mister . . . if I knew how to contact him, I'd do it in a heartbeat . . . because right now, I would like very much to have him here with us."

The man studied her face, obviously contemplating what she had said. "I believe you," he said. Then he turned to Harriet. "Mrs. Simms, I would like very much to have a tour of your house."

Harriet gave him a disbelieving look. "You want a tour of my house?"

"Yes. Please walk us through and explain the function of each area."

Harriet was still having difficulty grasping that he was asking for a tour of her house. "Where do you want to start?" she asked.

He pointed to the hallway that led away from the dining area and toward the northern end of the house. "The three of you should proceed along this hallway and explain each room to me."

Harriet reached for a set of folding doors on their right and said, "This is a coat closet."

The man said, "You may move on to the next door."

Myra and Moira were moving along in front, each in her own mind trying to determine the man's intentions.

The second door on their right was slightly ajar. Harriet pushed it open all the way and said, "This is a bathroom for day guests."

The man glanced inside, examined the doorknob and said, "You may move on."

She opened the first door on their left revealing a treadmill, an all-in-one home gym machine, and a window overlooking the front deck. She shrugged and said, "This is my exercise room."

He again examined the doorknob, stared at the window for a second; then backed out into the hallway and tilted his head to indicate the door behind him. "And over here?"

Myra and the women preceded him through the door into a large bedroom directly across the hall from the exercise room. He opened the door to a large walk-in closet, closed it again, glanced through the bathroom door, and then stared at the window that overlooked the back deck and Atlantic Ocean. Shaking his head slightly, he used the gun and motioned them back toward the hallway.

It was becoming obvious that the man was looking for something.

The next door was directly in front of them at the end of the hallway. It opened into an even larger bedroom that extended across the entire width of the house. It must have been obvious that this was the master bedroom because Harriet didn't say so and the man didn't ask. There was a door that opened onto the front deck and on the opposite side of the room another—actually French doors—that opened onto the deck overlooking the ocean. The man glanced at the doors and at the neatly made bed and then motioned them toward a wide opening where two mutually perpendicular walls would have joined had the opening not been there.

The opening led into a large, luxurious bathroom with a Jacuzzi mounted on a raised floor on the left and a separate shower built into the wall on the opposite side. The floor and shower were both made of travertine tiles and the floor had a beautiful inlaid mosaic at the center. Natural light from the ocean side flowed into the room through a large window made of solid glass blocks. There were two identical sinks mounted on what appeared to be antique water basin stands placed on two mutually perpendicular walls. Though the sinks did not have the words "his" and "hers" above them, that was obviously the intention. The Iraq war, however, had eliminated the need for the "his" sink.

The man grinned at Harriet and said, "You were not concerned with cost, were you?"

Harriet returned a faint smile.

"It is very nice," he said. "But it will not do."

"Will not do for what?"

He didn't answer her question; instead he asked, "What is downstairs?"

"You mean other than the garage?"

"Yes, other than the garage."

"A game room and a hot tub room . . ."

He nodded his head downward one time. "Please show me."

With Myra and the women leading the way, they all retraced their steps along the hallway back to the dining area, turned left through the living room area and headed for a set of stairs in the far corner. They passed an office space on the left that was enclosed behind double French doors, but he showed no interest in that. Myra and Moira hardly noticed the ocean view that was available at the top of the stairs: Their minds were distracted by apprehension, and by questions about this weird man who was spoiling their Sunday.

At the bottom of the stairs they turned right. The first room they passed housed the washer and dryer, but he showed no interest there. He pointed to a door farther down on the left and asked, "Where does that door go?"

"Nowhere," Harriet answered. "That's just an access door for electrical wiring and plumbing."

He opened the door and looked at the maze of wiring and pipes. After locating the telephone cable, he yanked it loose from its connections.

Harriet was furious. "Look, mister . . . I've tried to be nice. I don't know who you think you are, but you're trying my patience."

He waved the gun again and said, "I am the man with the gun."

They were now at the end of the hallway with the game room directly in front of them and the hot tub room on their right. The man glanced briefly at the pool table in the game room, same thing with the game room's outside door; then fixed his attention on the sliding glass door of the hot tub room.

"Let us look at this room," he said. He slid the movable half of the glass door to its open position and motioned the others inside.

The hot tub took up most of the room, but there were bathroom facilities lined up along the left wall near the entrance. First came a small shower stall followed by a toilet and then a sink. These were not closed in and were completely open to the view of anyone in the room.

The man rapped on the redwood wall with his knuckles; then pointed to the toilet and said, "Not much privacy there."

Harriet looked annoyed but didn't say anything. Moira had been trying to get her attention, but without success.

The man examined the contents of the cabinet beneath the sink, walked along each side of the hot tub to the back wall, looked into the shower stall again, and then seated himself on the steps that provided access to the tub.

He turned his attention to Harriet and said, "Who are the children in the photographs upstairs?"

She huffily replied, "My grandchildren."

"Do they visit you often?"

"Not often enough, but they're here from time to time."

"And do they have free run of the house when they are here?"

"Of course. What do you think?"

"So you allow them to play down here without supervision?"

"Why are you interested in my grandchildren?"

"I see that you keep the tub filled with water and I see that a child could easily climb these steps and fall into the tub. That would seem very careless of you."

"They're not allowed to play in here unsupervised. I keep the door locked when they're here."

"And how do you lock the door such that they cannot unlock it?"

"I had a pin installed at the top. When it's in place it prevents the movable part from sliding."

He smiled. "Ah, so." Then he stood and said, "Please demonstrate."

Harriet looked at Moira and Moira said, "Be nice to the man, Harriet."

Harriet begrudgingly demonstrated the locking feature while Myra and Moira remained in the room.

Once the pin was in place the man shook the door, apparently trying to shake the pin loose. When the pin stayed put he removed it himself and slid the door open again; then motioned for Harriet to go back inside. He followed her through the door and looked her over; then turned his attention to Moira. Both women were wearing dresses with no pockets. Apparently satisfied with their appearance, he ogled Myra. To her he said, "And what might you be concealing in your pockets, young lady?"

Myra was wearing tight jeans and an equally tight pullover top, both of which did a good job of showing off her lovely teenage figure. She raised her arms above her head and twirled her body around. "Does it look like I could be hiding anything in these clothes?"

He smiled and said, "No, I suppose not."

As he stepped out and started to slide the closed, Moira said, "Wait. . . . What are you planning to do?"

"I shall bring you more company," he said. "This party needs a young lady who *does* know how to contact Hawker. Fortunately for me she is not far from here."

Then he hesitated, slid the door open again and walked over to the toilet. With his eyes on the women, he stuck the gun under his belt and used both hands to lift the cover from the toilet's tank. With a grin, he backed through the door and threw the tank cover to the floor outside. When the cover hit the floor it made an unnerving racket and broke into several pieces.

Moira moved toward the door. "Wait. . . . My daughter needs her insulin from our car."

He shook his head as he tugged on the door. "Do not concern yourself with the insulin. It will not make a difference." Then he finished closing the door and inserted the pin.

As the man walked away toward the stairs, Harriet said, "That whole time he was just looking for a place to lock us up."

Moira nodded and said, "What do you suppose he meant when he said the insulin wouldn't make a difference?"

Myra gave her mother a disbelieving look. "Mom . . . you do know that's the guy Damon went looking for, don't you?"

"I guessed as much."

"And you do know what he was planning before Damon stopped him?"

Moira's face showed that she was beginning to get the picture.

Myra continued, "He's planning to send us to a place where I won't need the insulin."

"What are you two talking about?" Harriet asked.

Moira gave her a sad look. "I'm so sorry we drug you into this, Harriet. I had no idea this would happen. I didn't know that man was in this country even."

"Who is he?" Harriet asked. "And who's this Hawker he keeps talking about?"

"Damon Hawker is a physics professor that works with Thad." Moira stopped and looked at Myra.

Myra had been afraid that her mother would say too much. She quickly jumped on the opportunity to finish the explanation herself. "This guy is a Russian scientist named Ivan Petrov. On a recent visit to Russia, Damon literally destroyed an experiment Petrov was conducting. Petrov went crazy and is trying to get even with Damon. Actually, I'm probably not stating that correctly. It would be more correct to say that Petrov is trying to punish Damon. I'm quite sure that he plans to kill us with Damon watching. That's why he wants Damon here. The only thing I haven't figured out is how he plans to accomplish that . . . how he plans to arrange it so Damon will see it happening but not be able to stop it."

Moira repeated, "I'm so sorry, Harriet."

Myra quickly interjected, "Mom . . . forget sorry. We're gonna get out of here before he comes back."

"How?"

"I don't know yet. I'm working on it."

"We certainly can't get anybody's attention by yelling," said Harriet. "These inner walls are solid redwood boards and the exterior is solid brick. On top of that, there's insulation and soundproofing inside the walls. I never imagined that this room was going to become a prison for me. I thought I was doing a really good thing when I had that pin installed on the door. Now that pin is likely to be the death of me."

Myra scanned the room again. "Why doesn't this room have windows?" she asked.

"You know . . . I don't really know," said Harriet. "Barry designed it and we never discussed a window. I guess he just wanted privacy."

Myra examined the steps and saw that they were fastened securely to the hot tub. She then turned her attention to the door, and after a few seconds said, "Mom, come give me a boost up." She interlaced the fingers of her two hands and demonstrated how to build a step.

Moira provided the boost and lifted Myra high enough to examine the top of the door.

"Okay, put me down," said Myra.

"What were you looking for?" Moira asked.

"A hole. I thought they might have drilled all the way through when they installed the pin. If so, we might have been able to push the pin out from this side. But no such luck. There's no hole."

"What would you have used to push the pin out with?" Harriet asked.

"I don't know, but it doesn't matter since there's no hole. We need to concentrate on the only option we have left."

"What's that?"

"Breaking the glass. That's why Petrov took the toilet tank cover out. He wanted to remove anything that could be used for breaking the glass."

"That glass is supposed to be good stuff," said Harriet. "You'll never be able to break it with anything we have."

"Don't be negative, Harriet. Give me a little encouragement here."

"Sorry."

Myra looked behind the tub and found nothing. She then looked through the cabinet under the sink and found nothing useful. After walking around the room two or three times, she finally sat down on the steps with a sigh. "We have to assume the shortest amount of time for him to make that trip," she said. "That means he could be back in another fifteen or twenty minutes."

"Where do you think he went?" Moira asked.

"To get Teala. She's staying with Dennis. Straight across, they're only seven or eight miles from here. But he'll have to fight that Sunday afternoon traffic on Beach Boulevard."

"Who's Teala?" Harriet asked.

"She's Damon Hawker's fiancée," replied Myra. Then a thought struck her and she scrambled the two or three feet to the toilet. Feeling around behind the toilet bowl, she exclaimed, "All right!"

"What're you doing?" Moira asked.

"I'm removing this seat," she said. "It's gonna be our ticket out of here."

She was referring to the toilet seat and its lid. It was made of thick, solid oak.

Myra withdrew her hand from behind the toilet bowl and displayed a small object. "See that? That's what fastens the seat and lid to the bowl. I helped Dad change the seat in my bathroom one time and I just now remembered that it was fastened with plastic wing nuts that you tighten with your fingers. They're not actually wing nuts but it's the same idea."

She moved to the other side of the bowl and unscrewed the other nut; then lifted the seat and lid assembly into the air and proclaimed, "Voila."

After studying the assembly for a few seconds, Myra folded the lid away from the seat and took an overhand grip on the extreme front part of the seat. Standing a few feet from the glass door, she said, "Get behind the tub, ladies. I don't know what's gonna happen here."

She practiced her moves while waiting for Moira and Harriet to get positioned. Initially facing the glass, she twisted her upper torso around to her left without moving her feet and legs. The seat and lid assembly was held at arm's length, but not straight out because it was too heavy unless it was being swung. After a couple of gentle practice swings, she said, "Here goes." Then she swung the assembly around to her rear letting her upper body twist with it, which coiled her midsection into a tightly wound spring. Her upper torso reached its extreme point; then began to uncoil back to the front. She swung that seat and lid assembly with every ounce of strength she had and this time it was straight out at arm's length. At the critical moment, when her arms were about ninety degrees from where her toes were pointing, she released the assembly. It had been traveling in an arc, but its instantaneous velocity at the instant it was released was straight toward the glass. Now that it was free, it continued in a straight line and slammed into the glass.

The toilet seat didn't send the glass flying out into the hallway as one might expect. It bounced off the glass and fell to the floor inside. It had produced several cracks in the glass, however, and after a brief and anxious moment, the glass began falling to the floor.

The ladies cheered.

Myra picked up the seat and used it to punch more glass from the door to widen the opening. Then she stood to the side and motioned the others through. "Watch out for the glass."

Moira started to the left toward the stairs.

"Through the garage would be faster," said Harriet.

"We have to do more than get out of the house," said Moira. "We have to get out of the area and we'll need a car for that. Our car is blocking yours so we need my purse. And maybe he left my cell phone up there."

They all raced up the stairs and across the living room to the kitchen counter. The contents of Moira's purse were still strewn on the counter where she had dumped them, but her car keys were not there. Neither had he left the cell phone.

"That sneaky man took my keys," said Moira. "What're we gonna do now. We can't even push it out of the way because it's locked up."

Myra said, "Let's go, Mom. I have a key." She inserted a finger and a thumb into the watch pocket of her jeans and produced a single key. "I had a spare made after that time I locked the keys inside the car and I always make a point of carrying it any time I go out."

Moira smiled as she raked the items back into her purse. "That's exactly what I would expect from you," she said. To Harriet, she added, "Grab your house keys and lock your door on the way out, Harriet. Maybe that'll slow him down a little."

They raced down the three sets of steps and on to Moira's car. Myra didn't ask permission; she automatically assumed the driver's position since she had the key. She unlocked the doors and the others climbed in.

As they turned onto A1A, another car traveling in the opposite direction was slowing to make its turn onto the street they had just left. The other car's driver looked intently at them as he passed, and Myra got a good look at him. "That's him," she said. "And that's the same car that was parked near our house yesterday."

"Was Teala with him?" Moira asked.

Myra floored the accelerator. "Not unless he had her locked up in the trunk or tied up on the floor in the backseat. But I don't think he found her. He came back too soon."

"Be careful," said Moira. "It won't help anything if we wreck."

Myra looked into the rearview mirror and saw Petrov backing out onto A1A. "I'll try not to wreck us, but he's turning around and coming after us. Since we don't have a phone to call the police I'll have to get their attention with my driving."

As she approached an intersection where the traffic light was red, she checked carefully for other traffic; then barreled right through the intersection, running the red light. "That oughta get us some attention," she said.

Checking the rearview mirror again, she saw Petrov almost collide with another car when he tried to run the red light. That near-collision forced him to skid to a sideways stop in the middle of the intersection. But it didn't take him long to straighten up and resume the chase.

Myra made it through a couple of green lights, but because of her speed, she was now coming up behind the traffic in front. To make matters worse, they were approaching an intersection where the light had just turned red. All of the cars in front began stopping for the light.

Moira twisted around to look for Petrov. "He'll catch us for sure now," she said.

Myra did a sudden left turn into the parking lot of a shopping center. Once again she got lucky and Petrov had to wait for a string of cars to pass. Driving as fast as she could in the congested parking lot, she maneuvered away from the buildings and people and wound up on a street that ran perpendicular to A1A. After traveling west on that street for a short distance, she turned right onto the first street that looked like a major thoroughfare. She could no longer see Petrov in her rearview mirror, but she had no doubt he was still back there and had seen where she turned.

And she had been right: When she stopped briefly before turning west onto Beach Boulevard, she saw Petrov coming behind her again. After running two more red lights, passing illegally and speeding like a crazy teenager she still had no police on her tail.

Petrov was back there, though.

Moira was up front with Myra and Harriet was riding in the backseat. For the most part, the women weren't saying much. Considering the kind of driving Myra was doing, they didn't want to take a chance on distracting her. But eventually Moira ventured a thought: "I can't believe you're getting away with all this. If we didn't want the police to see you, they would be everywhere."

"If we can lose Petrov, we might be better off without the police," responded Myra. "It could open up a whole can of worms if they start asking too many questions."

Myra caught a green light at St. Johns Bluff Road and breezed right through; then ran another red light before encountering problems at Southside Boulevard. When she approached that intersection, the light was red and traffic was backed up. She knew if she stopped, Petrov would catch up to them, so she looked for an out. There was a strip mall on the right with an access road running behind it and connecting with Southside Boulevard. She whipped the car to the right through a traffic lane, causing another car to screech to a halt.

"Whoa," said Harriet. "That was close. Do you really have to drive this way? Surely he wouldn't shoot us right out here in public with everybody watching."

"That car wouldn't have hit us," said Myra. "The driver overreacted.

And Petrov doesn't care if he's seen. He's on a mission. The equation has changed, though. He won't try to capture us with all these people around. He'll just shoot us and be on his way. *Some* punishment for Damon would be better than none. And when he gets *us* . . . if he does . . . he'll go looking for more of Damon's friends."

"Seems like being friends with this Hawker person could be hazardous to one's health," said Harriet.

Myra quickly countered, "If you knew Damon Hawker better, you'd be proud to call him *your* friend also, even in a predicament like this."

Moira supported Myra's statement. "He truly is a remarkable person, Harriet."

Myra was forced to stop without being able to merge with the traffic on Southside Boulevard. Checking the rearview mirror, she saw that Petrov had just made the access road. She thought to herself: *Where are those police? Have they all taken the day off?*

The shoulder of the road was her only option. She began moving again, driving on the shoulder with her left blinker on, hoping someone would let her in. The other drivers were not in a charitable mood today. Finally, she caught a slight gap between two cars and forced her way in, eliciting a lot of horn honking. She kept her left blinker on and forced her way on into the left lane, angering even more drivers.

At the next crosscut through the median, she whipped left and was again stopped by traffic. This time it was the southbound traffic. She immediately realized that might have been a bad move because now she had nowhere to go. She checked the traffic in the direction she had come from and didn't see Petrov, but she knew he was there somewhere waiting for his opportunity.

Fortunately, she eventually caught a less-than-desirable break in the traffic and took it. A lack of boldness was not her weakness. Needless to say, more drivers were angered. Then she spotted Petrov traveling in the opposite direction. *Did he see her?* She didn't know, but she decided to change directions again at the next opportunity. She took the off-ramp that led back to Beach Boulevard. Merging with the Beach Boulevard traffic was not a problem, but her speed was limited to what everybody else was doing. There was no way she could pass and there was nowhere she could go except to flow with the traffic. The only comforting thought was that if Petrov was still on her tail, he would be in the same situation.

The next two lights were green, but then came Parental Home Road. The light at that intersection was red and all the traffic flowing with Myra was stopping. There were three westbound straight-through traffic lanes plus a left turn lane. Myra was in the left straight-through lane, sandwiched in between the traffic in the left turn lane and all the westbound traffic in the other two lanes. She knew the traffic light would switch to a left turn signal before it switched to green for her lane. If she had been thinking better, she would have moved into the left turn lane to prevent being trapped at a dead stop with the left turn traffic moving past her. But it was too late now. If Petrov knew where she was and got into the left turn lane, he could easily pull up right beside her. That thought caused her to glance at the rearview mirror as she was coming to a stop. And there he was, ten or fifteen cars back, trying to force his way into the left turn lane. She knew he would make it sooner or later.

Moira pointed to their left front to the opposite direction traffic. "Isn't that Dennis?"

Myra looked where her mother was pointing and saw Dennis' maroon Lincoln preparing to make a right turn onto Parental Home Road. "It certainly is," she replied. "And Teala is with him. That's why Petrov got back so quick. They weren't home. Now I *know* I want to be in the left turn lane. . . . Harriet, help me look for any gap between cars when traffic in that lane starts moving. If we stay here, Petrov will be able to pull right along beside us and start shooting."

She turned on her left blinker, cut her wheels to the left and moved the nose of the car as far as she could.

Sometimes life is just good: The left turn traffic began moving and one of the drivers actually waited and signaled Myra to go in front of him. Myra counted her blessings and wasted no time before accepting his offer. By this time, Dennis and Teala were well away from the intersection, but Myra knew where Dennis lived and knew that's where he was headed. She drove south on Parental Home Road as fast as the traffic would allow. She couldn't see Petrov in her mirror, but she knew he was back there.

There was still no sign of Petrov when she turned left onto Ebersol

Road. A few blocks later, just before a curve to the right, she turned left into Dennis' driveway. She was hoping the gate to the backyard would be open so she could drive back there and hide the car, but that wasn't to be. Not only was the gate not open; Dennis' Lincoln was parked in front of it. As Myra pulled up behind the Lincoln, Dennis appeared in the front doorway of his house.

Myra and the women jumped from the car and ran toward Dennis. Myra shouted, "The guy Damon went looking for is here. He's chasing us."

Dennis stepped into the yard and looked in the direction they had come from. "Are you sure?" he asked.

"Positive."

"Okay, go on inside. I'll give 'im a little surprise."

"He'll shoot you," said Moira.

Dennis pulled his jacket aside and revealed a pistol tucked under his belt. "I doubt that he's better with one of these than I am." Then he pulled the screen door open and waved them inside.

Once they were safely inside, he hastened to the other side of Moira's car and crouched down so he could see through the windows. After waiting there several minutes without seeing a single car on the street, he walked out to the street and looked in both directions. Still seeing no approaching cars, he went back into the house.

"Do you think we should call the police?" Moira asked.

Dennis shook his head. "Damon wouldn't want us to involve the police unless it was absolutely necessary. They would ask too many questions. Besides, they couldn't do any more for you than I can. I guarantee that nobody's going to harm you as long as you're with me. We do need to call Damon, though, and let him know his man is here."

Dennis called Hawker and Moira called her husband. Moira and Thad decided that he would drive to Jacksonville to escort them home, but it would be a couple of hours before he could get there. Hawker was already on his way back, but it would take him at least another three hours.

Myra was looking through a front window in the living room. "He's here," she said.

Dennis came from the kitchen into the living room. "Where?"

Myra pointed to the left front of the house. "Look to the left beyond where the road curves . . . that white sedan."

Dennis immediately spotted the car parked on the side of the road with its front to them. "I wonder how he knew to come around that way."

"I think he's been here at least twice already," said Myra. "The last time was a little while ago when he came looking for Teala but didn't find her. And he probably followed you two last night when you left our house."

Teala moved closer to the window. "Surely he knows we can see him sitting there."

"He wants us to see him," said Myra. "He wants us to call Damon. I haven't figured out how he plans to pull it off, but he wants Damon to watch us die."

"How can he be so sure we won't call the police?" Harriet asked.

Myra and Dennis looked at one another and Myra quickly said, "That's a good question. I guess he has his reasons."

Dennis went to his bedroom and came back a few minutes later with a revolver. He handed it to Teala and said, "There's no safety to worry about on this. All you have to do is point and pull the trigger. Lock the door behind me." Then he headed toward the front door.

"What're you gonna do?" Teala asked.

Dennis turned sideways as he opened the door. "I'm not gonna sit here and wait to play *his* game. I'm gonna make him play on *my* terms."

"Well he'd certainly be no match for your physical strength, but he'll probably just shoot you when he sees you coming."

"He would have to stick his arm out the window to do that. I'd see it coming in plenty of time to dive for cover."

"You know he's not gonna let you get close."

"He might. But either way I'll thwart his plans. He'll either run or let me get close. If he lets me get close, I'll hold a gun to his head until Damon gets here."

As Dennis left his driveway and began walking toward Petrov's rented car, he heard the engine start. That's what he was expecting—for Petrov to try to run rather than confront him. He had a Beretta stuck under his belt, positioned for a quick draw and hidden by the light jacket he was wearing. He would attempt to block Petrov's escape—at least up to a point.

But Petrov fooled him and remained where he was with the engine idling. Dennis continued his cautious approach, half expecting to see a gun thrust through the side window at any moment. He knew Petrov wouldn't try to shoot through the windshield.

He got close enough to clearly see the man's face. It looked exactly as Teala and Myra had described it. The man was sitting perfectly still, staring straight at Dennis with no expression of any kind on his face. His hands were not visible and Dennis wondered what they were doing.

Dennis paused briefly, trying to determine the status of the driver's side window. His guess was that Petrov wouldn't fire through it without first lowering the glass. Then a large bug crawled across the glass and gave Dennis his answer.

He started walking again, lining up for an approach to the driver's window. But he hadn't taken more than two steps when Petrov suddenly gunned the engine. The rear wheels spun with a fury, throwing grass, gravel and dirt from the one that was off the pavement, and smoke from the other one.

A split second later the car surged forward—straight for Dennis. But Dennis had already begun his reaction as soon as he heard the engine start to rev. He knew what was coming. He knew the man's plan was to kill him with the car instead of a gun. He dove to his left, hitting the ground just as the car sped past, clipping his ankle as it went. If that right rear wheel hadn't been off the pavement, he probably would have been dead.

He rolled to his right, drawing his pistol as he rolled. His thought was to shoot out the tires to prevent Petrov's escape, but when he aimed he was looking down the barrel at the house next to his. He changed his mind. He wasn't likely to miss, but if he did, a stray bullet might hit his neighbors. He wasn't willing to take that chance. So he watched as the car rounded the curve and drove out of sight.

As he pushed himself to a standing position, a surge of pain from his ankle almost caused him to fall again. He began limping back toward the house and saw the women coming to meet him. When they got closer, he scolded them. "I told everybody to stay inside."

"I don't remember you saying that," said Teala.

"Well you know that's what I meant when I told you to lock the door."

"That man deliberately tried to kill you," said Moira.

Dennis grinned. "I do believe that was his plan."

"You're limping," said Teala. "What did you hurt?"

"The car clipped my ankle when I dove out of its path."

"Well we'd better get you off of it and put an ice pack on it."

"It's not a big deal," said Dennis. "It'll be okay in a little while."

Teala took him by the arm. "Don't be macho. I want you mobile in case you have to tangle with Petrov again."

They all looked in both directions along the street, and seeing no sign of Petrov, went on into the house. Teala insisted that Dennis lie down on the couch and put his foot up on the couch's back. He removed his shoe and sock and followed her orders.

She felt around his ankle and said, "I don't feel any broken bones, but we'll put an ice pack on it to keep the swelling down. Where do you keep the aspirin?"

"In the cabinet left of the sink. Why? Do you have a headache?"

"No. The aspirin is for you . . . for inflammation."

Dennis grinned.

Myra was keeping watch through the front window.

Moira said to Harriet, "You'd better go home with us when Thad gets here. We'll bring you back after Damon . . . uh . . . clears up this situation."

Harriet had a quizzical look on her face. "All of you seem to have a lot of confidence in this Damon Hawker. What makes *him* so special?"

Moira looked at Teala; then back at Harriet. "He has some unusual skills."

An hour and fifteen minutes later Thad arrived in his SUV. Moira greeted him at the door. "You made pretty good time," she said.

He gave her a wry smile and said, "And I did it without getting a ticket."

"I think the police are taking the day off," said Myra. "We broke every law in the book getting here and didn't see a single police car."

"Well we'll be more careful on the way home," he said. "Our luck can't last forever."

Dennis had been trying to obey Teala's orders, but he stood now and assured her his ankle was okay.

Moira turned to Dennis. "Is it okay if I leave my car here? We'll pick it up when we bring Harriet back."

"Sure," said Dennis. "Just leave me the key so I can move it."

Myra fished the key out of her jeans pocket and gave it to him.

"Thanks for taking care of my girls," Thad said to Dennis.

Dennis grinned. "No problem, man. I enjoyed having a house full of women."

Thad loaded all of his girls—including the new one, Harriet—into his black SUV and headed home. Myra and Harriet rode in the backseat and Moira was up front with him. He fought the traffic on Beach Boulevard to I-95; then took that interstate to the beginning of I-10.

As they headed west on I-10, Moira said, "You would have been proud of Myra today."

"I'm always proud of Myra," said Thad. "But tell me all about it."

They gave him all the details of their ordeal, leaving out nothing.

"We sure spoiled whatever plans that crazy scientist had," said Myra. "And Dennis foiled him again. It wasn't exactly luck in either case, but our good luck can't hold out forever. Something needs to be done about that guy. It wouldn't surprise me at all to see him behind us right now."

She had been glancing back from time to time, but hadn't seen Petrov. That all changed when they exited I-10 onto US-301. The exit ramp is a U-shaped loop, and as they were completing the loop she looked back toward the interstate and saw Petrov exiting. "I was right," she said. "He just turned onto the exit ramp."

"Are you sure it's him?" Thad asked.

"Absolutely. It's the same car that was chasing us."

"We should let Hawker know where he is," said Thad. "Do you know his number?"

"No, but you can call Dennis and get him to relay the message."

He handed his cell phone to Moira and said, "You do it. Tell 'im we're on three-oh-one and we'll be taking twenty-four when we get to Waldo."

US-301 is a four-lane highway in that area, and passing and speeding are not much of a problem—unless one gets caught, that is. As soon as Thad was out of the congested area near the interstate ramps, he floored the accelerator pedal and passed every car in front of him. "We'll see if we can't lure him into the speed trap in Lawtey," he said to his girls. "He probably doesn't know about it. We'll slow down and obey the speed limit when we get there, but he probably won't because he'll be so far behind. Maybe the police will detain him."

"Remember what I told you earlier?" Myra said. "The police aren't working today."

"Well this little town has a completely different set of police. They don't play by the Jacksonville rules."

Thad slowed down when he reached the Lawtey city limits. There were cars in both lanes behind them, but they couldn't see Petrov. South of Lawtey, beyond the reduced-speed zone, Thad fell in with the other vehicles, matching their speed. *He* didn't want to be the one who got stopped.

After a few minutes, Myra said, "It didn't work. I see him in the left lane about five cars back."

"Okay . . . let's be logical about this," said Thad. "What will he do if he catches us? Or, is he even *trying* to catch us? Maybe he's just following to see where we go."

"He already knows where we live," said Myra. "I think he's positioning himself to maybe wreck us or something."

"I think you're right," said Thad. "I'm sure he doesn't just want to talk with us. Or he *may* be planning to go for us as we're trying to get from the car to the house. We'll be sitting ducks at that time."

Moira offered her two cents. "I think he made his intentions quite clear when he held a gun on us and locked us in that hot tub room."

"I think he's working from two different angles," said Myra. "He made it clear that he wanted Damon to be present for whatever he's planning, but I also think that if he can't arrange that, he'll go for any chance he gets to punish Damon by harming us or any of Damon's other friends."

"How did you get so wise in just sixteen years?" Thad asked Myra.

Myra smiled. "Don't blame me. I'm a product of you and Mom."

They got through Starke without Petrov being able to gain any ground. For some reason, the cars in the left lane had not been passing and that scenario was continuing south of Starke.

When they were nearing Waldo, Thad said, "I'm gonna make him play his hand before we get home. I don't want us to wind up like sitting ducks."

"Maybe we should try to find a policeman in Waldo," said Moira.

"These little towns typically have only one man to a car," said Thad. "If I understand everything I'm hearing about this crazy Russian, he would probably just shoot the policeman and again we'd be sitting ducks. I want him to show his hand while we're moving. He's not a professional killer, so he's not likely to be an expert with a firearm."

Harriet's mind had definitely—at least for a time—been taken off the loss of her husband. "Are your lives always this exciting?" she asked.

Remembering past experiences, Myra posed a thin smile. "We've had some close calls."

After they turned right in Waldo and headed for Gainesville, Myra said, "Well if you're wanting him to catch up to us, I think you're gonna get your wish. Only three other cars made the fork onto twenty-four and he's the third one back."

"I'll let the other two pass us when we get on the open highway," said Thad.

After getting beyond Waldo, he drove exactly the speed limit. He knew that nobody else did that and the other cars would soon be passing him. He was right: It didn't take the other drivers long to become impatient with his slowness. They both passed at the first opportunity. He held his speed and waited. As expected, Petrov began closing the gap between them.

Myra said, "He's coming, Dad."

Thad nodded. "I see that. Keep me posted on every move he makes."

"He's about one car length behind us now. I don't see a gun, but I doubt he'd try to shoot through the windshield anyway."

They began meeting a string of cars traveling in the opposite direction. On this two-lane highway, Petrov had no choice except to hold his position and wait.

Thad looked ahead beyond the approaching cars. "If he's going to do anything other than follow us, it should come after these cars pass."

He was right again: As soon as the last car was past, Petrov shifted to the other lane.

"He's starting around you, Dad."

"Okay, keep your eye on 'im."

"He's rolling the windows down. . . . Dad . . . he's picking up a gun. He's gonna shoot."

The front bumper of Petrov's rental sedan was just passing by Thad's window when Myra gave that warning. Thad suddenly swerved his large SUV to the left, slamming it into the front fender of Petrov's sedan. At the same instant, Petrov reacted instinctively and jerked his steering wheel away from the imminent collision. But his reaction was too severe: The sedan hit the shoulder on the left side of the road and went out of control, becoming slightly airborne and dropping into the ditch. It came to an almost instant stop when it hit the bottom of the ditch. The sudden deceleration was somewhat similar to a head-on collision at fifty miles an hour. The car would not be coming out of the ditch under its own power.

No other vehicles were in sight in either direction. Thad brought the SUV to a stop and looked back. Smoke was coming from the passenger-side window.

Moira grabbed Thad by the arm. "Don't you even think about going back there, Thad. That man was trying to kill you."

"You're right," said Thad. "That smoke is probably from the air bag deployment. If he was wearing his seat belt, he could be perfectly okay. . . . Give me the cell phone."

Thad dialed nine-one-one and reported that he had just seen a car crash into the ditch. He stated that he was afraid to go back and check on the driver because he was waving a gun around and driving crazy. He didn't tell the dispatcher that he knew who the driver was.

chapter 9

The Sun had gone down in Florida by the time Hawker returned from his trip to Russia. It had been a weird sensation watching the sky become lighter in the west at the same time he knew the Sun was actually going down. Dennis had called again and told him that Petrov was chasing Thad Wilson and family down US-301. He knew that Thad would have had more than enough time to get home, but the first thing he did was trace out that route anyway. Flying along the road between Waldo and Gainesville, he spotted a car in the ditch. Two police cars and an ambulance were parked on the side of the road with their lights flashing. The evening twilight gave the scene a psychedelic twist. He assumed the car was Petrov's rental because it matched the description he had been given.

Hawker definitely wanted to know Petrov's status so he landed and asked if he could be of assistance. He had been popping up everywhere over the past six months, so the police were not terribly surprised to see him. While he was asking his question, he glanced at the car and saw that Petrov was not there.

"I don't guess there's anything urgent here," said one of the policemen.

"Where's the driver?" Hawker asked.

"We don't know, but we'd certainly like to find him. We were told that he was waving a gun around."

"I'll check the area and see if I can locate him," said Hawker. He didn't tell them that he had no intention of turning Petrov over to the police.

The policeman pointed to Petrov's car. "We'll let a wrecker come get the car . . . although I suppose you could lift it out if we wanted you to."

Hawker didn't say so, but he preferred leaving the car in the ditch. He saluted the policeman and rose into the air to begin his search for Petrov. There was no sign of him anywhere in the vicinity of the wreck, but that didn't mean anything; he could be hiding in any one of a million different places. Hawker flew on to the Wilson home and checked the area there with the same result. He used the phone in his helmet to call Thad and was told that they were all okay.

"There's no way he can get past my alarm system without me knowing about it," said Thad. "And I won't hesitate to shoot him if he invades my home."

"I didn't know you owned a gun."

"I don't. I borrowed one from Dennis."

"I saw a car that looked like Petrov's in the ditch out on twenty-four."

"Yeah . . . we helped him put it there when he tried to take a shot at us."

"Good for you," said Hawker. "It sounds like you have everything under control. I'll go check on Dennis and Teala."

He called Dennis and found that they were also okay.

"I'll be there shortly," Hawker said. "I want to zip by the house and get a phone book."

When he got to Dennis' house he presented Dennis and Teala with the Gainesville area telephone book he had stopped for and asked them to start calling all hotels, motels and hospitals in that area. To Teala, he said, "You can tell 'em you're a nurse and you're trying to locate a man that might have been injured in an automobile accident. Give 'em his name and description and tell 'em he speaks with a Russian accent. While you're doing that I'm gonna go back and check all those same places with my enhanced hearing. I'll recognize his voice if I hear it."

"What will you do with him if you find him?" Teala asked.

"Put him on a deserted island for the time being. His neighbor may yet provide us with the evidence we need to have him locked up."

"What makes you think that?"

"It's a long story. I'll tell you all about it later. For now let's get busy and try to find him."

With that, he kissed her lightly and donned his helmet. Dennis opened the back door for him and said, "We'll call you if we get a lead."

Five minutes later Hawker was back in Gainesville. He floated in the shadows past hotel windows and listened for the sound of Petrov's voice. He knew it would not be an efficient use of his time to linger long in any one location since he had no idea where Petrov might be, so he listened while on the move. After several hours without success he returned to Dennis' house. They reported no success there either. He called Thad again and told him he would be at work the next day so Thad wouldn't have to take his class. He also asked if he and Teala could drive Moira's car back to Gainesville.

Thad was happy to have the car closer to home. "I'll bring Myra to your office in the morning," he said.

Hawker and Teala took almost two hours to drive home. She, of course, was staying at his house at least for the night. They would wait until the next day to make any further decisions: It was late and they were both tired.

The next day was Monday and Hawker had a class to teach. Not much coaxing was required to convince Teala to tag along with him. He had told her about Petrov trying to take a shot at the Wilsons.

"That guy is really persistent," she had said. "He must have something tough gnawing at his insides."

Then Hawker told her about his conversation with Petrov's neighbor in Russia.

They were now in Hawker's office at the university. He was explaining to her what he was planning for his class when Thad brought Myra in.

"I'm assuming you had an uneventful night," Hawker said.

Thad nodded. Then he grinned and said, "Looks like you're gonna have *two* good-looking women keeping you company today."

Hawker looked at Myra and Teala and smiled. "Yeah, I'm gonna put 'em to work helping me set up my demonstrations."

"I know Myra will enjoy that," said Thad. "But I don't know about Teala."

Teala smiled. "I'm improving." She knew Thad was thinking about the time many years ago when he was her physics professor.

Thad went on his way and left Hawker alone with his "good-looking" companions.

"Okay ladies," said Hawker. "I need to move some equipment to the classroom. Let's go to the lab."

With the bag containing Hawker's special suit nearby at all times, they moved several items to the classroom and prepared the physics demonstrations. For Myra, this was entertainment more than it was work. Teala sincerely tried to show an interest in what they were doing.

The equipment they had positioned across the front of the room included a sweeping, low-power laser beam, an ordinary flashing light, a microwave oven, a radio and a free-fall apparatus. The free-fall apparatus required more assembly than the rest of the equipment. It was used for measuring the acceleration due to gravity, and was basically a vertical metal pole several feet tall with two spaced electrical wires running from top to bottom. The pole was mounted on a frame that had three adjustable feet for leveling the device, and the two wires were connected to a high-voltage frequency generator. A metal plummet was held in place at the top of the pole between the two wires and then allowed to drop. As the plummet fell under the influence of gravity, high-voltage sparks jumped between the two wires via the plummet. To get to the inside wire, the sparks had to go through a waxed paper strip covering it. The distances between the holes created by the sparks—along with the known frequency of the sparks—were used by students to calculate the acceleration due to gravity. But Hawker wasn't using the apparatus for its intended purpose today.

As they were completing the wiring necessary to make everything work, Myra said, "It's easy to see the connection on the other demonstrations, but what does the free-fall apparatus have to do with electromagnetic radiation?"

Hawker shrugged. "Generally speaking, not much . . . but the sparks it produces *do* generate electromagnetic radiation. It's just a dramatic demonstration of one of the applications of electromagnetic radiation along with a method of producing it."

They completed the assembly and tested its operation.

"I remember using that thing when I was in your dad's class," said Teala. "I never quite got the hang of the calculations that went with the experiment."

When their preparations were all finished they went for a coffee break. Hawker was carrying the canvas bag as usual. When he began that practice he had worried that it might attract attention, but soon realized that it was not an unusual sight on a campus where many people carried a briefcase or some other container for their school related supplies.

All three were a little on edge, but Teala put it into words: "I keep expecting to see Petrov's face everywhere I look."

"I know," said Hawker. "Finding him is turning out to be more difficult than I anticipated. I don't have a clue where to start. I know he'll show up again eventually, but I'd much rather the encounter be on my terms."

Teala's voice took on a slightly accusative tone. "Considering all the capabilities that suit has, one would think you could put it on and find that guy before he hurts someone."

Hawker did feel some guilt and wondered if he was using his time wisely, but he responded with: "If you'll tell me exactly which feature of the suit I should use to find him, I'll hop right to it. But I'm not Superman you know . . . I don't have X-ray vision."

"Don't be touchy," she said. "I know you've done everything you can."

Back in the classroom with the students beginning to filter in, Myra and Teala took seats at the back of the room. Hawker was seated at his desk at the front, greeting the students as they entered. Two of his demonstrations were set up on his desk and the free-fall apparatus—being too tall to fit on a desk or table—was standing by the windows to his left.

He had been absent for his Wednesday and Friday classes the previous week because of his visit to the White House and the ensuing trip to Russia. An attractive young lady who frequently flirted with him lingered by his desk and asked, "Did you enjoy your vacation, Professor Hawker?"

"I need a vacation to recuperate from it," he answered.

Teala watched this exchange with much interest and thought about the time more than ten years ago when Hawker had been her tutor. She was also wishing she had not made that remark about finding Petrov during their coffee break. Hawker was worried enough already without her adding to it.

When it was time to start the class, Hawker got up from the desk and closed the door. Still standing he started his lecture: "Last time we covered the theory of electromagnetic radiation and we know there's an entire spectrum of frequencies that come under that heading, including light, radio waves and many others. Today I want to talk about some of the practical applications of electromagnetic radiation. Radio and television obviously fit that bill, but there are many other applications that might not be so obvious." He picked up a small item from his desk and began walking down the aisle between two rows of student desks. "You will note that several devices have been set up at the front of the room for a demonstration. With the exception of the free-fall apparatus on your right, all of these devices depend on electromagnetic radiation for their operation. In three of the cases, electromagnetic radiation is the product of the operation. You all have used the free-fall apparatus so you know its real purpose, but today we will use it as a radiation generator. . . ."

Hawker's lecture was interrupted by a man entering the room and closing the door behind him. Hawker's heart skipped a beat: The man who had entered was Petrov.

Petrov did not appear threatening; his hands were empty and down by his sides. But then he spoke. "Please, may I have everyone's attention, this is very important. Anyone who moves in any way will die. I am not joking." Then he reached inside his jacket and pulled out a pistol.

He continued, "I did not want to enter the room with a weapon in my hand because I feared it would cause some of you to die earlier than I had planned. We are going to play a game. Professor Hawker, I will start with you. Each time you move I will shoot one of your students. I will not be aiming for you."

Hawker was now standing about a third of the way down the aisle with his arms at his side. His special suit was in the bag by his desk; completely useless in this situation.

Petrov swept the room with his gun-free hand and said, "Now to the students. Many of you are going to die here today. That is not in question. The only question is who will die first and who will still be alive once I am dead. I hope you understand that the first person who moves will be the first one to die. Eventually, I will deplete my ammunition or someone will come through that door and shoot me. So your own actions will determine whether you live or die."

Hawker was hoping beyond hope that none of the students would panic and set Petrov off. He knew they were frightened and in a state of shock, but at least for the moment they were remaining still and quiet.

He noted that Petrov's pistol was a semiautomatic that probably held enough rounds to kill half of his class. Being careful not to move, he said, "Petrov, this is between you and me. Let's leave the students out of it."

Petrov displayed a condescending smile. "But Professor . . . do you not see that I want to punish you. A quick death for you would not be sufficient. We must prolong your suffering. What better way than for you to watch while your students die."

"But things don't have to go this way," said Hawker. "With your knowledge of nanotechnolgy and the immune system you could do great things for mankind. I could help you. You could become world-famous and achieve more wealth than you could use."

That caused Petrov to show anger. "Do you not think I could have had all that already if I desired it? No . . . that is not what I desire. Revenge is what motivates me. Revenge for the death of my son, and now revenge for the deaths of my men and the destruction of my work."

Hawker was almost afraid to say anything else. He certainly didn't want to agitate Petrov. "I know about your son," he said. "And I know that nothing can bring him back or make amends for your loss, but together maybe we could make something happen that would make his death serve a worthwhile purpose."

Petrov seemed to soften a bit. "He would have been about your age, Professor. Unfortunately, one of your military *cowboys* was so eager to score a kill that he didn't care that my son was a non-combatant and actually on a mission of mercy."

Hawker wanted to keep him talking without angering him again. "I'm actually in accord with your point of view on that. Let's go somewhere and talk this out. We can solve this problem without any more violence."

Petrov laughed. "Do not patronize me, Professor. I know what you are attempting. But I will say one other thing before the fun starts. I want the world to know why this has happened, so I will tell you what gave me the idea. . . . Your own government taught me that violence is the key to achieving one's goal. Perhaps it is teaching your young people the same lesson. Last night as I watched your television coverage of a shooting at another university it occurred to me that the same incident had been on every newscast I had seen since arriving in America. It became clear to me, that to get America's attention, I needed to shoot a few university students."

He paused as if for effect. "I suppose you could call me a copycat killer." Then he smiled. "Now the talking is finished."

Hawker had been considering his options while Petrov was talking. Although it seemed to contradict his stated intention, Petrov was now standing at the end of the aisle that Hawker occupied, giving him a clear shot at Hawker. Hawker believed that if he made a lunge at Petrov, Petrov couldn't get off more than one or two shots before he went down. One or two wounded students would be better than twelve or fifteen. But maybe he could even improve on those odds. He pressed the button on the device he had taken from his desk.

The device sent a remote control signal to a receiver connected to the free-fall apparatus. The plummet on the free-fall apparatus fell away from the electromagnet and downward, giving off a series of loud electric sparks as it went. The radiation from the sparks triggered another receiver that switched on the radio, the laser beam and the flashing light. The unexpected sounds and flashing lights diverted Petrov's attention for a brief instant, causing him to react without thinking: He shot at the man lunging toward him instead of shooting a student as he had promised.

Hawker felt something hit him in the chest. He didn't know exactly where, but it didn't matter. His momentum kept him going. Immediately after the chest impact, he felt a searing pain in his head. Then he collided with Petrov. They went down and everything went black for Hawker.

Like everyone else, Teala had been glued to her seat with her eyes on Petrov. When she saw Hawker lunge at him she grabbed her cell phone to dial 911. She saw Petrov point his gun at Hawker and shoot twice, but Hawker kept going. Then Hawker hit Petrov hard with his full body and they went down. She couldn't see what was happening but she heard more shots ring out over the noise the students were making as they scrambled for safety. While she was still waiting for the 911 dispatcher to answer, the shooting stopped.

She handed the phone to Myra and said, "This is nine-one-one. Tell 'em what's going on." Then she got out of her seat and crouched low while easing toward the front. She had to push students out of the way as she went.

When Hawker and Petrov came into view they were both lying still. Petrov was on his back with his right hand thrown out to the side. The gun was still in that hand but the hand was now relaxed. Hawker was lying on top of the pile with his left hand gripping Petrov's right arm and his right hand gripping Petrov's throat. Hawker's head was bloody and blood was running from underneath him and across Petrov's clothing.

Teala tried to turn Hawker over to check his injuries but couldn't budge him. She yelled to the students, "Somebody help me."

At that instant, the door was thrown open and a uniformed policeman burst into the room waving his gun around. He surveyed the scene on the floor; then swept his vision and gun across the room.

One of the students said, "There was only one shooter, officer."

The policeman eased closer to Petrov's gun hand while keeping a wary eye on everybody. He kicked the gun away and poised for a reaction, but there was none.

To Teala, he said, "Okay, lady . . . back away."

Teala didn't move; she was still tugging on Hawker.

The policeman grabbed her arm, and maybe he didn't mean it, but his gun was pointed right at her face. "I said move away."

A second policeman came through the door and saw the pile of bodies and blood and the struggle that was going on. He swept the room with his gun; then pointed it at Teala.

"You don't understand," said Teala. "I'm a nurse and this is my fiancé."

"I don't care who you are," retorted the policeman. "Back away."

Teala started sobbing as she moved back. "Please let me help him."

At that moment Ben Huron rushed into the room followed by two paramedics. Myra had finished talking with the 911 operator, and she moved forward and put an arm around Teala.

chapter 10

Hawker's next awareness was that of a party going on down the hall—or so it seemed. He could hear voices talking and laughing; faint at first and then louder. Then he realized there was something in his throat, and that he was violently shaking a rail on the side of his bed.

A feminine voice was saying, "You don't have to do that anymore, hon. I'm right here."

He felt a soft hand grip his arm and attempt to hold it still. A figure was slowly coming into focus. Then he was looking at the face of a nurse.

She smiled when she saw his open eyes and realized that he was seeing her. "For someone who was almost dead, you sure are a strong fellow," she said.

He couldn't speak because of the thing in his throat.

"You're in the recovery room at the hospital," she said. "You've had surgery."

He had stopped shaking the rail so she released his arm. But he immediately reached for the thing in his throat and she grabbed his arm again.

"You have to leave that alone," she said. "It's a breathing tube . . . and you need it to stay alive. . . . At least you *did*."

She held up her free hand and wiggled her fingers. "Wiggle your fingers for me if you understand what I'm saying."

He wiggled his fingers.

She released his arm again and said, "Yeah . . . I think they'll be taking that thing out of your throat when they see how well you're doing. There's a room full of people out there waiting to see you. Would you like that?"

He wiggled his fingers again. Then he was overcome by an irresistible urge to close his eyes. He didn't know how much time passed. When he opened his eyes again Ben, Teala and Myra were standing there. Teala had tears in her eyes. He wondered why she was crying; he didn't realize how he looked in all those bandages, and with the tubes coming out of his mouth and chest.

Ben said, "Welcome back."

With his right hand, Hawker made a motion as if he were holding a pen and writing. His left arm seemed to be restrained. Ben knew what Hawker wanted and pulled out a small notepad and a pen. He handed the pen to Hawker and held the notepad so Hawker could reach it.

Hawker scribbled: *Students? Petrov?*

Ben smiled. "None of the students were injured . . . thanks to you. And Petrov is dead." He could see the relief in Hawker's eyes. He also knew Hawker's aversion to killing, so he decided to wait until later to tell him *how* Petrov had died.

Hawker was covered with so much bandaging and other paraphernalia that Teala didn't have many choices where she could touch him. She took his right hand and tried not to show the pity she was feeling. "We won't stay too long. They're only letting three people at a time come in and there's a room full waiting to see you. Your students think you're the greatest hero that ever lived. But you can relax now . . . we all can. Petrov won't bother anybody anymore." She *also* had decided not to mention the fact that Hawker was the one who had killed Petrov.

Hawker began drifting again. He remembered seeing Myra standing there, but he couldn't remember if she had spoken to him. Maybe other people came afterwards; he wasn't sure. Maybe later that day, or maybe the next, the doctors removed his tubes. The removal process wasn't pleasant, but he was certainly glad to get rid of that thing in his throat.

He wasn't sure how much time had passed—it could have been two hours or two days—but sometime after the tubes had been removed, the lead surgeon that had operated on him came to visit. Hawker's head was clear now. He was fully aware of everything and everybody.

After the usual "How do you feel?" questions, the surgeon said, "You're lucky to be alive, young man. If your physical condition hadn't been so good, or if he had used a higher powered weapon, you wouldn't be with us now. Bones and muscles in your chest stopped the bullet a tiny fraction of an inch before it did irreparable damage. A little less muscle tissue and you wouldn't be here . . . at least not alive."

Hawker could talk now that his breathing tube was gone. "I always knew that all those push-ups would pay off some day," he said.

The surgeon grinned. "You've made a remarkable comeback. I don't think I've ever seen anybody bounce back from something like that so fast. We could let you go home in two or three days, but somebody would have to be with you twenty-four hours a day and I understand you live alone."

"I think I could arrange to have somebody there all the time," said Hawker. "How long would that have to continue?"

"At least a week . . . maybe longer."

"What about my head?"

"One of the bullets creased your skull. You may have some lingering pain and you may have a hair-part you don't want, but other than that, there was no permanent damage."

The doctor raised his eyebrows and grinned faintly. "We had a very special visitor while you were out of it."

"Yeah? . . . Who was that?"

"Would you believe the First Lady of the United States?"

Hawker's face became a question mark. "What was she doing here?"

"What do you think she was doing here? She was checking to see if you were okay. . . . No . . . that's not quite accurate. She wanted me to make *sure* you were going to be okay. She offered me any resource available to the U.S. government. I told her we had everything we needed right here and that I would do everything possible whether she was here or not. Her security detail was wreaking havoc in the hospital, but she refused to leave until I assured her that you would pull through and recover completely. I had to show a little more optimism than I actually had at the time. Would you please do me a favor and not get shot here in Gainesville anymore?"

Hawker grinned. "I'll do my best."

The surgeon reached into a pocket and pulled out a folded piece of paper. He handed it to Hawker and said, "She asked me to give you this."

Using the one hand that was functional, Hawker fumbled with the paper but wasn't having much success unfolding it. The doctor took it, unfolded it and handed it back.

The First Lady had written him a note: *I'm sorry I let you down. I'll try to make it up to you when you're well enough... FL*

He knew she felt responsible for Petrov getting into the country. He didn't blame her. There was only so much she could do. The rest of it would be up to the people who carried out her orders. He would have to call her as soon as he could retrieve the cell phone she had given him. It was locked in the glove box of Teala's car.

Ben came in shortly after the doctor left. "I guess this means you're gonna be wanting a few days off," he said.

"I *was* needing a rest," responded Hawker.

"That was a tough way to get it. . . . I guess the doctor told you about Lena Bradshaw's visit."

"Yeah. . . . I need the cell phone I left in Teala's car. Will you tell her if you see her?"

"I'll call her for you. She's back at work now, but she was camped out here until she was sure you would be okay."

"I've caused her a lot of grief."

Ben shook his head. "She doesn't blame you for the things that have happened." He pulled a chair up beside the bed. "You haven't asked about the suit."

"I was kinda hoping somebody would steal it," said Hawker. "It's caused enough problems for my friends . . . and now for my students."

"The suit didn't cause the problems," said Ben. "Bad guys did. Anyway, I grabbed the bag when I saw it sitting beside your desk and carried it around as if it were mine. I didn't want the police to make it part of the crime scene. It's in a bank vault now where nobody can get to it but me."

"It can stay there," said Hawker.

"We'll talk about it after you're well." Ben glanced toward the door as if expecting someone. "I'm sure the police will be in to talk with you soon now that you're coherent. Petrov wasn't carrying ID. They don't even know that he's from Russia yet. What're you gonna tell 'em?"

"What did the others tell 'em?"

"Nothing . . . other than what had happened in your classroom. The police didn't specifically ask Teala or Myra if they had seen Petrov before so they didn't volunteer the information."

"Who killed Petrov?"

Ben hesitated; then said, "You did. The campus police had to pry your fingers away from his neck. At first, they thought you were dead too."

Hawker closed his eyes. "That's four people I've killed now. All because of that suit."

Ben quickly countered with: "I'd like to point out that the *Shadow Messenger* didn't kill any of those people . . . Damon Hawker did. And he would have done the same if he had never seen the suit. In fact, if you could have been wearing the suit you probably wouldn't have had to kill any of them."

Then Ben shook Hawker's arm to get his attention. Hawker opened his eyes to see two men coming through the door. They were dressed in casual business attire including jackets and ties.

One of the men showed him a badge and asked, "Do you feel well enough to talk now?"

Apparently the man had been in before and thought Hawker knew who he was.

Hawker said, "Sure."

"Do you know the man who shot you?"

Hawker knew he would have to give them that much at least. "Yes," he said. "His name is Ivan Petrov. He's a Russian Scientist that I met once when I was in Russia."

"Why was he trying to kill you?"

"He wasn't there to kill me. He stated emphatically that the students were his target."

The second policeman glanced at a notepad he was holding and said, "But according to the students he also stated that he wanted to punish *you*."

"I think that he wanted to punish all Americans in general for the death of his son. That may be what he meant. He may have been using 'you' to mean all Americans."

The first policeman took over again. "Don't misunderstand us, Professor. We're not interested in charging you with a crime. We're convinced that your actions were justifiable, but we got the distinct impression that he was using 'you' in the singular. What did he have against you personally? Why did he choose your classroom?"

Hawker was facing a dilemma: He wasn't prepared to lie, but how much of what he knew could he safely tell these men? Now that they knew Petrov's name and where he was from, it wouldn't take too much digging to learn about the explosion at the pharmaceutical plant and the fact that Hawker was in Russia at the time.

As he had done many times in the past, Ben attempted to cover for Hawker. "Professor Hawker has intervened in many situations like this one over the years. He could have made many enemies."

The policeman gave Ben a stern look. "Excuse us, Dr. Huron, but we're well aware of Professor Hawker's reputation. We want *him* to answer the question." He turned back to Hawker. "The bad guy is dead. We have no intention of bringing charges against anyone, but we need to complete our investigation and close the books. What do you know that will help us?"

Hawker needed to stop the investigation from going too far. He decided to give them some facts that would perhaps satisfy them and stop them from digging too deep. "What I told you about Petrov hating all Americans was true. He blamed America for the death of his son and was planning a wholesale slaughter of Americans. I learned about his plans and was able to foil them. Before I give you any more details, I want you to promise that your report will state simply that Petrov was attempting to take revenge for the death of his son. I also want you to promise that you will close the investigation and not dig any deeper. If all of the details were made public, it could cause widespread panic and could seriously harm relations with Russia. It could even lead to war. This truly is a matter of national security and the details of how the aforementioned problem was solved should not go any further."

The two policemen looked at one another for a few seconds without speaking. Then the first one said, "I can't make any promises. We'll listen to what you have to say and if *we* decide that it should be kept secret, we will agree to end the investigation. But it's now *obvious* that you know more than you've told us. If you don't tell us the rest, you can bet we'll dig deeper. On top of that, we might change our minds and charge you with obstruction of justice."

"I doubt you could make that stick," said Hawker. "Justice has already been done in this case. There's nobody left for you to bring to justice."

"We'll think of something," retorted the policeman.

Hawker knew he would have to give them more. He just hoped he could satisfy them without telling them everything. He began, hesitantly choosing his words: "The U.S. was buying bird flu vaccine from Russia. Petrov was the lead scientist in the development of the vaccine, but he also had his own agenda. He was adding synthesized molecules to the vaccine that could be triggered later, killing everybody that had received it. The White House discovered there was a plot but didn't know the details. I was going to Russia on another matter so they asked me to check it out."

"Are you saying you work for the U.S. government . . . some kind of spy, or secret agent?"

"No . . . not at all. It's just that I'm a scientist and this involved highly technical stuff."

"Stuff that you just happened to be familiar with? I didn't know that physicists were experts when it comes to vaccines."

"I'm not an expert with vaccines, but he was using nanotechnology which I *have* studied. And the triggering equipment he planned to use is definitely within the realm of the physicist. The point is, I had to blow up an entire building to destroy the vaccine making equipment and supplies as well as the electronic equipment that would have been used to trigger the killer molecules. Although I'm not an agent of the U.S. government, the Russians wouldn't see it that way. They think some of their local terrorists did the job, but if you start asking questions and they find out I did it, they will assume that an American agent was sent to commit an act of terrorism on their soil."

The policeman gave a faint smile. "I think it's interesting that a man who is *not* a government agent is an expert in so many things including explosives."

"The explosive I used was natural gas and the evidence I had gathered was destroyed in the explosion. I sincerely hope that you can see the danger involved in stirring up this hornet's nest."

Both policemen remained silent, obviously thinking.

Hawker added, "And another thing to consider . . . thousands of Americans have already been injected with the vaccine. If they learned about this, it could cause a panic."

The policeman frowned. "Don't you think they have a right to know?"

"I won't argue that point, but I wouldn't tell 'em. If you stir this up and create a panic it'll be on your head, not mine. They're in no danger now that Petrov is dead, but I'm quite sure they wouldn't believe that."

Both policemen were silent again for a time; then the one that had been doing most of the talking said, "Anything else you want to tell us?"

Hawker attempted to shrug but was stopped by the pain. "What more would you want? I'm sure you can verify that we abruptly stopped importing vaccine from Russia and that the plant that was producing it exploded. But I implore you . . . let it go at that."

The policeman put his notepad away and said, "We'll get back to you." Then he nodded to his partner and the two of them left.

When they were out of hearing range, Hawker said to Ben, "What do you think they'll do?"

Ben shook his head. "Hard to tell, but you made a good case. And I think you did the right thing by telling them part of the story but not all of it."

Hawker's eyelids were growing heavy. He said, "I'm feeling sleepy, Ben. Don't be offended if I doze on you."

"Don't try to fight it," said Ben. "You need the rest."

When Hawker opened his eyes again Ben was gone and Teala was holding his hand. Her eyes were closed and she looked as if she had been crying. When he gently squeezed her hand she opened her eyes, smiled and said, "We foiled your plans, didn't we. You're not gonna get out of marrying me that easily."

Hawker managed a return smile. "Don't kid yourself, young lady. The prospect of marrying you is the only reason I stayed alive."

Then she started sobbing. "Oh, baby . . . I felt so bad when you got shot. I just knew you were dead."

He couldn't reach up to hug and console her, so he again gently squeezed her hand.

She squeezed back and said, "You asked me last week if your philosophy would be acceptable to Christians. I can't speak for all Christians, but I *do* know that if *anyone* goes to Heaven . . . *you* will."

She had to release his hand to reach for a tissue.

"How long have I been in here?" he asked. "I've lost track of time."

She sniffed and answered, "This is Wednesday, your third day."

He was looking at the clock on the wall. "So is it six in the morning, or six in the evening?"

"Evening," she said.

At that moment, a nurse came in with a tray. "We didn't want to wake you earlier," she said. "But we want you to try eating some real food."

That was when he realized he hadn't eaten in three days. He guessed the intravenous feeding plus the fact that he had been asleep most of the time kept him from noticing the adverse reaction he normally had from not eating.

Teala insisted on feeding him and he decided to take advantage of her mood while it lasted because she wasn't normally this accommodating. Spooning him a bite, she said, "Ben called and said you wanted your cell phone. I put it there on your night table." She motioned with her thumb. "I guess in this case it's an anytime table."

He swallowed and said, "Yeah, I want to call Mrs. Bradshaw. She left me a note. She feels guilty about Petrov getting into the country after I asked her to keep him out."

He ate all of his food with Teala patiently feeding him every bite.

"You did good," she said. "The doctor said you could go home Saturday morning if you continue improving the way you have been."

"When do you plan to eat?" he asked.

"I ate already. I went to the cafeteria while I was waiting for you to wake up."

"The surgeon told me someone would have to stay with me when I go home."

She gave him a playful smile. "So that was your plan, huh? . . . To get me living with you before we're married."

He gave her a devilish grin. "I could always stay here."

"Don't pout," she said. "I'll stay with you over the weekend and Myra has volunteered for Monday. By that time we'll have other people lined up for the rest of the week."

They talked about going to the courthouse together to apply for the marriage license and about the arrangements for their wedding. Teala eventually eased into mentioning some changes she would make to his house. That was something he had not thought about. He had lived alone for so many years that he had become accustomed to everything being arranged to meet *his* perceived needs. That would all change when she moved in. He was going to have to be considerate of her needs as well and be willing to compromise. But he was more than willing to accommodate her: He had waited a long time for this.

He didn't know when Teala left: He had fallen asleep. A nurse woke him up in the middle of the night to check his vital signs.

He was feeling better the next morning. He ate all of his breakfast without help and after he thought everybody was finished doing their chores on him he called the First Lady. She sounded happy to hear his voice.

"I'll take your calling me as a good sign," she said.

"I don't blame you," he replied. "You couldn't guard every gate yourself. Besides, it may be good that he came looking for me. He saved me the trouble of hunting him down."

"I hear the Russians lost one of their satellites," she said. "I wonder how that could have happened." Then she quickly added, "But I'm not asking you to tell me. I don't want to know."

He didn't want to talk about it either, so he said, "I appreciate you coming here to check on me and offering to help. I know it was a risk for you and it makes me feel special."

"You are special . . . and it wasn't that much of a risk because nobody knew I was going to be there."

At that moment a familiar face from his past appeared in the doorway of his hospital room. "Looks like I'm gonna have to cut this conversation short," he said. "Somebody just came in that I'll have to talk with."

"Okay, but I want us to get together after you're well enough. There are some things that I want to discuss with you." Then she disconnected without giving him the chance to respond.

Robert Ashe waited until Hawker finished talking on the phone; then moved on into the room and up to the bed. "Now I have a name to go with the face," he said. "But don't worry, your secret is just as safe now as it was before."

Hawker smiled and said, "Good to see you again. How've you been?"

"Better than you, apparently. Looks like the effects of that bullet are going to last a little longer than the effects of the bomb did."

"I was better protected from the bomb." Hawker hesitated; then asked, "How did you get in? I told 'em I didn't want to see reporters."

Ashe grinned. "I didn't mention that I was a reporter. I told 'em I was an old friend of yours."

"Well that's definitely true. I didn't think about you showing up here, or I would've made an exception in your case."

Robert Ashe had kept Hawker out of the hands of the Iraqi police earlier that year and had graciously shared his hotel room in Baghdad. He was the only reporter ever granted an interview by Hawker and the one that had given Hawker the name "Shadow Messenger." Hawker had trusted him enough to reveal his face but had not revealed his name.

"How're they treating you here?" said Ashe. "Do you need anything?"

"No, I'm doing fine. I should be going home in a couple of days."

"Needless to say, I'm glad to hear that you're going to be okay. I was a little worried when I first saw your picture in the paper. I was thinking what a loss to the world that would be if you didn't make it."

"Speaking of a loss to the world, I'm glad you're here," said Hawker. "There's a story that needs to be told and I think you're the guy to do it."

Ashe pulled up a chair and sat down. "I was hoping you would say something like that."

"It may not be the story you came here to get, but it's one the world needs to hear."

"I take it this won't be about you."

"You take it right. I would prefer that you don't even mention my name."

"I'll make you the same promise I made in Iraq. You tell me everything relevant to the story, but I won't write anything you don't want known."

Hawker nodded. "This is about the man I killed and what caused him to turn bad. It's also about what the world has lost as a result of all this."

"Sounds like my kind of story."

Hawker continued, "Ivan Petrov was a genius. He probably knew more about the human immune system than anybody alive. He had the knowledge and tools that could have cured cancer . . . not to mention many other diseases. But an event that happened about ten years ago deprived us all of the benefits that could have been reaped from his genius."

Hawker laid out the entire story, beginning with the death of Petrov's son, and carefully noted the things he didn't want to see in print. They were interrupted three times by people coming into the room, but managed to finish it before lunch.

When Hawker's lunch arrived, Ashe grinned and said, "I see you're still relying on room service for your meals."

When they had been together in Iraq, Ashe had always ordered room service for Hawker so that he could take off his helmet and eat in private. Ashe would then eat somewhere away from the hotel to conceal the fact that Hawker was sharing his room. Because of that arrangement they had never eaten a complete meal together.

Hawker grinned. "I'll share it with you if you're hungry enough to eat this stuff."

Ashe rose to his feet. "Thanks, but I need to get out of here and get to work on this story. Since I can't cite you as a source, I'll have to do some digging in the archives for some facts." He then shook Hawker's hand and added, "Get well. I'll be in touch."

Hawker was released from the hospital that following Saturday morning. Teala was there to drive him home and he asked her to stop along the way to buy him a couple of newspapers. He wanted a national paper for Robert Ashe's column and a local paper to get an idea of what the local police were doing. Robert Ashe had been a well respected journalist before he met Hawker, but his reports on the *Shadow Messenger* had gained him a certain prominence. His work was in demand and his article was there as promised:

DEATH OF A "MAD" SCIENTIST

By Robert Ashe

A few days ago a Russian scientist was killed in an American university classroom. He was killed by a professor who was trying to protect his students. But this article is not about the heroic act of the professor; it is about the mentality that triggered the sequence of events leading ultimately to that act—and about the ensuing consequences for all of us.

The Russian scientist's name was Ivan Petrov. He was truly a genius; he held the cure for cancer in his hands. He had synthesized molecules that could be injected into the human body and then controlled by external signals. These molecules could direct the immune system to kill specific diseased cells without harming healthy cells. His system would have worked on many diseases, not just cancer. Just imagine what that would mean to the world.

Ivan Petrov was also a loving father. He had been a loving husband until his wife died while giving birth to his only child. He then funneled all his love toward his son. According to sources who knew them, the two were as close as any father-son pair could be. The only division between them was the son's choice of a career: He wanted to serve in the military. The father was heartbroken but that did not diminish his love for his son.

Ten years and six months ago during the NATO intervention in the Kosovo war, Petrov's son was riding in a Russian convoy that was monitoring the situation on the ground. Although the Russians were lambasting NATO with their rhetoric, they were not involved in the fighting; they were engaged in negotiations to end the conflict. NATO racked up several notorious blunders—if they were all blunders—during their bombing raids: One that many people will recall was the bombing of the Chinese embassy in Belgrade. But the one that is pertinent to this story is the attack on the Russian convoy in which Petrov's son was riding. The attack was carried out by an American fighter jet and several members of the convoy were killed, including Petrov's son. The American pilot used as his defense the fact that the Serbian and Russian flags are similar. He said that he thought the flag he saw flying above the convoy was a Serbian flag. Other than temporarily losing his flying status, the pilot received no punishment. The American government apologized to Russia and offered compensation to the families.

Ivan Petrov was outraged. He refused the compensation and began a ten year quest for revenge against the United States. Instead of using his breakthroughs in immunology to cure disease he plotted ways to use them to avenge the death of his son. When that effort failed, he tried the more direct approach of shooting American university students. That leads us to the recent event mentioned at the beginning of this article. Petrov had to be stopped, but his death also put an end to contributions he could have made.

That brief lapse in judgment by the American pilot more than ten years ago snuffed out an innocent life which is bad enough, but it also changed another life forever. The redirection of that life—at least in all likelihood—deprived the world of the means for curing a wide range of diseases, including cancer. It also set the stage for a plot that would have resulted in the deaths of countless Americans. Fortunately, that plot was discovered and foiled.

The frequent reports of innocent civilians being killed by air strikes in Iraq and Afghanistan makes one wonder how many other lives are being changed in such a way that the world will lose out on other significant contributions. What was the urgency that made the American pilot shoot at the Russian convoy? The convoy was not shooting at him. In fact, the convoy wasn't shooting at anyone. Unfortunately, this shoot-first-and-ask-questions-

later attitude goes all the way to the top levels of U.S. government. Perhaps it is time for the U.S. to change its long-standing strategy and ask the questions first. Who knows—the world we save could be our own.

The local paper contained an update on the progress of the investigation into the incident at the university. The Gainesville Police Department had released a statement saying they had concluded the investigation of Petrov's death. They had determined that it was justifiable homicide and that it was a simple case of a father seeking revenge for the death of his son. That was the news Hawker had wanted to hear.

A few days later Hawker and Teala went together to the county courthouse to apply for a marriage license. Teala, who was driving, turned her head slightly and displayed a coy smile. "I got a letter from President Bradshaw today," she said.

Hawker looked at her in surprise. "Are you being serious?"

"Yes. He invited us to hold our wedding at the White House."

Hawker grinned. "That's his wife's doing. She still feels responsible for Petrov getting into the country."

"Well, Mr. Hawker . . . when I began my relationship with you I never dreamed I would be getting married in the White House."

"You're not," said Hawker. "We can't accept that invitation."

She frowned. "I was afraid you would say that."

"I know what it would mean to you, but we can't afford to draw any more attention to ourselves than we already have. The First Lady should know that."

Teala screwed up her face and continued her task of driving them to the courthouse.

They didn't get married in the White House, but they did get married. Teala insisted on a church wedding and Hawker relented on that. He decided he had already deprived her of enough. All of their friends from the university and from the *drop zone* were there, of course, but they were surprised at the number of other people who showed up. The church couldn't accommodate everybody. The doors and windows were opened and many people stood outside to listen to the ceremony. Teala made a beautiful bride and Hawker was finally a happy man.

author's note

The characters in this book are entirely fictional and are not based on any present or past employee of the University of Florida. Also, the opinions expressed by the characters are not taken from anything stated by an employee of the University of Florida. While the names of some places or organizations may be similar to actual entities, they are used in a fictitious manner.

about the author

J.G. Sumner is a retired educator with a degree in physics. During his thirty year career he taught engineering technologies, physics and mathematics at the college level. He also holds a private pilot license and was an active skydiver for more than thirty years. He now writes novels and does his own landscaping. He is the author of The Use of Power.